Praise for *The Storyteller*

"Enchanting . . . Mario Vargas Llosa more than justifies his visionary role and the novel itself."

—*The Boston Globe*

"Vargas Llosa has written a rich and warm novel in prose that is often eloquent, that has the ring of poetry."

—*The Newark Star-Ledger*

"Engrossing, engaging, and thought-provoking . . . An intricate weaving of political commentary and narrative style."

—*Minneapolis Star-Tribune*

"Original and satisfying."

—*Chicago Tribune*

"*The Storyteller* shows the confidence and command of a storyteller in complete control of his art."

—*San Francisco Chronicle*

Also by Mario Vargas Llosa

The Feast of the Goat
Death in the Andes
In Praise of the Stepmother
Aunt Julia and the Scriptwriter
The War of the End of the World
Conversation in the Cathedral
The Green House
A Fish in the Water (memoir)

The Storyteller

MARIO VARGAS LLOSA

Translated by Helen Lane

Picador

Farrar, Straus and Giroux

New York

 Printed in the United States of America. For information, address Picador, 175 Fifth Avenue, New York, N.Y. 10010.

Picador® is a U.S. registered trademark and is used by Farrar, Straus and Giroux under license from Pan Books Limited.

For information on Picador Reading Group Guides, as well as ordering, please contact the Trade Marketing department at St. Martin's Press.
Phone: 1-800-221-7945 extension 763
Fax: 212-677-7456
E-mail: trademarketing@stmartins.com

ISBN 0-312-42028-5

Originally published in Spanish as *El Hablador* by Seix Barral Biblioteca Breve

20 19 18 17 16 15 14 13 12

TO LUIS LLOSA URETA,
IN HIS SILENCE,
AND TO THE MACHIGUENGA
kenkitsatatsirira

ACKNOWLEDGMENTS

Like all the novels I have written, this one owes much to the help, voluntary or involuntary, of a number of institutions and individuals. I should like to mention the Summer Institute of Linguistics, the Dominican Mission to the Urubamba, and the CIPA (Centro de Investigación y Promoción Amazónica), and thank them for the hospitality offered me in the jungle; Vicente de Szyszlo and Luis Román, my excellent traveling companions in Amazonia; and Father Joaquín Barriales, O.P., the collector and translator of many Machiguenga songs and myths that appear in my book.

THE STORYTELLER

I CAME to Firenze to forget Peru and the Peruvians for a while, and suddenly my unfortunate country forced itself upon me this morning in the most unexpected way. I had visited Dante's restored house, the little Church of San Martino del Véscovo, and the lane where, so legend has it, he first saw Beatrice, when, in the little Via Santa Margherita, a window display stopped me short: bows, arrows, a carved oar, a pot with a geometric design, a mannequin bundled into a wild cotton cushma. But it was three or four photographs that suddenly brought back to me the flavor of the Peruvian jungle. The wide rivers, the enormous trees, the fragile canoes, the frail huts raised up on pilings, and the knots of men and women, naked to the waist and daubed with paint, looking at me unblinkingly from the glossy prints.

Naturally, I went in. With a strange shiver and the presentiment that I was doing something foolish, that mere curiosity was going to jeopardize in some way my well-conceived and, up until then, well-executed plan—to read Dante and Machiavelli and look at Renaissance paintings for a couple of months in absolute solitude—and precipitate one of those personal upheavals that periodically make chaos of my life. But, naturally, I went in.

The gallery was minute. A single low-ceilinged room in which, to make room for all the photographs, two panels had been added, every inch of them covered with pictures. A thin girl in glasses, sitting behind a small table, looked up at me. Could I visit the "Natives of the Amazon Forest" exhibition?

"Certo. Avanti, avanti."

There were no artifacts inside the gallery, only photos, fifty at least, most of them fairly large. There were no captions, but someone, perhaps the photographer himself, one Gabriele Malfatti, had written a few pages indicating that the photos had been taken during a two-week journey in the Amazon region of the departments of Cusco and Madre de Dios in eastern Peru. The artist's intention had been to describe, "without demagoguery or aestheticism," the daily life of a tribe which, until a few years ago, had lived virtually isolated from civilization, scattered about in units of one or two families. Only in our day had they begun to group together in those places documented by the exhibition, but many of them still remained in the forest. The name of the tribe was Hispanicized without spelling errors: the Machiguengas.

The photos were a quite faithful reflection of Malfatti's intention. There were the Machiguengas, aiming a harpoon from the bank of a river, or, half concealed in the undergrowth, drawing a bow in pursuit of capybaras or peccaries; there they were, gathering cassava in the tiny plots scattered around their brand-new villages, perhaps the first in their long history, clearing the forest with machetes, weaving palm leaves to roof their huts. A group of women sat lacing mats and baskets; another was making headdresses, hooking brightly colored parrot and macaw feathers into wooden circlets. There they were, decorating their faces and bodies in intricate designs with dye from the annatto tree, lighting fires, drying hides and skins, fermenting cassava for masato beer in canoe-shaped receptacles. The photos eloquently showed how few of them there were in the immensity of sky, water, and vegetation that surrounded them, how fragile and frugal their life was; their isolation, their archaic ways, their helplessness. It was true: neither demagoguery nor aestheticism.

What I am about to say is not an invention after the fact, nor yet a false memory. I am quite sure I moved from one photograph to the next with an emotion that at a certain moment turned to anxiety. What's happening to you? What might you come across in these pictures that would justify such anxiety?

From the very first photos I had recognized the clearings where Nueva Luz and Nuevo Mundo had been built—I had been in both less than three years before—and an overall view of the second of these had immediately brought back to my mind the feeling of impending catastrophe with which I lived through the acrobatic landing that morning as the Cessna belonging to the Institute of Linguistics avoided Machiguenga children. I even seemed to recognize some of the faces of the men and women with whom I had spoken, with Mr. Schneil's help. This became certainty when, in another photograph, I saw, with the same little bloated belly and the same bright eyes my memory had preserved, the boy whose mouth and nose had been eaten away by uta ulcers. He revealed to the camera, with the same innocence and unselfconsciousness with which he had shown it to us, that hole with teeth, palate, and tonsils which gave him the appearance of some mysterious wild beast.

The photograph I was hoping to see from the moment I entered the gallery was among the last. From the very first glance it was evident that the gathering of men and women, sitting in a circle in the Amazonian way—similar to the Oriental: legs crossed tailor-fashion, back held very straight—and bathed in the light of dusk fading to dark, was hypnotically attentive. They were absolutely still. All the faces were turned, like radii of a circumference, toward the central point: the silhouette of a man at the heart of that circle of Machiguengas drawn to him as to a magnet, standing there speaking and gesticulating. I felt a cold shiver down my spine. I thought: "How did that Malfatti get them to allow him to . . . How did he manage to . . . ?" I stooped, brought my face up very close to the photograph. I kept looking at it, smelling it, piercing it with my eyes and imagination, until I noticed that the girl in charge of the gallery had risen from her table and was coming toward me in alarm.

Making an effort to contain my excitement, I asked if the photographs were for sale. No, she didn't think so. They belonged to Rizzoli, the publishers. Apparently they were going to appear in a book. I asked her to put me in touch with the photographer. No, that wouldn't be possible, unfortunately: "Il signore Gabriele Malfatti è morto."

Dead? Yes. Of a fever. A virus he'd caught in the jungle, forse. Poor man! He was a fashion photographer: he'd worked for *Vogue* and *Uomo*, that sort of magazine, photographing models, furniture, jewelry, clothes. He'd spent his life dreaming of doing something different, more personal, such as taking this trip to the Amazon. And when at last he was able to do so, and they were just about to publish a book with his work, he died!

And now, le dispiaceva, but it was l'ora di pranzo and she had to close.

I thanked her. Before leaving to confront once again the wonders and the hordes of tourists of Firenze, I managed to cast one last glance at the photograph. Yes. No doubt whatsoever about it. A storyteller.

SAÚL ZURATAS had a dark birthmark, the color of wine dregs, that covered the entire right side of his face, and unruly red hair as stiff as the bristles of a scrub brush. The birthmark spared neither his ears nor his lips nor his nose, also puffy and misshapen from swollen veins. He was the ugliest lad in the world; but he was also a likable and exceptionally good person. I have never met anyone who, from the very outset, seemed as open, as uncomplicated, as altruistic, and as well-intentioned as Saúl; anyone who showed such simplicity and heart, no matter what the circumstances. I met him when we took our university entrance examinations, and we were quite good friends—insofar as it is possible to be friends with an archangel—especially during the first two years that we were classmates in the Faculty of Letters. The day I met him he informed me, doubled over with laughter and pointing to his birthmark: "They call me Mascarita—Mask Face. Bet you can't guess why, pal."

That was the nickname we always knew him by at San Marcos.

He came from Talara and was on familiar terms with everybody. Slang words and popular catch phrases appeared in every sentence he uttered, making it seem as though he were clowning even in his most personal conversations. His problem, he said, was that his father had made too much money with his general store back home; so much that one fine day he'd decided to move to Lima. And since they'd come to the capital his father had taken up Judaism. He wasn't very religious back in the Piura port town as far as Saúl could remember. He'd occasionally seen him reading the Bible, that, yes, but he'd never bothered to drill it into Mascarita that he belonged to a race and a religion that were different from those of the other boys of the town. But here in Lima, what a change! A real drag! Ridiculous! Chicken pox in old age, that's what it was! Or rather, the religion of Abraham and Moses. Pucha! We Catholics were the lucky ones. The Catholic religion was a breeze, a measly half-hour Mass every Sunday and Communion every first Friday of the month that was over in no time. But he, on the other hand, had to sit out his Saturdays in the synagogue, hours and hours, swallowing his yawns and pretending to be interested in the rabbi's sermon—not understanding one word—so as not to disappoint his father, who after all was a very old and very good man. If Mascarita had told him that he'd long since given up believing in God, and that, to put it in a nutshell, he couldn't care less about belonging to the Chosen People, he'd have given poor Don Salomón a heart attack.

I met Don Salomón one Sunday shortly after meeting Saúl. Saúl had invited me to lunch. They lived in Breña, behind the Colegio La Salle, in a depressing side street off the Avenida Arica. The house was long and narrow, full of old furniture, and there was a talking parrot with a Kafkaesque name and surname who endlessly repeated Saúl's nickname: "Mascarita! Mascarita!" Father and son lived alone with a maid who had come from Talara with them and not only did the cooking but helped Don Salomón out in the grocery store he'd opened in Lima. "The one that's got a six-pointed star on the metal grill, pal. It's called La Estrella, for the Star of David. Can you beat that?"

I was impressed by the affection and kindness with which Mascarita treated his father, a stooped, unshaven old man who suffered from bunions and dragged about in big clumsy shoes that looked like Roman buskins. He spoke Spanish with a strong Russian or Polish accent, even though, as he told me, he had been in Peru for more than twenty years. He had a sharp-witted, likable way about him: "When I was a child I wanted to be a trapeze artist in a circus, but life made a grocer of me in the end. Imagine my disappointment." Was Saúl his only child? Yes, he was.

And Mascarita's mother? She had died two years after the family moved to Lima. How sad; judging from this photo, your mother must have been very young, Saúl. Yes, she was. On the one hand, of course, Mascarita had grieved over her death. But, on the other, maybe it was better for her, having a different life. His poor old lady had been very unhappy in Lima. He made signs at me to come closer and lowered his voice (an unnecessary precaution, as we had left Don Salomón fast asleep in a rocking chair in the dining room and were talking in Saúl's room) to tell me:

"My mother was a Creole from Talara; the old man took up with her soon after coming to this country as a refugee. Apparently, they just lived together until I was born. They got married only then. Can you imagine what it is for a Jew to marry a Christian, what we call a goy? No, you can't."

Back in Talara it hadn't mattered because the only two Jewish families there more or less blended in with the local population. But, on settling in Lima, Saúl's mother faced numerous problems. She missed home—everything from the nice warm weather and the cloudless sky and bright sun all year round to her family and friends. Moreover, the Jewish community of Lima never accepted her, even though to please Don Salomón she had gone through the ritual of the lustral bath and received instruction from the rabbi in order to fulfill all the rites necessary for conversion. In fact—and Saúl winked a shrewd eye at me—the community didn't accept her not so much because she was a goy as because she was a little Creole from Talara, a simple woman with no education, who could barely read. Because the Jews of Lima had all turned into a bunch of bourgeois, pal.

He told me all this without a vestige of rancor or dramatization, with a quiet acceptance of something that, apparently, could not have been otherwise. "My old lady and I were as close as fingernail and flesh. She, too, was as bored as an oyster in the synagogue, and without Don Salomón's catching on, we used to play Yan-Ken-Po on the sly to make those religious Sabbaths go by more quickly. At a distance: she would sit in the front row of the gallery, and I'd be downstairs, with the men. We'd move our hands at the same time and sometimes we'd fall into fits of laughter that horrified the holier-than-thous." She'd been carried off by galloping cancer, in just a few weeks. And since her death Don Salomón's world had come tumbling down on top of him.

"That little old man you saw there, taking his nap, was

hale and hearty, full of energy and love of life a couple of years ago. The old lady's death left him a wreck."

Saúl had entered San Marcos University as a law student to please Don Salomón. As far as Saúl was concerned, he would rather have started giving his father a hand at La Estrella, which was often a headache to Don Salomón and took more out of him than was right at his age. But his father was categorical. Saúl would not set foot behind that counter. Saúl would never wait on a customer. Saúl would not be a shopkeeper like him.

"But why, papa? Are you afraid this face of mine will scare the customers away?" He recounted this to me amid peals of laughter. "The truth is that now that he's saved up a few shekels, Don Salomón wants the family to make its mark in the world. He can already see a Zuratas—me—in the diplomatic corps or the Chamber of Deputies. Can you imagine!"

Making the family name illustrious through the exercise of a liberal profession was something that didn't attract Saúl much either. What interested him in life? He himself didn't know yet, doubtless. He was finding out gradually during the months and years of our friendship, the fifties, in the Peru that, as Mascarita, myself, and our generation were reaching adulthood, was moving from the spurious peace of General Odría's dictatorship to the uncertainties and novelties of the return to democratic rule in 1956, when Saúl and I were third-year students at San Marcos.

By then he had discovered, without the slightest doubt, what it was that interested him in life. Not in a sudden flash, or with the same conviction as later; nonetheless, the extraordinary machinery had already been set in motion and little by little was pushing him one day here, another there, outlining the maze he eventually would enter, never to leave it again. In 1956 he was studying ethnology as well as law and had made several trips into the jungle. Did he already feel that spellbound fascination for the peoples of the jungle and for unsullied nature, for minute primitive cultures scattered throughout the wooded slopes of the ceja de montaña and the plains of the Amazon below? Was that ardent fellow feeling, sprung from the darkest depths of his personality, already burning within him for those compatriots of ours who from time immemorial had lived there, harassed and grievously harmed, between the wide, slow rivers, dressed in loincloths and marked with tattoos, worshipping the spirits of trees, snakes, clouds, and lightning? Yes, all that had already begun. And I became aware of it just after the incident in the billiard parlor two or three years after our first meeting.

Every so often, between classes, we used to go over to a run-down billiard parlor, which was also a bar, on the Jirón Azángaro, to have ourselves a game. Walking through the streets with Saúl showed how painful a life he must have led at the hands of insolent, nasty people. They would turn around or block his path as he passed, to get a better look at him, staring wide-eyed and making no effort to conceal the amazement or disgust that his face aroused in them, and it was not a rare thing for someone, children mostly, to come out with some insulting remark. He didn't appear to mind, and always answered their abuse with a bit of cheerful repartee. The incident as we entered the billiard parlor didn't provoke him, but it did me, since by nature I'm a far cry from an archangel.

The drunk was bending his elbow at the bar. The moment he laid eyes on us, he came staggering over and stood in front of Saúl with arms akimbo. "Son of a bitch! What a monster! What zoo did you escape from?"

"Well, which one would you say, pal? The only one around here, the one in Barranco, of course," Mascarita replied. "If you dash right over, you'll find my cage still open."

And he tried to make his way past. But the drunk stretched

out his hands, making hex signs with his fingers, the way children do when they're called bad names.

"You're not coming in here, monster." He was suddenly furious. "With a face like that, you should keep off the streets. You scare people."

"But if this is the only one I've got, what do you suggest I do?" Saúl said, smiling. "Come on, don't be a drag—let us by."

At that, I lost my patience. I grabbed the toper by the lapels and started shaking him. There was a show of fists, people milling round, some pushing and shoving, and Mascarita and I had to leave without having had our billiard game.

The next day I received a present from him. It was a small bone shaped like a diamond and engraved with a geometric design in a yellowish-brick color. The design represented two parallel mazes made up of bars of different sizes, separated by identical distances, the larger ones seemingly nestled inside the smaller ones. His brief accompanying letter, good-humored and enigmatic, went something like this:

Hi pal,

Let's see if this magic bone calms that impetuosity of yours and you stop punching poor lushes. The bone is from a tapir and the drawing is not the awkward scrawl it appears to be—just a few primitive strokes—but a symbolic inscription. Morenanchiite, the lord of thunder, dictated it to a jaguar, who dictated it to a witch-doctor friend of mine from the forests of the Alto Picha. If you think these symbols are whirlpools in the river or two coiled boa constrictors taking a nap, you may be right. But, above all, they represent the order that reigns in the world. Anyone who lets anger get the better of him distorts these lines, and when they're distorted they can no longer hold up the earth. You wouldn't want life, through your fault, to fall apart and men to return to the original chaos out of which Tasurinchi, the god of good, and Kientibakori, the god of evil, brought us by breathing us out, now would you, pal? So no more tantrums, and especially not because of me. Anyhow, thanks.

Ciao,

Saúl

I asked him to tell me more about the thunder and the tiger, the distorted lines, Tasurinchi and Kientibakori. He had me hanging on his words for an entire afternoon at his house in Breña as he talked to me of the beliefs and customs of a tribe scattered through the jungles of Cusco and Madre de Dios.

I was lying on his bed and he was sitting on a trunk with his parrot on his shoulder. The creature kept nibbling at his bright red hair and interrupting him with its peremptory squawks of "Mascarita!" "You be still now, Gregor Samsa," he soothed him.

The designs on their utensils and their cushmas, the tattoos on their faces and bodies, were neither fanciful nor decorative, pal. They were a coded writing that contained the secret names of people and magic formulas to protect things from damage and their owners from evil spells laid on them through such objects. The patterns were set by a noisy bearded deity, Morenanchiite, the lord of thunder, who in the middle of a storm passed on the key to a tiger from the heights of a mountain peak. The tiger passed it on to a medicine man, or shaman, in the course of a trance brought on by ayahuasca, the hallucinogenic plant, which, boiled into a brew, was drunk at all Indian ceremonies. That witch doctor of Alto Picha—"or, better put, a wise man, chum; I'm calling him a witch doctor so you'll understand what I'm talking about"—had explained to him the philosophy that had allowed the tribe to survive until now. The most important thing to them was serenity. Never to make mountains out of molehills or tempests in teapots. Any sort of emotional upheaval had to be controlled, for there is a fatal correspondence between the spirit of man and the spirits of Nature, and any violent disturbance in the former causes some catastrophe in the latter.

"A man throwing a fit can make a river overflow, and a murder make lightning burn down the village. Perhaps that bus crash on the Avenida Arequipa this morning was caused by your punching that drunk yesterday. Doesn't your conscience trouble you?"

I was amazed at how much he knew about the tribe. And even more so as I realized what a torrent of fellow feeling this knowledge aroused in him. He talked of those Indians, of their customs and myths, of their surroundings and their gods, with the respect and admiration that were mine when I brought up the names of Sartre, Malraux, and Faulkner, my favorite authors that year. I never heard him speak with such emotion even of Kafka, whom he revered, as he did of that tribe of Indians.

I must have suspected even then that Saúl would never be a lawyer, and I suspected also that his interest in the Amazonian Indians was something more than "ethnological." Not a professional, technical interest, but something much more personal, though hard to pin down. Surely more emotional than rational, an act of love rather than intellectual curiosity or the appetite for adventure that seemed to lurk in the choice of career made by so many of his fellow students in the Department of Ethnology. Saúl's attitude toward this new calling, the devotion he manifested for the world of the Amazon, were frequently the subject of conjecture on the campus of the San Marcos Faculty of Letters.

Was Don Salomón aware that Saúl was studying ethnology, or did he think he was concentrating on his law studies? The fact was that, even though Mascarita was still enrolled in the Faculty of Law, he never went to class. With the exception of Kafka, and *The Metamorphosis* in particular, which he had read countless times and virtually knew by heart, all his reading was now in the field of anthropology. I remember his consternation at how little had been written about the tribes and his complaints about how difficult it was to trace down material scattered in various monographs and journals that did not always reach San Marcos or the National Library.

It had all begun, he told me once, with a trip to Quillabamba during the national holidays. He had gone there at the invitation of a relative, a first cousin of his mother's and an uncle of his, who had emigrated from Piura to that region, had a small farm, and also dealt in timber. The man would go deep into the jungle in search of mahogany and rosewood, hiring Indians to clear trails and cut down trees. Mascarita had gotten on well with the Indians—most of them pretty well Westernized—and they had taken him with them on their expeditions and welcomed him in their camps up and down the vast region irrigated by the Alto Urubamba and the Alto Madre de Dios and their respective tributaries. He spent an entire night enthusiastically telling me what it was like to ride a raft hurtling through the Pongo de Mainique, where the Urubamba, squeezed between two foothills of the Cordillera, became a labyrinth of rapids and whirlpools.

"Some of the porters are so terrified they have to be tied to the rafts, the way they do with cows, to get them through the gorge. You can't imagine what it's like, pal!"

A Spanish missionary from the Dominican mission in Quillabamba had shown him mysterious petroglyphs scattered throughout the area; Saúl had eaten monkey, turtle, and grubs and gotten incredibly soused on cassava masato.

"The natives of the region believe the world began in the Pongo de Mainique. And I swear to you there's a sacred aura about the place, something indefinable that makes your hair stand on end. You can't imagine what it's like, pal. Really far out!"

This experience had consequences that no one could have envisaged. Not even Saúl himself, of that I'm sure.

He went back to Quillabamba for Christmas and spent the long year-end vacation there. He returned during the July vacation between terms and again the following December. Every time there was a break at San Marcos, even for only a few days, he'd head for the jungle in anything he could find: trucks, trains, jitneys, buses. He came back from these trips full of enthusiasm and eager to talk, his eyes bright with amazement at the treasures he'd discovered. Everything that came from there interested and excited him tremendously. Meeting the legendary Fidel Pereira, for instance. The son of a white man from Cusco and a Machiguenga woman, he was a mixture of feudal lord and aboriginal cacique. In the last third of the nineteenth century a man from a good Cusco family, fleeing from the law, went deep into those forests, where the Machiguengas had sheltered him. He had married a woman of the tribe. His son, Fidel, lived astride the two cultures, acting like a white when with whites and like a Machiguenga when with Machiguengas. He had several lawfully wedded wives, any number of concubines, and a constellation of sons and daughters, thanks to whom he ran all the coffee plantations and farms between Quillabamba and the Pongo de Mainique, putting the whole tribe to work and paying them next to nothing. But, in spite of that, Mascarita felt a certain liking for him:

"He uses them, of course. But at least he doesn't despise them. He knows all about their culture and is proud of it. And when other people try to trample on them, he protects them."

In the stories he told me, Saúl's enthusiasm made the most trivial happening—clearing a patch of forest or fishing for gamitana—take on heroic dimensions. But, above all, it was the world of the Indians with their primitive practices and their frugal life, their animism and their magic, that seemed to have bewitched him. I now know that those Indians, whose language he had begun to learn with the help of native pupils in the Dominican mission of Quillabamba—he once sang me a sad, repetitive, incomprehensible song, shaking a seed-filled gourd to mark the rhythm—were the Machiguengas. I now know that he had made the posters with their little drawings showing the dangers of fishing with dynamite that I had seen piled up in his house in Breña, to distribute to the whites and mestizos of the Alto Urubamba—the children, grandchildren, nephews, bastards, and stepsons of Fidel Pereira—in the hope of protecting the species of fish that fed those same Indians who, a quarter of a century later, would be photographed by the now deceased Gabriele Malfatti.

With hindsight, knowing what happened to him later—I have thought about this a lot—I can say that Saúl experienced a conversion. In a cultural sense and perhaps in a religious one also. It is the only concrete case I have had occasion to observe from close at hand that has seemed to give meaning to, to make real, what the priests at the school where I studied tried to convey to us during catechism through phrases such as "receiving grace," "being touched by grace," "falling into the snares of grace." From his first contact with the Amazon jungle,

Mascarita was caught in a spiritual trap that made a different person of him. Not just because he lost all interest in law and began working for a degree in ethnology, or because of the new direction his reading took, leaving precisely one surviving literary character, Gregor Samsa, but because from that moment on he began to be preoccupied, obsessed, by two concerns which in the years to come would be his only subjects of conversation: the plight of Amazonian cultures and the death throes of the forests that sheltered them.

"You have a one-track mind these days, Mascarita. A person can't talk with you about anything else lately."

"Pucha! That's true, old buddy. I haven't let you get a word in edgewise. How about a little lecture, if you're so inclined, on Tolstoy, class war, novels of chivalry?"

"Aren't you exaggerating a little, Saúl?"

"No, pal. As a matter of fact, I'm understating. I swear. What's being done in the Amazon is a crime. There's no justification for it, whatever way you look at it. Believe me, man, it's no laughing matter. Put yourself in their place, if only for a second. Where do they have left to go? They've been driven out of their lands for centuries, pushed farther into the interior each time, farther and farther. The extraordinary thing is that, despite so many disasters, they haven't disappeared. They're still there, surviving. Makes you want to take your hat off to them. Damn it all, there I go again! Come on, let's talk about Sartre. What gets my back up is that nobody gives a hoot in hell about what's happening to them."

Why did it matter to him so much? It certainly wasn't for political reasons, at any rate. Politics to Mascarita was the most uninteresting thing in the world. When we talked about politics I was aware that he was making an effort to please me, since at that time I had revolutionary enthusiasms and had taken to reading Marx and talking about the social relations of production. Such subjects bored Saúl as much as the rabbi's sermons did. Nor would it be accurate to say that these subjects interested him on the broad ethical grounds that the plight of the Indians in the jungle mirrored the social iniquities of our country, inasmuch as Saúl did not react in the same way to other injustices closer to home, which he may not even have noticed. The situation of the Andean Indians, for instance—and there were several million of them, instead of the few thousand in the Amazon jungle—or the way middle- and upper-class Peruvians paid and treated their servants.

No, it was only that specific expression of human lack of conscience, irresponsibility, and cruelty, to which the men, the trees, the animals, and the rivers of the jungle had fallen prey, that—for reasons I found hard to understand at the time, as perhaps he did, too—transformed Saúl Zuratas, erasing all other concerns from his mind and turning him into a man with a fixation. With the result that, if he had not been such a good person, so generous and helpful, I would very likely have stopped seeing him. For there was no doubt that he'd become a bore on the subject.

Occasionally, to see how far his obsession might lead him, I would provoke him. What did he suggest, when all was said and done? That, in order not to change the way of life and the beliefs of a handful of tribes still living, many of them, in the Stone Age, the rest of Peru abstain from developing the Amazon region? Should sixteen million Peruvians renounce the natural resources of three-quarters of their national territory so that seventy or eighty thousand Indians could quietly go on shooting at each other with bows and arrows, shrinking heads and worshipping boa constrictors? Should we forgo the agricultural, cattle-raising, and commercial potential of the region so that the world's ethnologists could enjoy studying at first hand kinship ties, potlatches, the rites of puberty, marriage, and death that these human oddities had been practicing, virtually unchanged, for hundreds of years? No, Mascarita, the country had to move forward. Hadn't Marx said that progress would come dripping blood? Sad though it was, it had to be accepted. We had no alternative. If the price to be paid for development and industrialization for the sixteen million Peruvians meant that those few thousand naked Indians would have to cut their hair, wash off their tattoos, and become mestizos—or, to use the ethnologists' most detested word, become acculturated—well, there was no way round it.

Mascarita didn't get angry with me, because he never got angry with anyone about anything, nor did he put on a superior I-forgive-you-for-you-know-not-what-you-say air. But I could feel that when I provoked him in this way I was hurting him as much as if I'd run down Don Salomón Zuratas. He hid it perfectly, I admit. Perhaps he had already achieved the Machiguenga ideal of never feeling anger so that the parallel lines that uphold the earth would not give way. Moreover, he would never discuss this subject, or any other, in a general way, in ideological terms. He had a built-in resistance to any sort of abstract pronouncement. Problems always presented themselves to him in concrete form: what he'd seen with his own eyes, and the consequences that anyone with an ounce of brains in his head could infer from it.

"Fishing with explosives, for example. People assume it's forbidden. But go have a look, pal. There isn't a river or a stream where the mountain people and the Viracochas—that's what they call us white people—don't save time by fishing wholesale with dynamite. Save time! Can you imagine what that means? Charges of dynamite blowing up schools of fish day and night. Whole species are disappearing, old man."

We were talking at a table in the Bar Palermo in La Colmena, drinking beer. Outside, the sun was shining, people hurried past, jalopies honked aggressively, and inside we were surrounded by the smoky atmosphere, smelling of frying oil and urine, typical of all the little cafés in downtown Lima.

"How about fishing with poison, Mascarita? Wasn't that invented by the tribal Indians? That makes them despoilers of the Amazon basin, too."

I said that so he'd fire his heavy artillery at me. And he did, of course. It was untrue, totally untrue. They did fish with barbasco and cumo, but only in the side channels and backwaters of the rivers, or in water holes that remained on islands after the floodwaters had receded. And only at certain times of year. Never in the spawning season, the signs of which they knew by heart. At those times they fished with nets, harpoons, or traps, or with their bare hands. You'd be goggle-eyed if you saw them, pal. On the other hand, the Creoles used barbasco and cumo all year round, and everywhere. Water poisoned thousands of times, decade after decade. Did I realize? Not only did they kill off all the fry at spawning time, but they were rotting the roots of trees and plants along the riverbanks as well.

Did he idealize them? I'm sure he did. And also, perhaps without meaning to, he exaggerated the extent of the disasters so as to reinforce his arguments. But it was evident that for Mascarita all those shad and catfish poisoned by barbasco and cumo, all the paiche destroyed by the fishers of Loreto, Madre de Dios, San Martín, or Amazonas, hurt him neither more nor less than if the victim had been his talking parrot. And, of course, it was the same when he spoke of the extensive tree felling done by order of the timber men—"My uncle Hipólito is one of them, I'm sorry to say"—who were cutting down the most valuable trees. He spoke to me at length of the practices of the Viracochas and the mountain people who had come down from the Andes to conquer the jungle and clear the woods with fires that burn over enormous areas of land, which after one or two crops become barren because of the lack of humus and the erosion caused by rain. Not to mention, pal, the extermination of animals, the frantic greed for hides and skins which, for example, had made of jaguars, lizards, pumas, snakes, and dozens of other species biological rarities on the point of vanishing. It was a long speech that I remember very well on account of something that cropped up at the end of the conversation, after we had polished off several bottles of beer and some cracklings (which he was extremely fond of). From the trees and the fish his peroration always circled back to the main reason for his anxiety: the tribes. At this rate they, too, would die out.

"Seriously, Mascarita, do you think polygamy, animism, head shrinking, and witch doctoring with tobacco brews represent a superior form of culture?"

An Andean boy was throwing bucketfuls of sawdust on the spittle and other filth lying on the red tile floor of the Bar Palermo as a half-breed followed behind him, sweeping up. Saúl looked at me for a long while without answering.

At last he shook his head. "Superior, no. I've never said or thought so, little brother." He was very serious now. "Inferior, perhaps, if the question is posed in terms of infant mortality, the status of women, polygamy or monogamy, handcrafts or industry. Don't think I idealize them. Not in the least."

He fell silent, as though distracted by something, perhaps the quarrel at a neighboring table that had flared up and died down rhythmically since we first sat down. But it wasn't that. Memory had distracted him. Suddenly he seemed sad. "Among the men who walk and those of other tribes there are many things that would shock you very much, old man. I don't deny that."

The fact, for instance, that the Aguarunas and the Huambisas of the Alto Marañón tear out their daughters' hymen at her menarche and eat it, that slavery exists in many tribes, and in some communities they let the old people die at the first signs of weakness, on the pretext that their souls have been called away and their destiny fulfilled. But the worst thing of all, the hardest to accept, perhaps, from our point of view, is what, with a little black humor, could be called the perfectionism of the tribes of the Arawak family. Perfectionism, Saúl? Yes, something that from the outset would appear as cruel to me as it had to him, old buddy. That babies born with physical defects, lame, maimed, blind, with more or fewer fingers than usual, or a harelip, were killed by their own mothers, who threw them in the river or buried them alive. Anybody would naturally be shocked by such customs.

He looked at me for a good while, silent and thoughtful, as if searching for the right words for what he wanted to say to me.

Suddenly he touched his enormous birthmark. "I wouldn't have passed the test, pal. They'd have liquidated me," he whispered. "They say the Spartans did the same thing, right? That little monsters, Gregor Samsas, were hurled down from the top of Mount Taygetus, right?"

He laughed, I laughed, but we both knew that he wasn't joking and that there was no cause for laughter. He explained to me that, curiously enough, though they were pitiless when it came to babies born defective, they were very tolerant with all those, children or adults, who were victims of some accident or illness that damaged them physically. Saúl, at least, had noticed no hostility toward the disabled or the demented in the tribes. His hand was still on the deep purple scab of his half-face.

"But that's the way they are and we should respect them. Being that way has helped them to live in harmony with their forests for hundreds of years. Though we don't understand their beliefs and some of their customs offend us, we have no right to kill them off."

I believe that that morning in the Bar Palermo was the only time he ever alluded, not jokingly but seriously, even dramatically, to what was undoubtedly a tragedy in his life, even though he concealed it with such style and grace: the excrescence that made him a walking incitement to mockery and disgust, and must have affected all his relationships, especially with women. (He was extremely shy with them; I had noticed at San Marcos that he avoided them and only entered into conversation with one of our women classmates if she spoke to him first.) At last he removed his hand from his face with a gesture of annoyance, as though regretting that he had touched the birthmark, and launched into another lecture.

"Do our cars, guns, planes, and Coca-Colas give us the right to exterminate them because they don't have such things? Or do you believe in 'civilizing the savages,' pal? How? By making soldiers of them? By putting them to work on the farms as slaves to Creoles like Fidel Pereira? By forcing them to change their language, their religion, and their customs, the way the missionaries are trying to do? What's to be gained by that? Being able to exploit them more easily, that's all. Making them zombies and caricatures of men, like those semi-acculturated Indians you see in Lima."

. . . 27 . . .

The Andean boy throwing bucketfuls of sawdust on the floor in the Palermo had on the sort of sandals—a sole and two cross-strips cut from an old rubber tire—made and sold by peddlers, and a pair of patched pants held up with a length of rope round his waist. He was a child with the face of an old man, coarse hair, blackened nails, and a reddish scab on his nose. A zombie? A caricature? Would it have been better for him to have stayed in his Andean village, wearing a wool cap with earflaps, leather sandals, and a poncho, never learning Spanish? I didn't know, and I still don't. But Mascarita knew. He spoke without vehemence, without anger, with quiet determination. He explained to me at great length what counterbalanced their cruelty (the price they pay for survival, as he put it): a view of Nature that struck him as an admirable trait in those cultures. It was something that the tribes, despite the many differences between them, all had in common: their understanding of the world in which they were immersed, the wisdom born of long practice which had allowed them, through an elaborate system of rites, taboos, fears, and routines, perpetuated and passed on from father to son, to preserve that Nature, seemingly so superabundant, but actually so vulnerable, upon which they depended for subsistence. These tribes had survived because their habits and customs had docilely followed the rhythms and requirements of the natural world, without doing it violence or disturbing it deeply, just the minimum necessary so as not to be destroyed by it. The very opposite of what we civilized people were doing, wasting those elements without which we would end up withering like flowers without water.

I listened to him and pretended to be taking an interest in what he was saying. But I was really thinking about his birthmark. Why had he suddenly alluded to it while explaining to me his feelings about the Amazonian Indians? Was this the key to Mascarita's conversion? In the Peruvian social order those Shipibos, Huambisas, Aguarunas, Yaguas, Shapras, Campas, Mashcos represented something that he could understand better than anyone else: a picturesque horror, an aberration that other people ridiculed or pitied without granting it the respect and dignity deserved only by those whose physical appearance, customs, and beliefs were "normal." Both he and they were anomalies in the eyes of other Peruvians. His birthmark aroused in them, in us, the same feelings, deep down, as those creatures living somewhere far away, half naked, eating each other's lice and speaking incomprehensible dialects. Was this the origin of Mascarita's love at first sight for the tribal Indians, the "chunchos"? Had he unconsciously identified with those marginal beings because of the birthmark that made him, too, a marginal being, every time he went out on the streets?

I suggested this interpretation to him to see if it put him in a better mood, and in fact he burst out laughing.

"I take it you passed Dr. Guerrita's psych course?" he joked. "I'd have been more likely to flunk you, myself."

And still laughing, he told me that Don Salomón Zuratas, being sharper than I was, had suggested a Jewish interpretation.

"That I'm identifying the Amazonian Indians with the Jewish people, always a minority and always persecuted for their religion and their mores that are different from those of the rest of society. How does that strike you? A far nobler interpretation than yours, which might be called the Frankenstein syndrome. To each madman his own mania, pal."

I retorted that the two interpretations didn't exclude each other. He wound up, highly amused, giving free play to his imagination.

"Okay, supposing you're right. Supposing being half Jewish and half monster has made me more sensitive to the fate of the jungle tribes than someone as appallingly normal as you."

"Poor jungle tribes! You're using them for a crying towel. You're taking advantage of them, too, you know."

"Well, let's leave it at that. I've got a class." He said goodbye as he got up from the table without a trace of the dark mood of a moment before. "But remind me next time to set you straight on those 'poor jungle tribes.' I'll tell you a few things that'll make your hair stand on end. What was done to them, for instance, in the days of the rubber boom. If they could live through that, they don't deserve to be called 'poor savages.' Supermen, rather. Just wait—you'll see."

Apparently he had spoken of his "mania" to Don Salomón. The old man must have come around to accepting the fact that, rather than in halls of justice, Saúl would bring prestige to the name Zuratas in university lecture halls and in the field of anthropological research. Was that what he had decided to be in life? A professor, a researcher? That he had the aptitude I heard confirmed by one of his professors, Dr. José Matos Mar, who was then head of the Department of Ethnology at San Marcos.

"Young Zuratas has turned out to be a first-rate student. He spent the three months of the year-end vacation in the Urubamba region, doing fieldwork with the Machiguengas, and the lad has brought back some excellent material."

He was talking to Raúl Porras Barrenechea, a historian with whom I worked in the afternoons, who had a holy horror of ethnology and anthropology, which he accused of replacing man by artifacts as the focal point of culture, and of butchering Spanish prose (which, let it be said in passing, he himself wrote beautifully).

"Well then, let's make a historian of the young man and not a classifier of bits of stone, Dr. Matos. Don't be selfish. Hand him on to me in the History Department."

The work Saúl did in the summer of '56 among the Machiguengas later became, in expanded form, his thesis for his bachelor's degree. He defended it in our fifth year at San Marcos, and I can remember clearly the expression of pride and deep personal happiness on Don Salomón's face. Dressed for the occasion in a starched shirt under his jacket, he watched the ceremony from the front row of the auditorium, and his little eyes shone as Saúl read out his conclusions, answered the questions of the jury, headed by Matos Mar, had his thesis accepted, and was draped in the academic sash he had thus earned.

Don Salomón invited Saul and me to lunch, at the Raimondi in downtown Lima, to celebrate the event. But he himself didn't touch a single mouthful, perhaps so as not to transgress the Jewish dietary laws inadvertently. (One of Saúl's jokes when ordering cracklings or shellfish was: "And besides, the idea of committing a sin as I swallow them down gives them a very special taste, pal. A taste you'll never know.") Don Salomón was bursting with pleasure at his son's brand-new degree.

Halfway through lunch he turned to me and begged me, in earnest tones, in his guttural Central European accent: "Convince your friend he should accept the scholarship." And noting the look of surprise on my face, he explained: "He doesn't want to go to Europe, so as not to leave me alone—as though I weren't old enough to know how to look after myself! I've told him that if he insists on being so foolish, he's going to force me to die so that he can go off to France to specialize with his mind at rest."

That was how I found out that Matos Mar had gotten Saúl a fellowship to study for a doctorate at the University of Bordeaux. Not wanting to leave his father all by himself, Mascarita had refused it. Was that really the reason why he didn't go off to Bordeaux? I believed it at the time; today I'm sure he was lying. I know now, though he confessed it to no one and kept his secret under lock and key, that his conversion had continued to work its way within him until it had taken on the lineaments of a mystical ecstasy, perhaps even of a seeking after martyrdom. I have no doubt, today, that he took the trouble to write a thesis and obtain a bachelor's degree in ethnology just to please his father, knowing the while that he would never be an ethnologist. Though at the time I was wearing myself out trying to land some sort of fellowship that would get me to Europe, I attempted several times to persuade him not to waste such an opportunity. "It's something that won't come your way again, Mascarita. Europe! France! Don't throw a chance like that away, man!" His mind was made up, once and for all: he couldn't go, he was the only one Don Salomón had in the world and he wasn't going to abandon him for two or three years, knowing what an elderly man his father was.

Naturally I believed him. The one who didn't believe him at all was the one who had secured him his fellowship and had such high academic hopes for him: his professor, Matos Mar. The latter appeared one afternoon, as was his habit, at Professor Porras Barrenechea's to exchange ideas and have tea and biscuits, and told him the news:

"You win, Dr. Porras. The History Department can fill the Bordeaux fellowship this year. Our candidate has turned it down. What do you make of all this?"

"As far as I know, it's the first time in the history of San Marcos that a student has refused a fellowship to France," Porras said. "What in the world got into the boy?"

I was there in the room where they were talking, taking notes on the myths of El Dorado and the Seven Cities of Cibola as set down by the chroniclers of the Discovery and the Conquest, and I put my oar in to say that the reason for Saúl's refusal was Don Salomón and his not wanting to leave him all by himself.

"Yes, that's the reason Zuratas gives, and I wish it were true," Matos Mar said, with a skeptical wave of his hand. "But I'm afraid there's something far deeper than that. Saúl's starting to have doubts about research and fieldwork. Ethical doubts."

Porras Barrenechea thrust his chin out and his little eyes had the sly expression they always had when he was about to make a nasty remark.

"Well, if Zuratas has realized that ethnology is a pseudoscience invented by gringos to destroy the Humanities, he's more intelligent than one might have expected."

But this did not raise a smile from Matos Mar.

"I'm serious, Dr. Porras. It's a pity, because the boy has outstanding qualities. He's intelligent, perceptive, a fine researcher, a hard worker. And yet he's taken it into his head, can you believe it, that the work we're doing is immoral."

"Immoral? Well, when it comes right down to it, who can tell what you're up to there among the good old chunchos, under cover of prying into their customs?" Porras laughed. "I myself wouldn't swear to the virtue of ethnologists."

"He's convinced that we're attacking them, doing violence to their culture," Matos Mar went on, paying no attention to him. "That with our tape recorders and ball-point pens we're the worm that works its way into the fruit and rots it."

He then recounted how, a few days before, there had been a meeting in the Department of Ethnology, at which Saúl Zuratas had flabbergasted everyone, proclaiming that the consequences of the ethnologists' work were similar to those of the activities of the rubber tappers, the timber cutters, the army recruiters, and other mestizos and whites who were decimating the tribes.

"He maintained that we've taken up where the colonial missionaries left off. That we, in the name of science, like them in the name of evangelization, are the spearhead of the effort to wipe out the Indians."

"Is he reviving the fanatical Indigenista movement to save Indian cultures that swept over the campus of San Marcos in the thirties?" Porras sighed. "I wouldn't be surprised. It comes in waves, like flu epidemics. I can already see Zuratas penning pamphlets against Pizarro, the Spanish Conquest, and the crimes of the Inquisition. No, I don't want him in the History Department! Let him accept the fellowship, take out French citizenship, and make his name furthering the Black Legend!"

I didn't pay much attention to what I heard Matos Mar say that afternoon amid the dusty shelves covered with books and busts of Don Quixote and Sancho Panza, in Porras Barrenechea's Miraflor house in the Calle Colina. And I don't think I mentioned it to Saúl. But today, here in Firenze, as I remember and jot down notes, this episode takes on considerable meaning in retrospect. That fellow feeling, that solidarity, that spell, or whatever it may have been, had by then reached a climax and assumed a different nature. In the eyes of the ethnologists—about whom the least that could be said was that, however shortsighted they might be, they were perfectly aware of the need to understand the jungle Indians' way of seeing in their own terms—what was it that Mascarita was defending? Was it something as chimerical as the recognition of their inalienable right to their lands, whereupon the rest of Peru would agree to place the jungle under quarantine? Must no one, ever, have the right to enter it, so as to keep those cultures from being contaminated by the miasmas of our own degenerated one? Had Saúl's purism concerning the Amazon reached such extremes?

The fact was that we saw very little of each other during our last months at San Marcos. I was all wrapped up in writing my thesis, and he had virtually given up his law studies. I met him very infrequently, on the rare occasions when he put in an appearance at the Department of Literature, in those days next door to the Department of Ethnology. We would have a cup of coffee, or smoke a cigarette together while talking under the yellowing palms outside the main building on campus. As we grew to adulthood and became involved in different activities and projects, our friendship, quite close in the first years, evolved into a sporadic and superficial relationship. I asked him questions about his travels, for he was always just back from or just about to set out for the jungle, and I associated this—until Matos Mar's remarks to Dr. Porras—with his work at the university or his increasing specialization in Amazonian cultures. But, except for our last conversation—that of our taking leave of each other, and his diatribe against the Institute of Linguistics and the Schneils—I think it is true to say that in those last months we never again had those endless dialogues, with both of us speaking our minds freely and frankly, that had been so frequent between 1953 and 1956.

If we had kept them up, would he have opened his heart to me and allowed me to glimpse what his intentions were? Most likely not. The sort of decision arrived at by saints and madmen is not revealed to others. It is forged little by little, in the folds of the spirit, tangential to reason, shielded from indiscreet eyes, not seeking the approval of others—who would never grant it—until it is at last put into practice. I imagine that in the process—the conceiving of a project and its ripening into action—the saint, the visionary, or the madman isolates himself more and more, walling himself up in solitude, safe from the intrusion of others. I for my part never even suspected that Mascarita, during the last months of our life at San Marcos—we were both adults by then—could be going through such an inner upheaval. That he was more withdrawn than other mortals or, more probably, became more reserved on leaving adolescence behind, I had indeed noticed. But I put it down entirely to his face, interposing its terrible ugliness between himself and the world, making his relationship with others difficult. Was he still the laughing, likable, easygoing person of previous years? He had become more serious and laconic, less open than before, it seems to me. But there I don't quite trust my memory. Perhaps he went on being the same smiling, talkative Mascarita whom I knew in 1953, and my imagination has changed him so as to make him conform more closely to the other one, the one of future years whom I did not know, whom I must invent, since I have given in to the cursed temptation of writing about him.

I am certain, however, that memory does not fail me as far as his dress and his physical appearance are concerned. That bright red hair, with its wild, uncombed tuft on the crown of his head, flaming and unruly, dancing above his bipartite face, the untouched side of it pale and freckled. Bright, shining eyes, and shining teeth. He was tall and thin, and I am quite sure that, except on his graduation day, I never spotted him wearing a tie. He always wore cheap coarse cotton sport shirts, over which he threw some bright-colored sweater in winter, and faded, wrinkled jeans. His heavy shoes never saw a brush. I don't think he confided in anyone or had any really intimate friends. His other friendships were most likely similar to the one between the two of us, very cordial but fairly superficial. Acquaintances, yes, many, at San Marcos, and also, doubtless, in the neighborhood where he lived. But I could swear that no one ever heard, from his own lips, what was happening to him and what he intended to do. If in fact he had planned it carefully, and it hadn't just happened, gradually, imperceptibly, the product of chance circumstances rather than the result of personal choice. I have thought about it a lot these last years, and of course I'll never know.

AFTER, the men of earth started walking, straight toward the sun that was falling. Before, they too stayed in the same place without moving. The sun, their eye of the sky, was fixed. Wide awake, always open, looking at us, warming the world. Its light was very strong, but Tasurinchi could withstand it. There was no evil, there was no wind, there was no rain. The women bore pure children. If Tasurinchi wanted to eat, he dipped his hand into the river and brought out a shad flicking its tail; or he loosed an arrow without aiming, took a few steps into the jungle, and soon came across a little wild turkey, a partridge, or a trumpet-bird brought down by his arrow. There was never any lack of food. There was no war. The rivers were full of fish, the forests of animals. The Mashcos didn't exist. The men of earth were strong, wise, serene and united. They were peaceable and without anger. Before the time afterwards.

Those who went came back, and entered the spirit of the best. That way, nobody used to die. "It's time I departed," Tasurinchi would say. He would go down to the riverbank and make his bed of leaves and dry branches, with a roof of ungurabi overhead. He would put up a fence of sharp-pointed canes all round to keep the capybaras prowling about on the shore of the river from eating his corpse. He would lie down, go away, and soon after come back, taking up his abode in the man who had hunted most, fought best, or faithfully followed the customs. The men of earth lived together. In peace and quiet. Death was not death. It was going away and coming back. Instead of weakening them, it made them stronger, adding to those who remained the wisdom and the strength of those who went. "We are and we shall be," said Tasurinchi. "It seems that we are not going to die. Those who went have come back. They are here. They are us."

Then why, if they were so pure, did the men of earth begin walking? Because one day the sun started falling. They walked so that it wouldn't fall any farther, to help it to rise. So Tasurinchi says.

That, anyway, is what I have learned.

Had the sun yet fought its war with Kashiri, the moon? Perhaps. It began blinking, moving, its light dimmed, and you could hardly see it. People started rubbing their bodies, shivering. That was the cold. That's how after began, it seems. Then, in the half darkness, confused, frightened, men fell into their own traps, they ate deer meat thinking it was tapir, they could not find the path from the cassava patch to their own house. Where am I? they said in despair, walking like blind men, stumbling. Where can my family be? What is happening to the world? The wind had begun to blow. Howling, buffeting, making off with the tops of the palm trees and pulling the lupunas up by the roots. The rain fell with a roar, causing floods. You could see herds of drowned huanganas, floating feet up in the current. Rivers changed course, rafts broke up on the dams, ponds turned into rivers. Souls lost their serenity. That was no longer going. It was dying. Something must be done, they said. Looking left and right, what? What shall we do? they said. "Start walking," Tasurinchi ordered. They were in total darkness, surrounded by evil. The cassava was beginning to give out, the water stank. Those who went no longer came back, frightened away by the disasters, lost between the world of the clouds and our world. Beneath the ground they walked on, they could hear the slow-moving Kamabiría, the river of the dead, flowing. Seeming to come closer, seeming to call to them. Start walking? "Yes," said the seripigari, falling into a tobacco trance. "Walk, keep walking. And remember this. The day you stop walking, you will disappear completely. Dragging the sun down with you."

That's how it started. Moving, walking. Keeping on, with or without rain, by land or by water, climbing up the mountain slopes or climbing down the ravines. Amid forests so dense that it was night in the daytime, and plains so bare they looked like pampas, without a single bush, like the head of a man that a little kamagarini devil has left completely bald. "The sun hasn't fallen yet," Tasurinchi encouraged them. "It trips and gets up again. Watch your step, it's dozed off. We must wake it up, we must help it. We have suffered evil and death, but we keep on walking. Would all the sparks in the sky be enough to count the moons that have passed? No. We are alive. We are moving."

So as to live walking, they had to travel light, stripping themselves of everything that was theirs. Dwellings, animals, seed, the abundance all round them. The little beach where they used to flip salty-fleshed turtles over on their backs, the forest bubbling with singing birds. They kept what was essential and started walking. Was their march through the forest a punishment? No, a celebration, rather, like going fishing or hunting in the dry season. They kept their bows and arrows, their horns full of poison, their hollow canes of annatto dye, their knives, their drums, the cushmas they were wearing, the pouches, and the strips of cloth to carry the children. The newborn were born walking, the old died walking. When the morning light dawned, the undergrowth was already rustling as they passed; they were already walking, walking, in single file, the men with their weapons at the ready, the women carrying the baskets and trays, the eyes of each and all fixed on the sun. We haven't lost our way yet. Our determination must have kept us pure. The sun hasn't fallen once and for all; it hasn't stopped falling yet. It goes and it comes back, like the souls of the fortunate. It heats the world. The people of the earth haven't fallen, either. Here we are. I in the middle, you all around me. I talking, you listening. We live, we walk. That is happiness, it seems.

But before, they had to sacrifice themselves for this world. Bear catastrophes, sufferings, evils that would have been the end of any other people.

That time, the men who walk halted to rest. In the night the jaguar roared and the lord of thunder rolled his hoarse thunder. There were bad omens. Butterflies invaded the huts and the women had to flap straw mats at them to chase them away from the trays of food. They heard the owl and the chícua screech. What is going to happen? they said, alarmed. During the night the river rose so high that at dawn they found themselves surrounded by roiling waters carrying along logs, small trees, weeds, and corpses being smashed to bits as they crashed against the banks. They hastily felled trees, improvised rafts and canoes before the flood swallowed the desolate island the earth had become. They had to shove their craft into the muddy waters and start paddling. They paddled and paddled, and while some pushed on the poles others cried out, signaling on the right a dam approaching, on the left the mouth of a whirlpool, and over there, over there, a flick of the tail of the cunning yacumama, lying very still beneath the water, waiting for the right moment to overturn the canoe and swallow the paddlers. Deep in the forest, the lord of demons, Kientibakori, crazy with joy, drank masato and danced in the middle of a crowd of kamagarinis. Many went, drowned in the flood when a tree trunk, invisible beneath the floodwaters, split open a raft and families were swept away.

Those didn't come back. Their bodies, bloated and nibbled at by piranhas, would sometimes turn up on a beach or dangling in shreds from the roots of a tree by the riverbank. Appearances don't deceive. The ones who went like that, went. Did the seripigaris know that then? Who knows whether wisdom had yet appeared? Once birds and beasts have eaten its shell, the soul can't find its way back, it seems. It stays lost in some world, it becomes a little kamagarini devil and goes down to join those below, or it becomes a little saankarite god and goes up to the worlds above. That's why, before, they mistrusted rivers, lakes, and even side channels that weren't very deep. That's why they plied the rivers only when all the other ways were closed. Because they didn't want to die, perhaps. Water is treacherous, it's said. To go away by drowning is to die, no doubt.

That, anyway, is what I have learned.

The bottom of the river in the Gran Pongo is strewn with our corpses. There must be a very great number of them. There they were breathed forth and there they no doubt return to die. That's where they must be, far below the surface, hearing the water moan as it crashes against the stones and dashes against the sharp rocks. That's why there are no turtles above the Pongo, in the mountain reaches. They're good swimmers, but even so, not one of them has ever been able to swim against the current in those waters. The ones that tried drowned. They, too, must be at the bottom now, hearing the shudders of the world above. That's where we Machiguengas started and that's where we'll end, it seems. In the Gran Pongo.

Others went fighting. There are many ways of fighting. Back then, the men who walk had paused to get back their strength. They were so tired they could hardly talk. They halted in a stretch of forest that seemed safe. They cleared it, built their houses, wove their roofs. It was a place high up and they thought the waters sent by Kientibakori to drown them wouldn't reach there, or if they did, they would see them in time and could escape. After clearing and burning off the forest, they planted cassava and sowed maize and plantain. There was wild cotton to weave cushmas, and tobacco plants, whose smell kept vipers away. Macaws came and chattered on their shoulders. Jaguar cubs sucked at the women's nipples. Women about to give birth went deep into the forest, bathed, and came back with infants who moved their hands and feet, whimpering, pleased by the gentle warmth of the sun. There were no Mashcos. Kashiri, the moon, caused no evils yet; he'd already been on earth, teaching people how to grow cassava. He had sown his bad seed, perhaps. People did not know. Everything seemed to be going well.

Then one night a vampire bit Tasurinchi as he slept. It sank its two fangs into his face, and even though he hit it with his fists, it wouldn't let him go. He had to tear it to pieces, smearing himself with its soft bones, sticky as shit. "It's a warning," said Tasurinchi. What did the warning say? Nobody understood it. Wisdom was lost or hadn't yet come. They didn't go away. They stayed there, frightened, waiting. Before the cassava and the maize grew, before the plantains bore fruit, the Mashcos came. They didn't sense their coming, they didn't hear the music of their monkey-skin drums. Suddenly arrows, darts, stones rained down on them. Suddenly great flames burned their houses down. Before they could defend themselves, the enemy had cut off many heads and carried off many women. And taken away all the baskets of salt they had gone to the Cerro to fill. Did the ones who went like that come back, or did they die? Who knows? They died perhaps. Their spirit went to give more fury and more strength to their despoilers, perhaps. Or are they still there, wandering helplessly about the forest?

Who knows how many have not returned? Those who were killed by arrows or stones, or fell trembling from poisoned darts and bad trances. Each time the Mashcos attacked and he saw the people set upon, Tasurinchi pointed to the sky, saying: "The sun is falling. We have done something wrong. We have become corrupt, staying so long in one place. Custom must be respected. We must become pure again. Let us keep walking." And wisdom returned, happily, just as they were about to disappear. So then they forgot about the fields they had sown, their houses, everything that could not be carried in their pouches. They put on their necklaces and their headdresses, burned the rest, and beating their drums, dancing and singing, they started walking. Once again, once again. Then the sun stopped falling down the sky worlds. Suddenly they felt it waking up, in a fury. "Now it's heating the world again," they said. "We're alive," they said. And they went on walking.

So, that time, the men who walk reached the Cerro. There it was. So high, so pure, rising, rising up to Menkoripatsa, the white world of the clouds. Five rivers flowed, dancing amid the salty stones. Around the Cerro were little groves of yellow ichu, with doves and partridges, with playful mice and ants that tasted of honey. The rocks were salt, the ground was salt, the river bottoms, too, were salt. The men of earth filled their baskets and their pouches and their nets, at peace, knowing that the salt would never run out. They were happy, it seems. They went away, they came back, and the salt had increased. There was always salt for those who went up to collect it. Many went up, Ashaninkas, Amueshas, Piros, Yaminahuas. The Mashcos went up. Everyone knew the Cerro. We arrived and the enemy was there. We didn't fight each other. There were no wars or massacres, only respect, they say. That, anyway, is what I have learned. And maybe it's true. Just as with the salt licks, just as with the water holes. In the hidden places in the forest where the earth is salty and they go to lick it, do animals fight each other? Who has ever seen a sajino attack a majaz, or a capybara bite a shimbillo at a salt lick? They don't do anything to each other. There they meet and there they stay, each one in its place, quietly licking the salt or the water from the ground until they've had their fill. Is it not a good thing to find a salt lick or a water hole? How easy it is to hunt the animals then. There they are, at peace, trustful, licking. They pay no attention to the stones; they don't flee when the arrows whistle. They fall easily. The Cerro was the salt lick of men, their great water hole. Perhaps it had its own magic. The Ashaninkas say that it is sacred, that spirits speak within the stone. That may be so; perhaps they talk together. They arrived with baskets and pouches and nobody hunted them. They looked at each other, that was all. There was salt and respect for everyone.

After, it was no longer possible to go up to the Cerro. After, they had to do without salt. After, anyone who went up there was hunted. Bound fast and carried off to the camps. That was the tree-bleeding. Get on with it, damn you! After, the earth was filled with Viracochas tracking down men. They carried them off to bleed trees and tote rubber. Get a move on, damn you! The camps were worse than the darkness and the rains, it seems; worse than the time of evil and the Mashcos. We were very lucky. Aren't we still walking? The Viracochas were cunning, they say. They knew people would go up with their baskets and nets to collect salt on the Cerro. They lay in wait for them with traps and shot at them. They carried off the ones who fell. Ashaninkas, Piros, Amahuacas, Yaminahuas, Mashcos. They had no preferences. Anyone who fell, if they had hands to bleed the tree, fingers to tear it open, stick a tin in it, and collect its milk, shoulders to carry, and feet to run with the balls of gum elastic to the camp. A few escaped perhaps. Very few, they say. It wasn't easy. You had to do more than run, you had to fly. Die, damn you! A bullet brought down the ones who tried to get away. One dead Machiguenga, damn you! "It's no use trying to escape from the camps," said Tasurinchi. "The Viracochas have their magic. Something is happening to us. We must have done something. The spirits protect them, and us they abandon. We are guilty of something. It's better to stick a chambira thorn into yourself or drink cumo juice. Going like that, from a thorn or poison, of your own free will, there's hope of coming back. Those who go from a rifle bullet don't come back. They stay floating on the river Kamabiría, dead amid the dead, forever." It seemed that men were going to disappear. But aren't we fortunate? Here we are. Still walking, still happy. After that time they never went to collect salt on the Cerro again. It must still be there, very high up, its pure soul looking the sun in the face.

That, anyway, is what I have learned.

Tasurinchi, the one who lives at the bend in the river, the one who used to live by the lagoon where, at low water, in the dry season, so many turtles turn up half dead, is walking. I went and saw him. I blew my hunting horn from a long way off to let him know I was coming to visit him, and then when

I was closer I let him know by shouting: "I've come! I've come!" My little parrot repeated: "I've come! I've come!" He didn't turn up to greet me, so I thought he might have gone to live somewhere else and my journey there had been for nothing. No, his house was still there, alongside the bend in the river. I stood in front of it with my back turned, waiting for him to receive me. I had to wait a long time. He was down at the river, hollowing out a tree trunk to make himself a canoe.

While I waited for him I watched his wife. Seated at her loom close by, she was dyeing strands of wild cotton with pounded palillo roots. She didn't get up or look at me. She went on working as though I hadn't arrived or were invisible. She was wearing more necklaces than the last time. "Do you wear that many necklaces so as to keep the little kamagarini devils away, or so that the machikanari witch can't cast spells on you?" I asked her. But she didn't answer and went on dyeing the strands of cotton as though she hadn't heard me. She was also wearing many ornaments on her arms and ankles and on the shoulders and the front of her cushma. Her headdress was a rainbow of macaw, toucan, parrot, cashew bird, and pavita kanari feathers.

At last Tasurinchi arrived. "I'm here," I said to him. "Are you there?" "Here I am," he answered, pleased to see me, and my parrot repeated: "I am, I am." Then his wife rose to her feet and unrolled two mats for us to sit on. She brought a pot of freshly roasted cassava that she emptied out onto plantain leaves, and a little jar of masato. She, too, seemed pleased to see me. We went on talking till the next moon, without stopping.

His wife was heavy with child and this time it would be born at the right time and wouldn't be lost. A little god had told the seripigari so, in a trance. And he had told him that this time, if the child died before it was born, like the other times, it would be the woman's fault and not a kamagarini's. In that trance the seripigari found out many things. The other times the children were born dead because she'd swallowed a brew to make them die inside her and push them out before it was time. "Is that so?" I asked his wife. And she answered: "I don't remember. Perhaps so. Who knows?" "Yes, it's true," Tasurinchi assured me. "I've warned her that if the child is born dead this time, I'll kill her." "If it's born dead he'll thrust a poisoned dart in me and leave my body down by the riverside so the capybaras will eat me," his wife confirmed. She laughed. She wasn't afraid but, rather, seemed to be making mock of us.

I asked Tasurinchi why he so badly wanted his wife to bear a child. It wasn't the child he cared about; he was worried about her. "Isn't it strange that all her children are born dead?" he said. He asked her again in front of me: "You pushed them out dead because you drank a brew?" She repeated what she had said to me: "I don't remember." "Sometimes I think she's not a woman but a she-devil, a sopai," Tasurinchi confessed to me. It's not just because of this business about children that he thinks she's got a different sort of soul. It's also all those bracelets, necklaces, headdresses, and ornaments she wears. And it's true. I've never seen anyone with so many things on their body or on their cushma. Who knows how she can walk with all that weighing her down? "Look at what she's got on now," Tasurinchi said. He made the woman come close and pointed: seed bangles, rows of necklaces of partridge bones, capybara teeth, monkey femurs, majaz fangs, caterpillar skins, and many other things I can't remember. "She says the necklaces protect her from the bad sorcerer, the machikanari," Tasurinchi told me. "But sometimes, looking at her, it seems more likely she's a machikanari herself, concocting a spell against someone." She laughed and said she didn't think she was a witch or a she-devil, but only a woman, just like the others.

Tasurinchi wouldn't mind being by himself if he killed his wife. "Rather that than go on living with someone who can steal every last piece of my soul," he explained. But I thought that wouldn't happen, since according to what the seripigari found out in the trance, the child would be born walking this time. "Maybe that's how it will be," I heard his wife say, laughing uproariously without raising her eyes from the strands of cotton. They are well, both of them. Walking. Tasurinchi gave me this little net woven of wild cotton fibers. "To catch fish with," he said. He also gave me some cassava and maize. "Aren't you afraid to journey alone?" he asked me. "We Machiguengas always go through the forest in company, because of what we might meet on the way." "I have company, too," I said. "Can't you see my little parrot?" "Parrot, parrot," the little parrot repeated.

I told all this to Tasurinchi, the one who used to live by the Mitaya and now lives in the forest up the Yavero. Lost in thought, reflecting, he commented: "I don't understand it. Is he afraid his wife is a sopai because she pushes out dead children? The women here must be she-devils too, then, because they give birth not only to dead babies but to toads and lizards as well sometimes. Who has taught that a woman is a bad witch because she wears many necklaces? It is a teaching unknown to me. The machikanari is an evil sorcerer because he serves the breather-out of demons, Kientibakori, and because the kamagarinis, who are his little devils, help him prepare spells, just as the seripigari, who is a good sorcerer, is helped by the little gods that Tasurinchi breathed out to cure evils, to undo spells, and to discover the truth. But both the machikanaris and the seripigaris wear necklaces, as far as I know."

At that, the women burst out laughing. It couldn't be true that they push out dead babies, for there was an ant-heap of little ones, there in that hut by the Yavero. "There are many mouths," Tasurinchi complained. Before, by the Mitaya, fish always fell into the nets, even though the land wasn't good for growing cassava. But where he's settled now, far up one of the streams that empty into the Yavero, there are no fish. It's a dark place, full of toads and armadillos. Damp earth that rots plants.

I've always known that armadillo meat must not be eaten because the armadillo has an impure mother and brings harm; spots come out all over the body of anybody who eats it. But there they ate it. The women skinned an armadillo and then roasted its meat, cut up in small chunks. Tasurinchi put a piece in my mouth with his fingers. I was so scared I had a hard time swallowing it down. It doesn't seem to have done me any harm. If it had, I might not be here walking, perhaps.

"Why did you go so far, Tasurinchi?" I asked him. "I had trouble finding you. What's more, the Mashcos live in this region, quite close to here." "You went around to my place on the Mitaya and didn't meet up with Viracochas?" he said in surprise. "They're everywhere down there. Especially on the riverbank opposite where I used to live."

Strangers started using the river, going up and coming down, coming down and going up, many moons ago. There were Punarunas, come down from the sierra, and many Viracochas. They weren't just passing through. They stayed. They've built cabins and cut down trees. They hunt animals with guns that thunder in the forest. Some men who walk also came with them. The ones who live high up, on the other side of the Gran Pongo, the ones who have already given up being men and have more or less taken up Viracocha ways of dressing and talking. They'd come down to help them, there along the Mitaya. They came to visit Tasurinchi. Trying to persuade him to go to work with them, clearing the forest and carrying stones for a road they were opening up along the river. "The Viracochas won't hurt you," they encouraged him, saying: "Bring the women along too, to prepare your food for you. Look at us—have they done us any harm, would you say? It's no longer like the tree-bleeding. In those days, yes, the Viracochas were devils. They wanted to bleed us like they bled the trees. They wanted to steal our souls. It's different now. With these, you work as long as you like. They give you food, they give you a knife, they give you a machete, they give you a harpoon to fish with. If you stay on, you can have a gun."

The ones who had been men seemed happy, perhaps. "We're lucky people," they said. "Look at us, touch us. Don't you want to be like us? Learn, then. Do like us, then." Tasurinchi allowed himself to be persuaded. "All right," he said, "I'll go have a look." And crossing the river Mitaya, he went with them to the Viracochas' camp. And discovered, there and then, that he'd fallen into a trap. He was surrounded by devils. What made you realize that, Tasurinchi? Because the Viracocha who was explaining to him what it was he wanted him to do—and it wasn't easy to understand—suddenly, just like that, showed the filth of his soul. How so, Tasurinchi? What happened? The Viracocha had been asking him: "Are you any good with a machete?" when all of a sudden he broke off, just like that, with his face all puckered up. He opened his mouth wide, and achoo! achoo! achoo! Three times running, it seems. His eyes got all teary, red as a candle flame. Tasurinchi had never been that scared in his whole life. I'm seeing a kamagarini, he thought. That's what its face looks like; that's the noise it makes. I'm going to die, this very day. As he was thinking, It's a devil, a devil, he felt little drops all over him, as though he'd just come out of the water. The cold made his bones creak, and he saw himself from inside, as in a trance. He had to make the greatest effort of his life, he said, to force himself to move. His legs wouldn't obey him, he was shaking so hard. At last he was able to move. The Viracocha was talking again, not realizing he'd given himself away. A stream of green snot ran out his nostrils. He went on talking as though nothing had happened—the way I'm talking right now. He was surprised, no doubt, to see Tasurinchi running away, leaving him standing there with his words in his mouth. Those who had been men and were standing close by tried to stop Tasurinchi. "Don't be scared, nothing's going to happen to you," they said, trying to deceive him. "He's sneezing, that's all. It doesn't kill them. They've got their own medicine." Tasurinchi got into his canoe, pretending: "Yes, all right. I've got to go home, but I'll be back, wait for me." His teeth were still chattering, it seems. They're devils, he thought. I'm going to die today, perhaps.

As soon as he reached the other side of the river, he gathered the women and children together: "Evil has come. We are surrounded by kamagarinis," he told them. "We must go far away. Let us go. It may not be too late. We may still be able to walk." That's what they did, and now they are living in this gorge, deep in the forest, a long way from the Yavero. According to him the Viracochas won't come that far. Nor the Mashcos either; even they couldn't get used to a place like this. "Only we men who walk can live in places like this," he said with pride. He was pleased to see me. "I was afraid you'd never come this far to visit me," he said. The women, picking about in each other's hair, kept saying: "We're lucky we escaped. What would have become of our souls otherwise?" They, too, seemed pleased to see me. We ate and drank and talked for many moons. They didn't want me to leave. "How can you go?" said Tasurinchi. "You're not through talking yet. Keep on talking. You've a lot to tell me still." If he'd had his way, I'd be there in the Yavero forest still, talking.

He's not finished building his house yet. But he's already cleared the land, cut the poles and the palm fronds, and gathered bundles of straw for the roof. He had to fetch all this from farther down because where he is there aren't any palm trees or straw. A young man who wants to marry one of his daughters is living nearby and helping Tasurinchi find a plot of ground higher up where he can plant cassava. It's full of scorpions and they're getting rid of them by blowing smoke down the holes of their hiding places. There are also many bats at night. They've already bitten one of the children who left the fireside in his sleep. He says that up there the bats go out to look for food even when it's raining, something that's never been seen anywhere else. The Yavero is country where the animals have different habits. "I'm still getting to know them," Tasurinchi told me. "Life gets difficult when a person goes to live somewhere else," I said. "So it does," he said. "Luckily we know how to walk. Luckily we've been walking for such a long time. Luckily we're always moving from one place to another. What would have become of us if we were the sort of people who never move! We'd have disappeared who knows where. That's what happened to many in the days of the tree-bleeding. There are no words to express how fortunate we are."

"Next time you visit Tasurinchi, remind him that it's the man who goes achoo! who's a devil and not the woman who gives birth to dead children or wears many bright-colored necklaces," Tasurinchi mocked, making the women laugh. And he told me this story that I'm going to tell you. It happened many moons ago, when the first White Fathers started turning up on this side of the Gran Pongo. They were already settled on the other side, farther up. They had houses in Koribeni and Chirumbia, but they hadn't come this way, downstream. The first one to cross the Gran Pongo went to the river Timpía, knowing that there were men who walk there. He'd learned how to speak. He spoke, it seems. You could understand what he meant. He asked lots of questions. He stayed on there. They helped him to burn off the land, put his house up, clear a field. He came and went. He brought food, fishhooks, machetes. The men who walk got on well with him. They seemed happy. The sun was in its place, peaceful. But on returning from one of his journeys the White Father had changed his soul, even though his face was the same. He'd become a kamagarini and brought evil. But nobody noticed, and because of that, nobody started walking. They'd lost wisdom, perhaps. That, anyway, is what I have learned.

The White Father was lying on his straw mat and they could see him making faces. Achoo! Achoo! When they came to ask him "What's the matter? Why are you puckering your face up like that? What's that noise?" he answered, "It's nothing, it'll soon be over." Evil had entered everyone's soul. Children, women, old men. And also, so they say, macaws, cashew birds, little mountain pigs, partridges, all the animals they had. They, too: Achoo! Achoo! At first they laughed, thinking it was some sort of playful trance. They beat their chests and pushed each other in fun. And screwing up their faces: Achoo! Snot ran out their noses, spittle out their mouths. They spat and laughed. But they could no longer start walking. The time had passed.

Their souls, broken in pieces, had begun leaving their bodies through the tops of their heads. All they could do was resign themselves to what was going to happen.

They felt as though a fire had been lighted inside their bodies. They were burning up, they were aflame. They bathed in the river, but instead of putting out the fire, the water made it worse. Then they felt a terrible chill, as though they'd been in a downpour all night. Though the sun was there, looking with its yellow eye, they shivered, frightened, dizzy, as in a trance or a drunken stupor, not seeing what they saw, not recognizing what they knew. Raging, sensing that the evil was deep within them, like a chigger under the nail. They had not heeded the warning, they had not started walking at the first achoo! from the White Father. Even the lice died, it seems. The ants, the beetles, the spiders that went near there died, they say. Nobody, ever, has gone back to live in that place by the river Timpía. Though no one really knows where it is now, because the forest grew over it again. It's best not to go anywhere near it, to go around it, avoiding it altogether. You can recognize it by a white mist that stinks and a piercing whistle. Do the souls of those who go like that come back? Who knows? Maybe they come back, or maybe they keep floating on the Kamabiría, the watery way of the dead.

I am well, walking. Now I am well. The evil was in me a while ago and I thought the time had come for me to put up my shelter of branches on the riverbank. I had set out to visit Tasurinchi, the blind one who lives by the river Cashiriari. Suddenly everything started streaming out of me as I walked. I didn't realize it till I saw my dirtied legs. What evil is this? What has entered my body? I went on walking, but I still had a long way to go to reach the Cashiriari. When I sat down to rest, the shivers came over me. I wondered what I could do, and casting my eyes all round, I finally saw a datura tree and tore off all the leaves I could reach. I made a brew and sprinkled it on my body. I warmed the water in the pot again. I heated the stone the seripigari had given me till it was red-hot and put it in. I breathed the steam from it till sleep came over me. I was like that for many moons, who knows how many, lying on my straw mat without the strength to walk, without even strength enough to sit up. Ants crawled over my body and I didn't brush them off. When one came close to my mouth I swallowed it, and that was my only food. Between dreams I heard the little parrot calling me: "Tasurinchi! Tasurinchi!" Half asleep, half awake, and always cold, so cold. I felt great sadness perhaps.

Then some men appeared. I saw their faces above me, leaning over to look at me. One pushed me with his foot and I couldn't speak to him. They weren't men who walk. They weren't Mashcos either, happily. Ashaninkas, I think they were, because I could understand some of what they said. They stood there looking at me, asking me questions I didn't have the strength to answer, even though I heard them, far away. They seemed to be having an argument as to whether I was a kamagarini or not. And also about what it was best to do if you met up with a little devil in the forest. They argued and argued. One said it would bring evil on them to have seen someone like me on their path and the prudent thing to do was to kill me. They couldn't agree. They talked it over and thought for a long time. Luckily for me, they finally decided to treat me well. They left me some cassavas, and seeing I hadn't strength enough to pick them up, one of them put a bit in my mouth. It wasn't poison; it was cassava. They put the rest in a plantain leaf and placed it in this hand. Maybe I dreamed it all. I don't know. But later, when I felt better and my strength came back, there were the cassavas. I ate them, and the little parrot ate, too. Now I could continue my journey. I walked slowly, stopping every so often to rest.

When I arrived at the place by the river Cashiriari where Tasurinchi, the blind one, lives, I told him what had happened to me. He breathed smoke on me and prepared a tobacco brew. "What happened to you was that your soul divided itself into many souls," he explained to me. "The evil entered your body because some machikanari sent it or because, quite by accident, you crossed its path. The body is merely the soul's cushma. Its wrapping, like a worm's. Once the evil had gotten inside, your soul tried to defend itself. It ceased to be one and became many so as to confuse the evil, which stole the ones it could. One, two, several. It can't have taken many or you'd have gone altogether. It was a good thing to bathe in tohé water and breathe its steam, but you should have done something more cunning. Rubbed the top of your head with annatto dye till it was red all over. Then the evil couldn't have gotten out of your body with its load of souls. That's where it gets out, that's its door. The annatto blocks its path. Feeling itself a prisoner inside, it loses its strength and dies. It's the same with bodies as with houses. Don't devils who enter houses steal souls by escaping through the crown of the roof? Why do we weave the slats in the top of the roof so carefully? So the devil can't escape, taking the souls of those who are asleep along with him. It's the same with the body. You felt weak because of the souls you'd lost. But they've already come back to you and that's why you're here. They must have escaped from Kientibakori, taking advantage of his kamagarinis' carelessness, and come back looking for you—aren't you their home?—and found you there in the same place, gasping, dying. They entered your body and you were born again. Now, inside of you, all the souls are back together again. Now they're just one soul again."

That, anyway, is what I have learned.

Tasurinchi, the blind one, the one who lives by the Cashiriari, is well. Though he can see almost nothing most of the time, he can still work his fields. He's walking. He says he sees more in his trance now than before he went blind. What happened to him was a good thing, perhaps. He thinks so. He's managing things so his blindness bothers him and his family as little as possible. His youngest son, who was crawling last time I came to visit him, has gone. A viper bit him in the leg. When they noticed, Tasurinchi prepared a brew and did what he could to save him, but a long time had gone by. He changed color, turned as black as huito dye, and went.

But his mother and father had the joy of seeing him once again.

This is how it came about.

They went to the seripigari and told him they were very unhappy because of the child's going. They said to him: "Find out what's become of him, which of the worlds he's in. And ask him to come visit us, even if it's just one time." That's what the seripigari did. In the trance, his soul, guided by a saankarite, traveled to the river of pure souls, the Meshiareni. There he found the child. The saankarites had bathed him, he had grown, he had a house, and soon he would have a wife as well. Telling him how sad his mother and father still were, the seripigari persuaded him to come back to this earth to visit them one last time. He promised he would, and he did.

Tasurinchi, the blind one, said that a young man dressed in a new cushma suddenly appeared in the house by the Cashiriari. They all recognized him even though he was no longer a child but a young man. Tasurinchi, the blind one, knew it was his son because of the pleasant odor he gave off. He sat down among them and tasted a mouthful of cassava and a few drops of masato. He told them about his journey, from the time his soul escaped from his body through the top of his head. It was dark, but he recognized the entrance to the cavern leading down to the river of dead souls. He cast himself into the Kamabiría and floated on the dense waters without sinking. He didn't have to move his hands or his feet. The current, silvery as a spiderweb, bore him slowly along. Around him, other souls were also journeying on the Kamabiría, that wide river along whose banks rise cliffs steeper than those of the Gran Pongo, perhaps. At last he arrived at the place where the waters divide, dragging over their precipice of rapids and whirlpools those who descend to the Gamaironi to suffer. The current itself sorted the souls out. With relief, the son of Tasurinchi the blind one felt the waters bearing him away from the falls; he was happy, knowing that he would continue journeying along the Kamabiría with those who were going to rise, by way of the river Meshiareni, to the world above, the world of the sun, Inkite. He still had a long way to go to reach it. He had to make his way past the end of this world, the Ostiake, into which all rivers flow. It is a swampy region, full of monsters. Kashiri, the moon, sometimes goes there to plot his mischief.

They waited till the sky was free of clouds and the stars were reflected brightly in the water. Then Tasurinchi's son and his traveling companions could ascend the Meshiareni, which is a stairway of bright stars, to Inkite. The saankarites received them with a feast. He ate a sweet-tasting fruit that made him grow and they showed him the house where he would live. And now, on his return, they would have a wife waiting for him. He was happy, it seems, in the world above. He didn't remember being bitten by the viper.

"Don't you miss anything on this earth?" his kinfolk asked him. Yes. Something. The bliss he felt when his mother suckled him. The blind one from the Cashiriari told me that, asking permission to do so, the youth went to his mother, opened her cushma, and very gently sucked her breasts, the way he used to as a newborn babe. Did her milk come? Who knows? But he was filled with bliss, perhaps. He said goodbye to them, pleased and satisfied.

The two younger sisters of Tasurinchi's wife have also gone. Punarunas who appeared round about the Cashiriari carried her off and kept her for many moons, making her cook and using her as a woman. It was the time when she ought to have been pure, with her hair cut short, not eating, not talking to anyone, her husband not touching her. Tasurinchi said he did not shame her for what had happened to her. But she was tormented by the fate that had befallen her. "I don't deserve to be spoken to now," she said. "I don't even know whether I deserve to live." She slowly walked down to the shore of the river just as night was falling, made her bed of branches, and plunged a chambira thorn into herself. "She was so sad I suspected she'd do that," Tasurinchi, the blind one, told me. They wrapped her in two cushmas so the vultures wouldn't peck at her, and instead of casting her adrift in a canoe on the river or burying her, they suspended her from a treetop. A wise thing to do, for her bones are licked by the sun's rays morning and evening. Tasurinchi showed me where, and I was amazed. "That high! How did you get way up there?" "I may not be able to see, but you don't need eyes to climb a tree, only legs and arms, and mine are still strong."

The other sister of the wife of Tasurinchi, the blind one by the Cashiriari, fell down a ravine coming back from the cassava patch. Tasurinchi had sent her to check the traps he puts around the farm, which the agoutis always fall into, he says. The morning went by and she didn't come back. They went out to look for her and found her at the bottom of the ravine. She'd rolled down; perhaps she'd slipped, perhaps the ground gave way beneath her feet. But that surprised me. It's not a deep ravine. Anyone could jump or roll to the bottom without killing himself. She died before, perhaps, and her empty body, without a soul, rolled down to the bottom of the ravine. Tasurinchi, the Cashiriari blind one, says: "We always thought that girl would go without any explanation." She spent her life humming songs that nobody had ever heard. She had strange trances, she spoke of unknown places, and apparently animals would tell her secrets when there was nobody around to hear them. According to Tasurinchi, those are sure signs that someone will go soon. "Now that those two have gone, there's more food to share around. Aren't we lucky?" he joked.

He has taught his littlest sons to hunt. He makes them practice all day long because of what might happen to him. He asked them to show me what they had learned. It's quite true, they can already handle a bow and a knife, even the ones who are just beginning to walk. They're good at making traps and fishing as well. "As you can see, they won't run short of food," Tasurinchi said to me. I like the spirit he shows. He's a man who never loses heart. I stayed with him for several days, going with him to set out his fishhooks and lay his traps, and I helped him clear his field of weeds. He worked bent double, pulling them out as though his eyes could see. We also went to a lake where there are súngaro fish, but we didn't catch anything. He never tired of listening to me. He made me repeat the same stories. "That way, once you've gone, I can tell myself all over again what you're telling me now," he said.

"What a miserable life it must be for those who don't have people who talk, as we do," he mused. "Thanks to the things you tell us, it's as though what happened before happens again, many times." One of his daughters had fallen asleep as I spoke. He woke her with one shake, saying: "Listen, child! Don't waste these stories. Know the wickedness of Kientibakori. Learn the evils his kamagarinis have done us and can still do us."

We now know many things about Kientibakori that those who came before didn't know. We know he has many intestines, like inkiro the tadpole. We know he hates us Machiguengas. He has tried many times to destroy us. We know he breathed out all the badness there is, from the Mashcos to the evil. Sharp rocks, dark clouds, rain, mud, the rainbow—he breathed them out. And lice, fleas, chiggers, poisonous snakes and vipers, mice and toads. He breathed out flies, gnats, mosquitoes, bats and vampires, ants and turkey buzzards. He breathed out the plants that burn the skin and those that can't be eaten; and the red earth that's good for making pots but not for growing cassava. This I learned by the river Shivankoreni, from the mouth of the seripigari. The one who knows the most about the things and the beings breathed out by Kientibakori, perhaps.

The time he was closest to destroying us was that time. It was no longer the time of abundance, nor was it that of the tree-bleeding. After the first and before the second, it seems. A kamagarini disguised as a man appeared and said to the men who walk: "The one who really needs help is not the sun. But rather Kashiri, the moon, who is the father of the sun." He gave them his reasons, which set them to thinking. Wasn't the sun so strong it made people's eyes water if they dared look at it directly without blinking? So what help did it need? The old story about its falling and then rising again was a trick. Kashiri, on the other hand, with his faint, gentle light was always fighting against the darkness, under difficult conditions. If the moon weren't there at night, watching in the sky, the darkness would be total, a thick blackness: men would fall down the precipice, would step on vipers, wouldn't be able to find their canoes or go out to plant cassava or hunt. They'd be prisoners in just one place, and the Mashcos could surround them, shoot them down with arrows, cut off their heads, and steal their souls. If the sun fell altogether, it would be night, perhaps. But as long as there was the moon it would never be entirely night, just half darkness, and life would go on, perhaps. So shouldn't men help Kashiri instead? Wasn't this to their advantage? If they did, the light of the moon would be brighter and night would be less dark, a half light, good to walk by.

The one who said those things appeared to be a man but he was a kamagarini. One of the ones that Kientibakori breathed out to go about this world sowing misfortune. The ones before did not recognize him. Even though he arrived in the midst of a great storm, the way little devils always arrive in the villages. The ones before didn't understand that, perhaps. If someone appears as the lord of thunder is roaring and rain is falling in torrents, it's not a man, it's a kamagarini. We know now. They hadn't learned that yet. They allowed themselves to be persuaded. And, changing their habits, they started doing by night what they had done by day before and by day what they had done by night. Thinking that Kashiri, the moon, would be brighter that way.

Once the eye of the sun appeared in the sky, they took refuge beneath their roofs, saying to each other: "It's time to rest." "It's time to light the fires." "It's time to sit and listen to the one who talks." That's what they did: they rested while the sun shone, or they gathered around to listen to the storyteller till darkness began to fall. Then, shaking off their drowsiness, they said: "The time has come to live." They traveled by night, they hunted by night, they built their dwellings by night, they cleared the forest and cleaned the weeds and the underbrush from the cassava fields by night. They got used to this new way of life. To the point that they could no longer bear being out of doors in the daylight. The heat of the sun burned their skin and the fire of its eye blinded them. Rubbing themselves, they said: "We cannot see. How terrible this light is. We hate it." On the other hand, their eyes had grown used to the dark and they could see in the night the way you and I can see in the daytime. They said: "It's quite true. Kashiri, the moon, is grateful to us for the help we give him." They started calling themselves not men of the earth, as before, or men who walk, or men who talk. But men of darkness.

Everything was going very well, perhaps. They seemed happy, perhaps. Life went on without anything happening. They felt at peace. Those who went came back, and one way or another, there was always enough food. "We were wise to do what we did," they said. But they were mistaken, it seems. They had lost wisdom. They were all turning into kamagarinis, but they didn't know it. Until certain things started happening to them. One fine day Tasurinchi woke up covered with fish scales, with a tail where his feet had been. He looked like an enormous carachama. Yes, the fish that lives in water and on land, the fish that swims and walks. Dragging himself painfully along, he took refuge in the pond, muttering mournfully that he couldn't bear life on land because he missed the water. A few moons later, when he woke up, wings had sprouted where Tasurinchi's arms used to be. He gave a little hop, and they saw him take off and disappear above the trees, beating his wings like a hummingbird. A snout and tusks grew on Tasurinchi, and his sons, not recognizing him, shouted excitedly: "A sajino! Let's eat it!" When he tried to tell them who he was, all he could do was snort and grunt. He had to make his escape trotting clumsily on his four stumpy legs he hardly knew how to use, pursued by a hungry horde aiming arrows and stones at him. "Let's catch it, let's chase it down!" they said.

The earth was running short of men. Some had turned into birds, some into fish, others into tortoises or spiders, and went to live the life of little kamagarini devils. "What is happening to us? What misfortunes are these?" the ones who survived asked themselves, bewildered. They were helpless with fear and blind, but they didn't know it. Once again, wisdom had been lost. "We are about to disappear," they moaned. They were sad, perhaps. And then, amid all the confusion, the Mashcos fell upon them and there was a great massacre. They cut off the heads of many and carried off their women. It seemed that there would be no end to the catastrophes. And then it all of a sudden occurred to one of them, in his despair: "Let's go visit Tasurinchi."

He was a seripigari, old by then, who lived by the river Timpía, behind a waterfall. He listened to them but said nothing. He went with them to the place where they lived. His eyes gummy with sleep, he contemplated the hopelessness and disorder that reigned in the world. He fasted for several moons, silent, concentrating, meditating. He prepared the brews for the trance. He pounded green tobacco in a mortar, pressed the leaves through a sieve, poured water on them, and put the pot on to boil till the brew thickened and bubbled. He pounded the roots of ayahuasca, pressed out the dark juice, boiled it, and let it cool. They put out the fire and covered the hut all around with plantain leaves so it would be totally dark inside. The seripigari breathed smoke on them one by one, all of them; he chanted and they answered him, chanting. Then he swallowed his brews, still chanting. They waited, breathless. He went on waving his bundle of leaves and chanting. They didn't understand what he was saying. At last, when he'd become a spirit, they saw his shadow climb up the center pole of the hut and disappear through the roof, out the very same place the devil goes when carrying off souls. Not long after, he came back. He had the same body as before, but it was no longer him; it was a saankarite. He scolded them furiously. He reminded them of what they had been, of what they had done, all the many sacrifices since they had started walking. How could they have allowed themselves to be taken in by the tricks of their immemorial enemy? How could they have betrayed the sun for Kashiri, the moon? By changing their way of life they had upset the order of the world, disoriented the souls of those who had gone. In the darkness they were living in, the souls were unable to recognize them, didn't know whether or not they were the right ones. That's why the misfortunes occurred, perhaps. The spirits of those who went and came back, confused by the change, went away again. They wandered in the forest, orphaned, moaning in the wind. The kamagarini got inside bodies that had been abandoned, that had lost the support of their souls, and corrupted them; that was why they sprouted feathers, scales, claws, snouts, spurs. But there was still time. Degeneration and impurity had been brought upon them by a devil living among them, dressed as a man. They went out to hunt him down, determined to kill him. But the kamagarini had fled to the depths of the forest. At last they understood. Ashamed, they went back to doing as they had done before, until the world, life, became what they really were and should be. Sorrowful, repenting, they started walking. Shouldn't each one do what he was meant to do? Was it not their task to walk, helping the sun to rise? They fulfilled their obligation, perhaps. Are we fulfilling ours? Are we walking? Are we living?

Among all the many different kamagarinis that Kientibakori breathed out, the worst little devil is the kasibarenini, it seems. Small as a child, if he turns up somewhere in his earth-colored cushma, it's because there's somebody sick there. He's out to take possession of his soul so as to make him do cruel things. That's why sick people should never be left alone, not for a single moment. The slightest inattention and the kasibarenini has things his way. Tasurinchi says that's what happened to him. The one who's living by the river Camisea now. Tasurinchi. According to him, a kasibarenini was to blame for what happened over there in Shivankoreni, where everybody's still furious, remembering. I went to see him on the little beach along the Camisea where he'd put up his hut. He was alarmed when he caught sight of me. He grabbed his shotgun. "Have you come to kill me?" he said. "Watch out, look here at what I have in my hand." He wasn't angry, just sad. "I've just come to visit you," I soothed him. "And to talk to you if you care to listen. If you'd rather I went away, I'll go." "How could I not want you to talk to me?" he replied, unrolling two straw mats. "Come, come. Eat all my food, take all my cassavas. Everything is yours." He complained bitterly because they wouldn't let him go back to Shivankoreni. If he even goes near the place, his former kinfolk come out to meet him with stones and arrows, screaming at him: "Devil, cursed devil!"

Worse still, they've asked a bad sorcerer, a machikanari, to bring evil on him. Tasurinchi caught him trying to hide in his house to steal a lock of his hair or something belonging to him, so as to be able to make him fall sick and die a horrible death. He could have killed the machikanari, but all he did was make him run away by shooting his gun off in the air. According to him, this proves his soul is pure again. "It's not right that they should hate me so," he says. He told me he'd gone to visit Tasurinchi, upriver, to bring him food and presents. Offering to clear a new field for him in the forest, he asked him to give him any one of his daughters as a wife. Tasurinchi insulted him: "Nit, shit, traitor, how dare you come round here? I'm going to kill you right now." And he'd gone after him with a machete.

Tearfully, he lamented his fate. He said it wasn't true that he was a kasibarenini devil disguised as a man. He'd been one for a time, perhaps, before. But now he's just the same as any of the Machiguengas of Shivankoreni who won't let him come near. His misfortune began that time when he had the evil. He was so thin and so weak he couldn't get up from his mat. Nor could he speak. He opened his mouth and his voice didn't come out. I must be turning into a fish, he thought. But he could see and hear what was happening around him, in the other huts of Shivankoreni. He was deeply alarmed when he saw that everyone was taking off the bracelets and the ornaments they were wearing on their wrists, arms, and ankles. He could hear them saying: "He's going to die soon, but his spirit will pull out his veins, and while we're asleep he'll tie us down with them at the places on our bodies where we wore ornaments." He tried to reassure them, to tell them that he'd never do that to them, and, what was more, that he wasn't dying. But his voice wouldn't come out. And that was when he spied him, out in the pouring rain. He roamed all about the village, harmless enough, or so he made it appear. A youngster in an earth-colored cushma, amusing himself playing with datura seeds and imitating the hovering wings of a hummingbird with his hands. It never occurred to Tasurinchi that he could be a little devil, so he wasn't worried when his family set out for the lake to fish. Then, once he saw he was alone, the kasibarenini changed himself into an ant and entered Tasurinchi's body by way of the little opening inside the nose through which tobacco juice is sniffed. There and then he felt cured of the evil, there and then his strength came back, and the flesh on his bones. Yet at the same time he felt an irresistible urge to do what he did next. Just like that, running, howling, beating his chest like a monkey, he started burning down the huts of Shivankoreni. He says it wasn't him but the little devil who set fire to the straw and ran from one place to the other with burning candles, roaring and leaping for joy. Tasurinchi remembers how the parrots squawked and how he choked in the clouds of smoke as before him, behind him, to the right, to the left, everything went up in flames. If the others hadn't arrived on the scene, Shivankoreni would no longer exist. He says that as soon as he saw people come running he regretted what he had done. He had to run away in terror, saying to himself: "What's happening to me?" They wanted to kill him, chasing after him screaming: "Devil, devil!"

But, according to Tasurinchi, all this is an old story. The little devil that made him set fire to Shivankoreni was sucked out of him by a seripigari of Koribeni: he drew it out through his armpit, and then he vomited it up. Tasurinchi saw it: it had the form of a little white bone. He says that since then he's become just like me, or any of you, again. "Why do you think they won't let me live in Shivankoreni?" he asked me. "Because they don't trust you," I explained to him. "They all remember that day you cured yourself and then went and burned down their houses. And what's more, they know you've been living over there on the other side of the Gran Pongo, among the Viracochas." Because Tasurinchi doesn't wear a cushma, but a shirt and trousers. "There among them, I felt like an orphan," he told me. "I dreamed of returning to Shivankoreni. And now that I'm here, my kinfolk make me feel like an orphan, too. Will I always live alone like this, without a family? The one thing I want is a woman to roast cassavas and bear children."

I stayed with him for three moons. He's a close-mouthed, moody man who sometimes talks to himself. Someone who's lived with a kasibarenini devil inside his body can't ever be the same as he was before, perhaps. "Your coming to visit me is the beginning of a change, perhaps," he said to me. "Do you think the men who walk will let me walk with them soon?" "Who knows?" I answered. "There's nothing sadder than to feel that one is somebody who's no longer a man," he said as we parted. As I walked along the Camisea I spied him in the distance. He had climbed up a hillock and his eyes were following me. I could remember his surly, forlorn face, though I could no longer see it.

That, anyway, is what I have learned.

I FIRST became acquainted with the Amazon jungle halfway through 1958, thanks to my friend Rosita Corpancho. Her function at the University of San Marcos was vague; her power unlimited. She prowled among the professors without being one of them, and they all did whatever she asked; thanks to her wiles, doors of officialdom stuck shut were opened and paths of bureaucracy smoothed.

"There's a place available for someone on an expedition to the Alto Marañón that's been organized by the Institute of Linguistics for a Mexican anthropologist," she said to me one day when I ran into her on the campus of the Faculty of Letters. "Would you like to go?"

I had finally managed to obtain the fellowship to Europe I'd coveted and was to leave for Spain the following month. But I accepted without a moment's hesitation.

Rosita is from Loreto, and if you listen carefully you can still catch in her voice an echo of the delightful singsong accent of eastern Peru. She protected and promoted—as no doubt she still does—the Summer Institute of Linguistics, an organization which, in the forty years of its existence in Peru, has been the object of virulent controversy. I understand that as I write these lines it is packing its bags to leave the country. Not because it has been expelled (though this was on the verge of happening during General Velasco's dictatorship), but on its own initiative, since it considers that it has fulfilled the mission that brought it to Yarinacocha, its base of operations on the banks of the Ucayali, some ten kilometers from Pucallpa, from which it has spread into nearly all the remote folds and corners of Amazonia.

What exactly is the purpose of the Institute? According to its enemies, it is a tentacle of American imperialism which, under cover of doing scientific research, has been engaged in gathering intelligence and has taken the first steps toward a neocolonialist penetration of the cultures of the Amazonian Indians. These accusations stem, first and foremost, from the Left. But certain sectors of the Catholic Church—mainly the jungle missionaries—are also hostile to it and accuse it of being nothing more than a phalanx of Protestant evangelists passing themselves off as linguists. Among the anthropologists, there are those who criticize it for perverting the aboriginal cultures, attempting to Westernize them and draw them into a mercantile economy. A number of conservatives disapprove of the presence of the Institute in Peru for nationalist and Hispanist reasons. Among these latter was my professor and academic adviser back in those days, the historian Porras Barrenechea, who, when he heard that I was going on that expedition, solemnly cautioned me: "Be careful. Those gringos will try to buy you." He couldn't bear the thought that, because of the Institute, the jungle Indians would probably learn to speak English before they did Spanish.

Friends of the Institute, such as Rosita Corpancho, defended it on pragmatic grounds. The work of the linguists—studying the languages and dialects of Amazonia, compiling lexicons and grammars of the various tribes—served the country, and besides, it was supervised, in theory at least, by the Ministry of Education, which had to approve of all its projects and received copies of all the material it collected. As long as that same Ministry or Peruvian universities didn't take the trouble to pursue such research themselves, it was to Peru's advantage that it was being undertaken by others. Moreover, the infrastructure set up by the Institute in Amazonia, with its fleet of hydroplanes and its system of radio communication between the headquarters at Yarinacocha and the network of linguists living with the tribes, was also of benefit to the country, since teachers, civil servants, and the military forces in remote jungle localities were in the habit of making use of it, and not just in cases of emergency.

The controversy has not ended, nor is it likely to end soon.

That expedition of just a few short weeks' duration which I was lucky enough to be able to join made such a great impression on me that, twenty-seven years later, I still remember it in abundant detail and still write about it. As I am doing now, in Firenze. We went first to Yarinacocha and talked with the linguists and then, a long way from there, to the region of the Alto Marañón, visiting a series of settlements and villages of two tribes of the Jíbaro family: the Aguarunas and the Huambisas. We then went up to Lake Morona to visit the Shapras.

We traveled in a small hydroplane, and in some places in native canoes, along narrow river channels so choked with tangled vegetation overhead that in bright daylight it seemed dark as night. The strength and the solitude of Nature—the tall trees, the mirror-smooth lagoons, the immutable rivers—brought to mind a newly created world, untouched by man, a paradise of plants and animals. When we reached the tribes, by contrast, there before us was prehistory, the elemental, primeval existence of our distant ancestors: hunters, gatherers, bowmen, nomads, shamans, irrational and animistic. This, too, was Peru, and only then did I become fully aware of it: a world still untamed, the Stone Age, magico-religious cultures, polygamy, head-shrinking (in a Shapra village of Moronacocha, the cacique, Tariri, explained to us, through an interpreter, the complicated technique of steeping and stuffing with herbs required by the operation)—that is to say, the dawn of human history.

I am quite sure that throughout the entire trip I thought continually of Saúl Zuratas. I often spoke about him with his mentor, Dr. Matos Mar, who was also a member of the expedition; it was on this journey, in fact, that we became good friends. Matos Mar told me that he had invited Saúl to come with us, but that Zuratas had refused because he strongly disapproved of the work of the Institute.

Thanks to this expedition, I was better able to understand Mascarita's fascination with this region and these people, to get some idea of the forcefulness of the impact that changed the course of his life. But, besides that, it gave me firsthand experience that enabled me to justify many of the differences of opinion which, more out of instinct than out of real knowledge, I had had with Saúl over Amazonian cultures. Why did he cling to that illusion of his: wanting to preserve these tribes just as they were, their way of life just as it was? To begin with, it wasn't possible. All of them, some more slowly, others more rapidly, were being contaminated by Western and mestizo influences. Moreover, was this chimerical preservation desirable? Was going on living the way they were, the way purist anthropologists of Saúl's sort wanted them to do, to the tribes' advantage? Their primitive state made them, rather, victims of the worst exploitation and cruelty.

In an Aguaruna village, Urakusa, where we arrived one evening, we saw through the portholes of the hydroplane the scene which had become familiar each time we touched down near some tribe: the eyes of the entire population of men and women, half naked and daubed with paint, attracted by the noise of the plane, followed its maneuvers as they slapped at their faces and chests with both hands to drive away the insects. But in Urakusa, besides the copper-colored bodies, the dangling tits, the children with parasite-swollen bellies and skins striped red or black, a sight awaited us that I have never forgotten: that of a man recently tortured. It was the headman of the locality, whose name was Jum.

A party of whites and mestizos from Santa María de Nieva—a trading post on the banks of the Nieva River that we had also visited, put up in a Catholic mission—had arrived in Urakusa a few weeks before us. The party included the civil authorities of the settlement plus a soldier from a frontier post. Jum went out to meet them, and was greeted by a blow that split his forehead open. Then they burned down the huts of Urakusa, beat up all the Indians they could lay their hands on, and raped several women. They carried Jum off to Santa María de Nieva, where they submitted him to the indignity of having his hair cut off. Then they tortured him in public. They flogged him, burned his armpits with hot eggs, and finally hoisted him up a tree the way they do paiche, large river fish, to drain them off. They left him there for several hours, then untied him and let him go back to his village.

The ostensible reason for this savagery was a minor incident that had taken place in Urakusa between the Aguarunas and a detachment of soldiers passing through. But the real reason was that Jum had tried to set up a cooperative among the Aguaruna villages of the Alto Marañón. The cacique was a quick-witted and determined man, and the Institute linguist working with the Aguarunas encouraged him to take a course at Yarinacocha so as to become a bilingual teacher. This was a program drawn up by the Ministry of Education with the aid of the Institute of Linguistics. Men of the tribes who, like Jum, seemed capable of setting up an educational project in their villages were sent to Yarinacocha, where they took a course—a fairly superficial one, I imagine—given by the linguists and Peruvian instructors, to enable them to teach their people to read and write in their own language. They then returned to their native villages with classroom aids and the somewhat optimistic title of bilingual teacher.

The program did not attain the goal it had set—making the Amazonian Indians literate—but, as far as Jum was concerned, it had unforeseeable consequences. His stay in Yarinacocha, his contacts with "civilization" caused the cacique of Urakusa to discover—by himself or with the help of his instructors—that he and his people were being iniquitously exploited by the bosses with whom they traded. These bosses, whites or Amazonian mestizos, periodically visited the tribes to buy rubber and animal skins. They themselves fixed the price of what they bought, and paid for it in kind—machetes, fishhooks, clothing, guns; the price of these articles was also set to suit their own whim or convenience. Jum's stay at Yarinacocha made him realize that if, instead of trading with the bosses, the Aguarunas took the trouble to go sell their rubber and hides in the cities—at the offices of the Banco Hipotecario, for instance—they would get far better prices for what they had to sell and could buy for far less the same articles that the bosses sold them.

Discovering the value of money had tragic consequences for Urakusa. Jum informed the bosses that he would no longer trade with them. This decision meant pure and simple ruin for the Viracochas of Santa María de Nieva who had received us so warmly, and who were themselves nothing more than a handful of miserable whites and mestizos, most of them illiterate and barefoot, living in conditions nearly as wretched as those of their victims. The fierce extortions they practiced on the Aguarunas did not make them rich; they earned barely enough to survive. Exploitation in this part of the world was carried out at a level little short of subhuman. That was the reason for the punitive expedition, and as they tortured Jum they kept repeating: "Forget the cooperative."

All this had just happened. Jum's wounds were still oozing pus. His hair had not grown back in. As they translated this story for us in the peaceful clearing of Urakusa—Jum could get out little more than a few hoarse sentences in Spanish—I thought: "I must talk this over with Saúl." What would Mascarita say? Would he admit that in a case like this it was quite obvious that what was to Urakusa's advantage, to Jum's, was not going backward but forward? That is to say, setting up their own cooperative, trading with the towns, prospering economically and socially so that it would no longer be possible to treat them the way the "civilized" people of Santa María de Nieva had done. Or would Saúl, unrealistically, deny that this was so, insist that the true solution was for the Viracochas to go away and let the inhabitants of Urakusa return to their traditional way of life?

Matos Mar and I stayed awake all that night, talking about Jum's story and the horrifying condition of the weak and the poor in our country that it revealed. Invisible and silent, Saúl Zurata's ghost took part in our conversation; both of us would have liked to have him there, offering his opinion and arguing. Matos Mar thought that Jum's misfortune would provide Mascarita with further arguments to support his theory. Didn't the entire episode prove that coexistence was impossible, that it led inevitably to the Viracochas' domination of the Indians, to the gradual and systematic destruction of the weaker culture? Those savage drunkards from Santa María de Nieva would never, under any circumstances, lead the inhabitants of Urakusa on the path to modernization, but only to their extinction; their "culture" had no more right to hegemony than that of the Aguarunas, who, however primitive they might be, had at least developed sufficient knowledge and skill to coexist with Amazonia. In the name of age-old prior occupation, of history, of morality, it was necessary to recognize the Aguarunas' sovereignty over these territories and to expel the foreign intruders from Santa María de Nieva.

I didn't agree with Matos Mar; I thought Jum's story was more likely to bring Saúl around to a more practical point of view, to accepting the lesser evil. Was there the slightest chance that a Peruvian government, of whatever political persuasion, would grant the tribes extraterritorial rights in the jungle? Obviously not. That being the case, why not change the Viracochas so that they'd treat the Indians differently?

We were stretched out on a floor of beaten earth, sharing a mosquito net, in a hut reeking of rubber (it was the storeroom of Urakusa), surrounded by the breathing of our slumbering companions and the unfamiliar sounds of the jungle. At the time, Matos Mar and I also shared socialist ideas and enthusiasms, and in the course of our talk together, the familiar subject of the social relations of production, which like a magic wand served to explain and resolve all problems, naturally cropped up. The problem of the Urakusas, that of all the tribes, should be seen as part of the general problem resulting from the class structure of Peruvian society. By substituting for the obsession with profit—individual gain—the idea of service to the community as the incentive to work, and reintroducing an attitude of solidarity and humanity into social relations, socialism would make possible that coexistence between modern and primitive Peru that Mascarita thought impossible and undesirable. In the new Peru, infused with the science of Marx and Mariátegui, the Amazonian tribes would, at one and the same time, be able to adopt modern ways and to preserve their essential traditions and customs within the mosaic of cultures that would go to make up the future civilization of Peru. Did we really believe that socialism would ensure the integrity of our magico-religious cultures? Wasn't there already sufficient evidence that industrial development, whether capitalist or communist, inevitably meant the annihilation of those cultures? Was there one exception anywhere in the world to this terrible, inexorable law? Thinking it over—in the light of the years that have since gone by, and from the vantage point of this broiling-hot Firenze—we were as unrealistic and romantic as Mascarita with his archaic, anti-historical utopia.

That long conversation with Matos Mar under the mosquito net, watching the dark pouches hanging from the palm-leaf roof sway back and forth—by daybreak they had mysteriously disappeared, and turned out to be balls of hundreds of spiders that curled up together in the huts at night, by the warmth of the fire—is one of the undying memories of that journey. Another: a prisoner of an enemy tribe whom the Shapras of Lake Morona allowed to wander peacefully around the village. His dog, however, was shut up in a cage and was watched very closely. Captors and captive were evidently in agreement as to the symbolic import of this; in the minds of both parties the caged animal kept the prisoner from running away and bound him to his captors more securely—the force of ritual, of belief, of magic—than any iron chain could have. And yet another: the gossip and fantastic tales we heard all during the journey concerning a Japanese adventurer, rogue, and feudal lord called Tushía, who was said to live on an island in the Pastaza River with a harem of girls he'd abducted from all over Amazonia.

But, in the long run, the most haunting memory of that trip—one that on this Florentine afternoon is almost as searing as the summer sun of Tuscany—is doubtless the story I heard a couple of linguists, Mr. and Mrs. Schneil, tell in Yarinacocha. At first I had the impression that I had never heard the name of that tribe before. But suddenly I realized that it was the same one that Saúl had told me so many stories about, the one he had come in contact with on his first trip to Quillabamba: the Machiguengas. Yet, except for the name, the two didn't seem to have much in common.

Little by little I began to understand the reason for the discrepancy. Though it was the same tribe—numbering between four and five thousand—the Machiguengas were a people split apart. This explained the differences between the two groups and their different relationships with the rest of Peru. A dividing line, whose chief topographical feature was the Pongo de Mainique, separated the Machiguengas scattered about in the ceja de montaña—a wooded region below the high sierra where whites and mestizos were numerous—from the Machiguengas of the eastern region, on the far side of the Pongo, where the Amazonian plain begins. A geographical accident, the narrow gorge between mountains where the Urubamba becomes a raging torrent, filled with foam, whirlpools, and deafening tumult, separated the Machiguengas above, who were in contact with the white and mestizo world and had begun the process of acculturation, from the others, scattered through the forests of the plain, living in near-total isolation and preserving their traditional way of life more or less unchanged. The Dominicans had established missions—such as Chirumbia, Koribeni, and Panticollo—among the former, and in that region there were also Viracocha farms, where a few Machiguengas worked as hired hands. This was the domain of the famous Fidel Pereira and the Machiguenga world described in Saúl's stories: the one most Westernized and most exposed to the outside.

The other part of the community (but, under such conditions, could one speak of a community?), scattered over the enormous area of the Urubamba and Madre de Dios basins, kept itself jealously isolated, even at the end of the fifties, and resisted any form of contact with the whites. The Dominican missionaries had not reached them, and, for the moment at least, there was nothing in that region to attract the Viracochas. But even this sector was not homogeneous. Among these primitive Machiguengas there was an even more archaic small group or fraction, hostile to the others, known by the name of Kogapakori. Centered on the region bathed by two tributaries of the Urubamba, the Timpía and the Tikompinía, the Kogapakori went about stark-naked, though some of the men wore phallic sheaths made of bamboo, and attacked anyone who entered their territory, even those who were ethnically related. Their case was exceptional, for, compared with other tribes, the Machiguengas were traditionally peaceful. Their gentle and docile nature had made them choice victims of the rubber boom, during the great manhunts to provide Indian labor for the rubber camps, at which time the tribe had been literally decimated and on the point of disappearing. For the same reason they had always come off the losers in skirmishes with their age-old enemies the Yaminahuas and the Mashcos, especially the latter, famous for their bellicosity. These were the Machiguengas the Schneils told us about. For two years and a half they had been working to make themselves accepted by the groups with which they had succeeded in making contact, yet they still encountered distrust and even hostility on their part.

Yarinacocha at dusk, when the red mouth of the sun begins to sink behind the treetops and the greenish lake glows beneath the indigo sky where the first stars are beginning to twinkle, is one of the most beautiful sights I have ever seen. We were sitting on the porch of a wooden house contemplating, over the Schneils' shoulders, the horizon line of the darkening forest. It was a magnificent sight. But I think we all felt uncomfortable and depressed. For the story they told us—they were young, with that healthy, candid, puritanical, hardworking air about them that all the linguists wore like a uniform—was a dismal one. Even the two anthropologists of the group, Matos Mar and the Mexican, Juan Comas, were surprised at the depths of prostration and pessimism to which, according to the Schneils, the broken-spirited Machiguenga people had been reduced. From what we heard, the tribe seemed to be virtually falling apart.

These Machiguengas had hardly been studied. Except for a slim volume published in 1943 by a Dominican, Father Vicente de Cenitagoya, and a few articles by other missionaries on their customs and their language, which had appeared in the journals of the Order, no serious ethnographic study of them existed. They belonged to the Arawak family and there was some confusion between them and the Campas of the Ene, Perené, and Gran Pajonal Rivers, since their languages had common roots. Their origin was a total mystery; their identity, blurred. Vaguely referred to as Antis by the Incas, who expelled them from the eastern part of the Cusco region but were never able to invade their jungle territory or subjugate them, they appear in the Chronicles and Relations of the Colony under such arbitrarily assigned designations as Manaríes, Opataris, Pilconzones, until nineteenth-century travelers at last started calling them by their name. One of the first to refer to them in this way was a Frenchman, Charles Wiener, who in 1880 came across "two Machiguenga corpses, ritually abandoned in the river," which he decapitated and added to his collection of curiosities collected in the Peruvian jungle. They had been on the move since time immemorial and it was unlikely that they had ever lived together in settled communities. The fact that they had been displaced at frequent intervals by more warlike tribes and by whites—during the various booms: the rubber, gold, rosewood, and agricultural colonization "fevers"—toward ever more unhealthy and infertile regions, where the survival of a large group was impossible, had accentuated their fragmentation and brought on the development among them of an individualism bordering on anarchy. Not one Machiguenga village existed. They did not have caciques and did not appear to acknowledge any authority other than that of each father in his own family. They lived in tiny units of ten people or so at most, scattered over the enormous region that included all the jungle zone of Cusco and Madre de Dios. The poverty of the area forced these human units to keep continually on the move, maintaining a considerable distance between each other so as not to exhaust the game. Due to the erosion and impoverishment of the soil, they had to shift the location of their cassava patches at the end of every two years of cultivation at most.

What the Schneils had been able to discover of their mythology, beliefs, and customs suggested that they had always led a very hard life and afforded a few glimpses of their history.

They had been breathed out by the god Tasurinchi, creator of everything that existed, and did not have personal names. Their names were always temporary, related to a passing phenomenon and subject to change: the one who arrives, or the one who leaves, the husband of the woman who just died, or the one who is climbing out of his canoe, the one just born, or the one who shot the arrow. Their language had expressions only for the quantities one, two, three, and four. All the others were covered by the adjective "many." Their notion of paradise was modest: a place where the rivers had fish and the woods had game. They associated their nomad life with the movement of the stars through the firmament. There was a high incidence of self-inflicted death among them. The Schneils told us of several cases they had witnessed: Machiguenga men and women—mostly the latter—who took their own lives by plunging chambira thorns into their hearts or into their temples, or by swallowing potions of deadly poison, for pointless reasons: an argument, an arrow that had missed, a reprimand by one of their kin. The most trivial frustration could lead a Machiguenga to kill himself. It was as though their will to live, their instinct for survival, had been reduced to a minimum.

The slightest illness brought on death. They were terrified of head colds, as were many of the tribes of Amazonia—sneezing in front of them always meant frightening them—but, and in this they differed from the other tribes, they refused to take care of themselves once they fell ill. At the least headache, bleeding, or accident, they prepared themselves for death. They would not take medicine or let themselves be looked after. "What's the use, if we must go in one way or another?" they would say. Their witch doctors or medicine men—the seripigaris—were consulted and called upon to exorcize bad spirits and evils of the soul; but as soon as these manifested themselves as bodily ills, they regarded them as more or less incurable. A sick person making his way to the riverbank to lie down and await death was a frequent sight.

Their wariness and mistrust of strangers were extreme, as were their fatalism and timidity. The sufferings the community had endured during the rubber boom, when they were hunted by the "suppliers" of the camps or by Indians of other tribes who could thereby pay their debts to the bosses, had left a mark of terror in their myths and legends of that period, which they referred to as the tree-bleeding. Perhaps it was true, as a Dominican missionary, Father José Pío Aza—the first to study their language—maintained, that they were the last vestiges of a Pan-Amazonian civilization (attested, so he claimed, by the mysterious petroglyphs scattered throughout the Alto Urubamba) which had suffered defeat after defeat since its encounters with the Incas and was gradually dying out.

Making the first contacts had been very difficult for the Schneils. A full year after these first attempts had gone by before he, and only he, had succeeded in being received by a Machiguenga family. He told us what a touch-and-go experience it had been, how anxious and hopeful he had been that morning, at one of the headwaters of the Timpía river, as, stark-naked, he had approached the solitary hut, made of strips of bark and roofed with straw, which he had already visited on three occasions, leaving presents—without meeting anybody, but feeling behind his back the eyes of Machiguengas watching him from the forest—and seen that this time the half dozen people who lived there did not run away.

From then on, the Schneils had spent brief periods—either one of them at a time or the two of them together—with that family of Machiguengas or others living along the Alto Urubamba and its tributaries. They had accompanied groups of them when they went fishing or hunting in the dry season, and had made recordings that they played for us. An odd crackling sound with sudden sharp notes and, now and again, a guttural outpouring that they informed us were songs. They had a transcription and translation of one of these songs, made by a Dominican missionary in the thirties; the Schneils had heard it again, a quarter of a century later, in a ravine of the Sepahua River. The text admirably illustrated the state of mind of the community as it had been described to us. So much so that I copied it out. Since then I have always carried it with me, folded in four in a corner of my billfold, as a charm. It can still be deciphered:

Opampogyakyena shinoshinonkarintsi
Sadness is looking at me
opampogyakyena shinoshinonkarintsi
sadness is looking at me
ogakyena kabako shinoshinonkarintsi
sadness is looking hard at me
ogakyena kabako shinoshinonkarintsi
sadness is looking hard at me
okisabintsatana shinoshinonkarintsi
sadness troubles me very much
okisabintsatana shinoshinonkarintsi
sadness troubles me very much
amakyena tampia tampia tampia
air, wind has brought me
ogaratinganaa tampia tampia
air has borne me away
okisabintsatana shinoshinonkarintsi
sadness troubles me very much
okisabintsatana shinoshinonkarintsi

sadness troubles me very much
amaanatyomba tampia tampia
air, wind has brought me
onkisabintsatenatyo shinonka
sadness troubles me very much
shinoshinonkarintsi
sadness
amakyena popyenti pogyentima pogyenti
the little worm, the little worm has brought me
tampia tampia tampia
air, wind, air

Though they had a working knowledge of the Machiguenga language, the Schneils were still a long way from mastering the secrets of its structure. It was an archaic tongue, vibrantly resonant and agglutinative, in which a single word made up of many others could express a great overarching thought.

Mrs. Schneil was pregnant, which was the reason the two of them had returned to the base at Yarinacocha. As soon as their first child was born, the couple would return to the Urubamba. Their son or daughter, they said, would be brought up there and would master Machiguenga more thoroughly, and perhaps sooner, than they would.

The Schneils, like all the other linguists, had degrees from the University of Oklahoma, but they and their colleagues were motivated above all by a spiritual goal: spreading the Glad Tidings of the Bible. I don't know what their precise religious affiliation was, since there were members of a number of different churches among the linguists of the Institute. The ultimate purpose that had led them to study primitive cultures was religious: translating the Bible into the tribes' own languages so that those peoples could hear God's word in the rhythms and inflections of their own tongue. This was the aim that had led Dr. Peter Townsend to found the Institute. He was an interesting person, half evangelist and half pioneer, a friend of the Mexican president Lázaro Cárdenas and the author of a book about him. The goal set by Dr. Townsend still motivates the linguists to continue the patient labor they have undertaken. I have always been both moved and frightened by the strong, unshakable faith that leads men to dedicate their lives to that faith and accept any sacrifice in its name; for heroism and fanaticism, selfless acts and crimes alike can spring from this attitude. But as far as I could gather in the course of that journey, the faith of the linguists from the Institute seemed benign enough. I still remember that woman, little more than a girl, who had lived for years among the Shapras of the Morona, and that family settled among the Huambisas, whose children—little redheaded gringos—splashed about naked along the banks of the river together with the copper-colored children of the village, talking and spitting in the very same way they did. (The Huambisas spit as they talk, to prove they're telling the truth. As they see it, a man who doesn't spit as he talks is a liar.)

They lived, admittedly, in primitive conditions among the tribes, but at the same time they could rely on an infrastructure that protected them: planes, radio, doctors, medicines. Even so, their profound conviction and their ability to adapt were exceptional. Save for the fact that they wore clothes, while their hosts went around nearly naked, the linguists we visited who had settled in with the tribes lived in much the same way they did: in identical huts or virtually in the open air, in the most precarious of shelters, sharing the frugal diet and Spartan ways of the Indians. All of them had that taste for adventure—the pull of the frontier—that is so frequent an American trait, shared by people of the most diverse backgrounds and occupations. The Schneils were very young, their married life was just beginning, and as we gathered from our conversation with them, they did not regard their coming to Amazonia as something temporary but, rather, as a vital, long-term commitment.

What they told us of the Machiguengas kept running through my mind all during our travels through the Alto Marañón. It was something I wanted to talk over with Saúl: I needed to hear his criticisms and comments on what the Schneils reported. And, besides, I had a surprise for him: I had learned the words of that song by heart and would recite it to him in Machiguenga. I could imagine his astonishment and his great burst of friendly laughter . . .

The tribes we visited in the Alto Marañón and Moronacocha were very different from those of the Urubamba and the Madre de Dios. The Aguarunas had contact with the rest of Peru and some of their villages were undergoing a process of outbreeding whose results were visible at first glance. The Shapras were more isolated, and until recently—chiefly because they were headhunters—they had had a reputation for violence; but one did not find among them any of those symptoms of depression or moral disintegration that the Schneils had described in the Machiguengas.

When we returned to Yarinacocha on our way back to Lima, we spent one last night with the linguists. It was a working session, during which they questioned Matos Mar and Juan Comas as to their impressions. At the end of the meeting I asked Edwin Schneil if he was willing to talk with me a while longer. He took me to his house, where his wife made us a cup of tea. They lived in one of the last cabins, where the Institute ended and the jungle began. The regular, harmonious, rhythmical chirring of insects served as background music to our chat, which went on for a long time, with Mrs. Schnëil occasionally joining in. It was she who told me of the river cosmogony of the Machiguengas, in which the Milky Way is the river Meshiareni, plied by innumerable great and minor gods in their descent from their pantheon to the earth, and by the souls of the dead as they mount to paradise. I asked them whether they had photographs of the families they had lived with. They said they didn't, but showed me many Machiguenga artifacts. Large and small monkey-skin drums, cane flutes and a sort of panpipe, made of reeds of graduated lengths bound together with vegetable fibers, which, when placed against the lower lip and blown across, produced a rich scale of sounds ranging from a shrill high note to a deep bass one. Sieves made of cane leaves cut in strips and braided, like little baskets, to filter the cassava used to make masato. Necklaces and bangles of seeds, teeth, and bones. Anklets, bracelets. Headpieces of parrot, macaw, toucan, and cockatoo feathers set into circlets of wood. Bows, arrowheads of chipped stone, horns used to store the curare used for poisoning their arrows and the dyes for their tattooing. The Schneils had made a number of drawings on cardboard, copying the designs the Machiguengas painted on their faces and bodies. They were geometrical; some very simple, others like complicated labyrinths. They explained that they were used according to the circumstances and the social status of a person. Their function was to attract good luck and ward off bad luck. These were for bachelors, these for married men, these for going hunting, and as for others, they weren't quite sure yet. Machiguenga symbolism was extremely subtle. There was one design, an X-shape like a Saint Andrew's Cross inscribed in a half circle, which, apparently, they painted on themselves when they were going to die.

It was only at the end, when I was looking for a break in

the conversation so as to take my leave, that, quite incidentally, there arose the subject which, seen from afar, blots out all the others of that night and is surely the reason why I am now devoting my days in Firenze, not so much to Dante, Machiavelli, and Renaissance art, as to weaving together the memories and fantasies of this story. I don't know how it came up. I asked a lot of questions, and some of them must have been about witch doctors and medicine men (there were two sorts: the good ones, seripigaris, and the bad ones, machikanaris). Perhaps that was what led up to it. Or perhaps my asking them about the myths, legends, and stories they had collected in their travels brought about the association of ideas. They didn't know much about the magic practices of the seripigaris or the machikanaris, except that both, like the shamans of other tribes, used tobacco, ayahuasca, and other hallucinogenic plants, such as kobuiniri bark, during their trances, which they called la mareada, the very same word they used for being drunk on masato. The Machiguengas were naturally loquacious, superb informants, but the Schneils had not wanted to press them too hard on the subject of sorcery, for fear of violating their sense of privacy.

"Yes, and besides the seripigaris and the machikanaris, there is also that curious personage who doesn't seem to be either a medicine man or a priest," Mrs. Schneil said all of a sudden. She turned uncertainly toward her husband. "Well, perhaps a bit of both, wouldn't you say, Edwin?"

"Ah, you mean the . . ." Mr. Schneil said, and hesitated. He uttered a long, loud guttural sound full of *s*'s. Remained silent, searching for a word. "How would you translate it?"

She half closed her eyes and bit a knuckle. She was blond, with very blue eyes, extremely thin lips, and a childish smile.

"A talker, perhaps. Or, better yet, a speaker," she said at

last. And uttered the same sound again: harsh, sibilant, prolonged.

"Yes." He smiled. "I think that's the closest. Hablador: a speaker."

They had never seen one. And their punctilious discretion—their fear of rubbing their hosts the wrong way—had stopped them from asking for a detailed account of the functions the hablador fulfilled among the Machiguengas; whether there were several of them or only one; and also, though they tended to discard this theory, whether, rather than an actual, concrete person, they were talking of some fabulous entity such as Kientibakori, chief of demons and creator of all things poisonous and inedible. It was certain, however, that the word "hablador" was uttered with a great show of respect by all the Machiguengas, and each time someone uttered it in front of the Schneils the others had changed the subject. But they didn't think it was a question of a taboo. For the fact was that the strange word escaped them very frequently, seeming to indicate that the hablador was always on their minds. Was he a leader or teacher of the whole community? No, he didn't seem to exercise any specific power over that loose, scattered archipelago, Machiguenga society, which, moreover, lacked any sort of authorities. The Schneils had no doubts on that score. The only headmen they had ever had were those imposed by the Viracochas, as in the little settlements of Koribeni and Chirumbia, set up by the Dominicans, or at the time of the haciendas and the rubber camps, when the bosses designated one of them as cacique so as to control them more easily. Perhaps the hablador exercised some sort of spiritual leadership or was responsible for carrying out certain religious practices. But from the allusions that they had caught, an odd sentence here, an answer there, they had gathered that the function of the hablador was above all what his name implied: to speak.

An odd thing had happened to Mrs. Schneil a few months before, near the Kompiroshiato River. The Machiguenga family she was living with—eight people: two old men, a grown man, four women, and a young girl—suddenly disappeared, without a word of explanation to her. She was very surprised, since they had never done anything of the sort before. All eight of them reappeared a few days later, as mysteriously as they had disappeared. Where had they gone off to like that? "To hear the hablador," the young girl said. The meaning of the sentence was quite clear, but Mrs. Schneil didn't find out any more, for nobody volunteered any further details, nor did she ask for any. But the eight Machiguengas had been extremely excited and whispered together endlessly during the following days. Seeing them engrossed in their interminable conclaves, Mrs. Schneil knew they were remembering the hablador.

The Schneils had made conjectures and carpentered up theories. The hablador, or habladores, must be something like the courier service of the community. Messengers who went from one settlement to another in the vast territory over which the Machiguengas were dispersed, relating to some what the others were doing, keeping them informed of the happenings, the fortunes and misfortunes of the brothers whom they saw very rarely or not at all. Their name defined them. They spoke. Their mouths were the connecting links of this society that the fight for survival had forced to split up and scatter to the four winds. Thanks to the habladores, fathers had news of their sons, brothers of their sisters, and thanks to them they were all kept informed of the deaths, births, and other happenings in the tribe.

"And of something more besides," Mr. Schneil said. "I have a feeling that the hablador not only brings current news but also speaks of the past. He is probably also the memory of the community, fulfilling a function similar to that of the jongleurs and troubadours of the Middle Ages."

Mrs. Schneil interrupted to explain to me that it was difficult to be sure of that. The Machiguenga verb system was complicated and misleading, among other reasons because it readily mixed up past and present. Just as the word for "many"—tobaiti—was used to express any quantity above four, "now" also included at least today and yesterday, and the present tense of verbs was frequently used to recount events in the recent past. It was as though to them only the future was something clearly defined. Our conversation turned to linguistics and ended with a string of examples of the humorous and unsettling implications of a form of speech in which before and now were barely differentiated.

I was deeply moved by the thought of that being, those beings, in the unhealthy forests of eastern Cusco and Madre de Dios, making long journeys of days or weeks, bringing stories from one group of Machiguengas to another and taking away others, reminding each member of the tribe that the others were alive, that despite the great distances that separated them, they still formed a community, shared a tradition and beliefs, ancestors, misfortunes and joys: the fleeting, perhaps legendary figures of those habladores who—by occupation, out of necessity, to satisfy a human whim—using the simplest, most time-hallowed of expedients, the telling of stories, were the living sap that circulated and made the Machiguengas into a society, a people of interconnected and interdependent beings. It still moves me to think of them, and even now, here, as I write these lines, in the Caffè Strozzi in old Firenze, under the torrid July sun, I break out in goose pimples.

"And why is it you break out in goose pimples?" Mascarita

said. "What is it you find so fascinating? What's so special about habladores?"

A good question. Why hadn't I been able to get them out of my mind since that night?

"They're a tangible proof that storytelling can be something more than mere entertainment," it occurred to me to say to him. "Something primordial, something that the very existence of a people may depend on. Maybe that's what impressed me so. One doesn't always know why one is moved by things, Mascarita. They strike some secret chord, and that's that."

Saúl laughed and clapped me on the shoulder. I had been speaking seriously, but he took it as a joke.

"Oh, I see. It's the literary side that interests you," he exclaimed. He sounded disappointed, as though that aspect diminished the value of my curiosity. "Well, don't let your imagination run away with you. I'll bet it's those gringos who told you that story about storytellers. Things just can't be the way they seem to be to them. I assure you the gringos understand the Machiguengas even less than the missionaries do."

We were in a little café on the Avenida España, having bread and cracklings. It was several days after my return from Amazonia. As soon as I got back I had looked for him around the university and left messages for him at La Estrella, but I hadn't been able to contact him. I was afraid I'd be off to Europe without having said goodbye to Saúl when, on the eve of my departure for Madrid, I ran into him as I got off a bus on a corner of the Avenida España. We went to that little café, where he'd treat me, he said, to a farewell meal of crackling sandwiches and ice-cold beer, the memory of which would stay with me during the whole time I was in Europe. But the memory that remained etched on my mind was, rather, his evasive answers and his incomprehensible lack of interest in a subject—the Machiguenga storytellers—which I'd thought he'd be all excited about. Was it really lack of interest? Of course not. I know now that he pretended not to be interested and lied to me when, on being backed into a corner by my questions, he assured me that he'd never heard a word about any such storytellers.

Memory is a snare, pure and simple: it alters, it subtly rearranges the past to fit the present. I have tried so many times to reconstruct that conversation in August 1958 with my friend Saúl Zuratas in the seedy café on the Avenida España, with its broken-down chairs and rickety tables, that by now I'm no longer sure of anything, with the exception, perhaps, of his enormous birthmark, the color of wine vinegar, that attracted the stares of the customers, his rebellious crest of red hair, his red-and-blue-checkered flannel shirt, and his heavy hiking shoes.

But my memory cannot have entirely invented Mascarita's fierce diatribe against the Summer Institute of Linguistics, which still rings in my ears twenty-seven years later, or my stunned surprise at the contained fury with which he spoke. It was the only time I ever saw him like that: livid with anger. I discovered that day that the archangelic Saúl, like other mortals, was capable of letting himself go, in one of those rages that, according to his Machiguenga friends, could destabilize the universe.

I said as much in the hope of distracting him. "You're going to bring on an apocalypse with your tantrum, Mascarita."

But he paid no attention to me. "Those apostolic linguists of yours are the worst of all. They work their way into the tribes to destroy them from within, just like chiggers. Into their spirit, their beliefs, their subconscious, the roots of their way of being. The others steal their vital space and exploit them or push them farther into the interior. At worst, they kill them physically. Your linguists are more refined. They want to kill them in another way. Translating the Bible into Machiguenga! How about that!"

He was so agitated I didn't argue. Several times, listening to him, I had to bite my tongue so as not to contradict him. I knew that, in Saúl Zurata's case, his objections to the Institute were not frivolous or motivated by political prejudice; that, however questionable they might seem to me, they represented a point of view long pondered and deeply felt. Why did the work of the Institute strike him as more insidious than that of the bearded Dominicans and the little Spanish nuns of Quillabamba, Koribeni, and Chirumbia?

He had to postpone his answer, as the waitress came up at that moment with a fresh batch of bread and cracklings. She set the platter down on the table and stood for a long moment looking, fascinated, at Saúl's birthmark. I saw her cross herself as she went back to her stove.

"You're mistaken. I don't find it more insidious," he finally answered sarcastically, still beside himself. "They, too, want to steal their souls, of course. But the jungle is swallowing up the missionaries, the way it did Arturo Cova in *The Vortex*. Didn't you see them on your trip? Half dead of hunger, and, what's more, very few of them. They live in such need they're in no state to evangelize anybody, luckily. Their isolation has dulled their catechistic spirit. They survive, and that's all. The jungle has clipped their claws, pal. And the way things are going in the Catholic Church, there soon won't be any priests at all, not even for Lima, let alone Amazonia."

The linguists were a different matter altogether. They were backed by economic power and an extremely efficient organization which might well enable them to implant their progress, their religion, their values, their culture. Learn the aboriginal languages! What a swindle! What for? To make the Amazonian Indians into good Westerners, good modern men, good capitalists, good Christians of the Reformed Church? Not even that. Just to wipe their culture, their gods, their institutions off the map and corrupt even their dreams. Just as they'd done to the redskins and the others back in their own country. Was that what I wanted for our jungle compatriots? To make them into what the original inhabitants of North America now were? Servants and shoeshine boys for the Viracochas?

He paused, noticing that three men at the next table had stopped talking to listen to him, their attention attracted by his birthmark and his rage. The unmarked side of his face was congested, his mouth was half open and his lower lip pushed forward and trembling. I got up to go urinate without really needing to, hoping my absence would calm him. The señora at the stove asked me, with lowered voice as I passed, whether what was wrong with his face was very serious. I whispered that it was only a birthmark, no different from the mole you have on your arm, señora. "Poor thing, it makes you feel sorry for him just looking at it," she murmured.

I returned to our table and Mascarita tried his best to smile as he lifted his glass: "To your good health, friend. Forgive me for getting so worked up."

But in fact he hadn't calmed down and was obviously still tense and about to explode again. I told him his expression reminded me of a poem, and I recited in Machiguenga the lines I remembered of the song about sadness.

I managed to make him smile, for a moment.

"You speak Machiguenga with a slight California accent," he joked. "How does that happen, I wonder?"

But a while later he lashed out at me again on the subject

that was keeping him on hot coals. Without meaning to, I had stirred up something that distressed and deeply wounded him. He spoke without stopping, as if holding his breath.

Up till now nobody had succeeded, but it was possible that the linguists would get away with it. In four hundred, five hundred years of trying, all the others had failed. They had never been able to subjugate those tiny tribes they despised. I must have read about it in the Chronicles I was doing research on at Porras Barrenechea's. Hadn't I, pal? What happened to the Incas every time they sent armies to the Antisuyo. To Túpac Yupanqui, especially. Hadn't I read about it? How their warriors disappeared in the jungle, how the Antis slipped through their fingers. They hadn't subjugated a single one, and out of spite, the people of Cusco began to look down on them. That's why they invented all those disparaging Quechua words for the Amazonian Indians: savages, degenerates. Yet, despite all that, what had happened to the Inca empire, the Tahuantinsuyo, when it was forced to confront a more powerful civilization? The barbarians of the Antisuyo, at least, went on being what they had been. Wasn't that so? And had the Spaniards been any more successful than the Incas? Hadn't all their "expeditions" into Anti territory been a total failure? They killed them whenever they could lay their hands on them, but that rarely happened. Were the thousands of soldiers, adventurers, outlaws, and missionaries who descended on the Oriente between 1500 and 1800 able to bring one single tribe under the dominion of illustrious Christian and Western civilization? Did all this mean nothing to me?

"I'd rather you told me what it means to you, Mascarita," I said.

"That these cultures must be respected," he said softly, as though finally beginning to calm down. "And the only way to respect them is not to go near them. Not touch them. Our culture is too strong, too aggressive. It devours everything it touches. They must be left alone. Haven't they amply demonstrated that they have the right to go on being what they are?"

"You're an Indigenist to the nth degree, Mascarita," I teased him. "Just like the ones in the thirties. Like Dr. Luis Valcárcel when he was young, wanting all the colonial churches and convents demolished because they represented Anti-Peru. Or should we bring back the Tahuantinsuyo? Human sacrifice, quipus, trepanation with stone knives? It's a laugh that Peru's last Indigenist turns out to be Jewish, Mascarita."

"Well, a Jew is better prepared than most people to defend the rights of minority cultures," he retorted. "And, after all, as my old man says, the problem of the Boras, of the Shapras, of the Piros, has been our problem for three thousand years."

Is that what he said? Could one at least infer something of the sort from what he was saying? I'm not sure. Perhaps this is pure invention on my part after the event. Saúl didn't practice his religion, or even believe in it. I often heard him say that the only reason he went to the synagogue was so as not to disappoint Don Salomón. On the other hand, some such association, whether superficial or profound, must have existed. Wasn't Saúl's stubborn defense of the life led by those Stone Age Peruvians explained, at least in part, by the stories he'd heard at home, at school, in the synagogue, through his inevitable contacts with other members of the community, stories of persecution and of dispersion, of attempts by more powerful cultures to stamp out Jewish faith, language, and customs, which, at the cost of great sacrifice, the Jewish people had resisted, preserving their identity?

"No, I'm not an Indigenist like the ones of the thirties.

They wanted to restore the Tahuantinsuyo, and I know very well that there's no turning back for the descendants of the Incas. The only course left them is integration. The sooner they can be Westernized, the better: it's a process that's bogged down halfway and should be speeded up. For them, it's the lesser evil now. So you see I'm not being utopian. But in Amazonia it's different. The great trauma that turned the Incas into a people of sleepwalkers and vassals hasn't yet occurred there. We've attacked them ferociously but they're not beaten. We know now what an atrocity bringing progress, trying to modernize a primitive people, is. Quite simply, it wipes them out. Let's not commit this crime. Let's leave them with their arrows, their feathers, their loincloths. When you approach them and observe them with respect, with a little fellow feeling, you realize it's not right to call them barbarians or backward. Their culture is adequate for their environment and for the conditions they live in. And, what's more, they have a deep and subtle knowledge of things that we've forgotten. The relationship between man and Nature, for instance. Man and the trees, the birds, the rivers, the earth, the sky. Man and God, as well. We don't even know what the harmony that exists between man and those things can be, since we've shattered it forever."

That he did say. Surely not in those words. But in a form that could be transcribed that way. Did he speak of God? Yes, I'm certain he spoke of God, because I remember asking him, surprised at what he said, trying to make a joke of what was eminently serious, if that meant that now we, too, had to begin believing in God.

He remained silent, head bent. A bluebottle fly had found its way into the café and was buzzing about, bumping against the sooty walls. The señora behind the counter never stopped looking at Mascarita. When Saúl raised his head, he seemed embarrassed. His tone of voice was even more serious now.

"Well, I no longer know whether I believe in God or not, pal. One of the problems of our ever-so-powerful culture is that it's made God superfluous. For them, on the contrary, God is air, water, food, a vital necessity, something without which life wouldn't be possible. They're more spiritual than we are, though you may not believe it. Even the Machiguengas, who by comparison with the others are relatively materialistic. That's why what the Institute is doing is so damaging, taking away their gods and replacing them with their own, an abstract God who's of no use to them at all in their daily life. The linguists are the smashers of idols of our time. With planes, penicillin, vaccination, and whatever else is needed to destroy the jungle. And since they're all fanatics, when something happens to them such as happened to those gringos in Ecuador, they feel even more inspired. Nothing like martyrdom to spur on fanatics, don't you agree, pal?"

What had happened in Ecuador, some weeks before, was that three American missionaries of some Protestant church had been murdered by a Jíbaro tribe with which one of them was living. The other two happened to be passing through the region. No details were known. The corpses, beheaded and pierced with arrows, had been found by a military patrol. Since the Jíbaros are headhunters, the reason for the decapitation was obvious. It had stirred up a great scandal in the press. The victims were not members of the Institute of Linguistics. I asked Saúl, intuitively anticipating what his answer would be, what he thought of those three corpses.

"I can assure you of one thing at least," he said. "They were beheaded without cruelty. Don't laugh! Believe me, it's true. With no desire to make them suffer. In that respect, the tribes are all alike, regardless of how different they may be otherwise. They kill only out of necessity. When they feel threatened, when it's a question of kill or be killed. Or when they're hungry. But the Jíbaros aren't cannibals. They didn't kill them to eat them. The missionaries either said something or did something that suddenly made the Jíbaros feel they were in great danger. A sad story, I grant you. But don't draw hasty conclusions. It has nothing in common with Nazi gas chambers or with dropping the atomic bomb on Hiroshima."

We sat there together for a long time, perhaps three or four hours. We ate a lot of crackling sandwiches and finally the woman who owned the café served us a dish of corn-flour pudding, "on the house." As we left, unable to contain herself and pointing at Saúl's birthmark, she asked "whether his affliction caused him great pain."

"No, señora, it doesn't hurt at all, fortunately. I'm not even aware that I have such a thing," Saúl replied, smiling.

We walked along together for a while, still talking of the one subject of the afternoon, of that I'm certain. As we said goodbye on the corner of the Plaza Bolognesi and the Paseo Colón, we embraced.

"I really must apologize," he said, suddenly remorseful. "I've chattered like a parrot and didn't let you open your mouth. You didn't even have a chance to tell me what you're planning to do in Europe."

We agreed to write to each other, if only a postcard now and then, to keep in touch. I wrote three times in the following years, but he never answered me.

That was the last time I saw Saúl Zuratas. The image floats unchanged above the tumultuous surge of the years, the gray air, the overcast sky, and the penetrating damp of a Lima winter serving as a backdrop. Behind him, a confusion of cars, trucks, and buses coiling around the monument to Bolognesi, and Mascarita, with the great dark stain on his face, his flaming red hair, and his checkered shirt, waving goodbye and shouting: "We'll see if you come back a real Madrileño, lisping your *z*'s and using archaic second-person plurals. Have a good trip, and lots of luck to you over there, pal!"

Four years went by without any news of him. None of the Peruvians who came through Madrid or Paris, where I lived after finishing my postgraduate studies, was ever able to tell me anything about Saúl. I thought of him often, in Spain especially, not only because of my liking for him but also because of the Machiguengas. The story the Schneils had told me about habladores kept coming back to my mind, enticing me, exciting my imagination and desire as a beautiful girl might. I had only morning classes at the university, and each afternoon I used to spend several hours at the National Library, on Castella, reading novels of chivalry. One day I remembered the name of the Dominican missionary who had written about the Machiguengas: Fray Vicente de Cenitagoya. I looked in the catalogue, and there was the book.

I read it in one sitting. It was short and naïve. The Machiguengas, whom the good Dominican frequently called savages and chided paternally for being childish, lazy, and drunken, as well as for their sorcery—which Fray Vicente called "nocturnal sabbaths"—seemed to have been observed from outside and from a considerable distance, even though the missionary had lived among them for more than twenty years. But Fray Vicente praised their honesty, their respect for their given word, and their gentle ways. Moreover, his book confirmed certain information I had which finally convinced me. They had a natural inclination, little short of unhealthy, toward listening to and telling stories, and they were incorrigible gossips. They couldn't stay still, felt no attachment whatsoever to the place where they lived, and seemed possessed by the demon of movement. The forest cast a sort of spell over them. Using all sorts of blandishments, the missionaries attracted them to the settlements of Chirumbia, Koribeni, and Panticollo. They wore themselves out trying to get the Machiguengas to settle down. They gave them mirrors, food, seed: they taught them the advantages of living in a community, for their health, for their education, for their very survival. They seemed persuaded. They put up their huts, cleared their fields, agreed to send their children to the little mission school, and appeared themselves, painted and punctual, at the evening Rosary and the morning Mass. They seemed well on their way along the path of Christian civilization. Then all of a sudden, one fine day, without saying thank you or goodbye, they vanished into the forest. A force more powerful than they drove them: an ancestral instinct impelled them irresistibly toward a life of wandering, scattered them through the tangled virgin forests.

That same night I wrote to Mascarita sending him my comments on Father Cenitagoya's book. I told him I'd decided to write something about Machiguenga storytellers. Would he help me? Here in Madrid, out of homesickness perhaps, or because I had constantly found myself mulling over our conversations in my mind, I no longer found his ideas as absurd or unrealistic as I once had. In any case, I would try to make my story as authentic and as intimate a portrayal of the Machiguenga way of life as I could. Would you lend me a hand, pal?

I set to work, brimming over with enthusiasm. But the result was lamentable. How could I write about storytellers without having at least a superficial knowledge of their beliefs, myths, customs, history? The Dominican monastery in the Calle Claudio Coello gave me invaluable help. It had a complete collection of *Misiones Dominicanas*, the journal of the missionaries of the Order in Peru, and in it I found numerous articles on the Machiguengas and also Father José Pío Aza's excellent studies of the language and folklore of the tribe.

But perhaps I learned most from the talk I had with a bearded missionary in the vast resounding library of the monastery, where the high ceiling echoed back what we were saying. Fray Elicerio Maluenda had lived for many years in the Alto Urubamba, and had become interested in Machiguenga mythology. He was a keen-minded, very learned old man, with the rather rustic manners of one who has spent his life out-of-doors, roughing it in the jungle. Every so often, as though to make a greater impression on me, he larded his pure Spanish with a peculiar-sounding Machiguenga word.

I was delighted with what he told me of the cosmogony of the tribe, full of complex symmetries and Dantesque echoes—as I discover now in Firenze, reading the *Commedia* in Italian for the first time. The earth was the center of the cosmos and there were two regions above it and two below, each one with its own sun, moon, and tangle of rivers. In the highest, Inkite, lived Tasurinchi, the all-powerful, the breather-out of people, and through it, bathing fertile banks with fruit-laden trees, flowed the Meshiareni, or river of immortality, that could be dimly made out from the earth, for it was the Milky Way. Below Inkite floated the weightless region of clouds, or Menkoripatsa, with its transparent river, the Manaironchaari. The earth, Kipacha, was the abode of the Machiguengas, a wandering people. Beneath it was the gloomy region of the dead, almost all of whose surface was covered by the river Kamabiría, plied by the souls of the deceased before taking up their new abode. And last of all, the lowest and most terrible region, that of the Gamaironi, a river of black waters where there were no fish, and of wastelands where there was nothing to eat, either. This was the domain of Kientibakori, creator of filthy things, the spirit of evil and the chief of a legion of demons, the kamagarinis. The sun of each region was less powerful and less bright than the one above. The sun of Inkite was motionless, a radiant white. The sun of Gamaironi was dark and frozen. The hesitant sun of earth came and went, its survival mythically linked to the conduct of the Machiguengas.

But how much of this—and the many other details that Fray Maluenda had given me—was true? Hadn't the admirable missionary added to or adapted much of the material he had collected? I queried Mascarita on the subject in my second letter. Again there was no answer.

I must have sent him the third one a year or so later, since by then I was in Paris. I took him to task for his stubborn silence and confessed that I'd given up the idea of writing about the habladores. I filled any number of composition books with my scribblings and spent many hours in the Place du Trocadéro, in the library of the Musée de l'Homme and in front of its display cases, trying in vain to understand the storytellers, to intuit what they were like. The voices of the ones that I'd contrived sounded all wrong. So I had resigned myself to writing other stories. But what was he doing? How was he getting on? What had he been doing all this time, and what were his plans?

It was not until the end of 1963, when Matos Mar turned up in Paris, to speak at an anthropological congress, that I heard of Mascarita's whereabouts. What I learned left me flabbergasted.

"Saúl Zuratas went to live in Israel?"

We were in the Old Navy in Saint-Germain-des-Prés, drinking hot grog to withstand the cold of a depressing ash-gray December evening. We sat smoking as I eagerly plied him with questions about friends and developments in far-off Peru.

"Something to do with his father, it seems," Matos Mar said, bundled up in such a bulky overcoat and heavy scarf he looked like an Eskimo. "Don Salomón, from Talara. Did you know him? Saúl was very fond of him. Remember how he refused that fellowship to Bordeaux so as not to leave him alone? Apparently the old man took it into his head to go off to Israel to die. And devoted as he was to his father, Mascarita of course let him have his way. They decided the whole thing very suddenly, from one day to the next, more or less. Because, when Saúl told me, they'd already sold the little shop in Breña, La Estrella, and had their bags all packed."

And did Saúl like the idea of settling in Israel? Because once there, he'd have to learn Hebrew, do his military service, reorganize his life from A to Z. Matos Mar thought he might have been exempted from military service because of his birthmark. I searched my memory trying to remember whether I'd ever heard Mascarita mention Zionism, returning to the Homeland, Alyah. Never.

"Well, maybe it wasn't a bad thing for Saúl, starting all over again from zero," Matos Mar reflected. "He must have adapted to Israel, since all this happened some four years ago, and as far as I know, he hasn't come back to Peru. I can well imagine him living in a kibbutz. The truth of the matter is that Saúl wasn't getting anywhere in Lima. Ethnology and the university had both been a disappointment to him, for reasons I never quite understood. He never finished his doctoral dissertation. And I think even his love affair with the Machiguengas was a thing of the past. 'Aren't you going to miss your naked savages there in Urubamba?' I asked him when we said goodbye. 'Of course not,' he said. 'I can adapt to anything. And there must be plenty of people who go around naked in Israel, too.' "

Unlike Matos Mar, I didn't think Saúl would have found Alyah easy going. Because he was, viscerally, a part of Peru, too torn and revolted by Peruvian affairs—one of them at least—to cast everything aside overnight, the way one changes shirts. I often tried to imagine him in the Middle East. Knowing him, I could readily foresee that in his new country the Palestine question and the occupied territories would confront Saúl Zuratas, the Israeli citizen, with all sorts of moral dilemmas. My mind wandered, trying to see him in his new surroundings, jabbering away in his new language, going about his new job—what was it?—and I prayed to Tasurinchi that no bullet might have come Mascarita's way in the wars and border incidents in Israel since he'd arrived there.

A MISCHIEVOUS kamagarini disguised as a wasp stung the tip of Tasurinchi's penis while he was urinating. He's walking. How? I don't know, but he's walking. I saw him. They haven't killed him. He could have lost his eyes or his head, his soul could have left him after what he did there among the Yaminahuas. Nothing happened to him, it seems. He's well, walking, content. Not angry, laughing, perhaps. Saying "What's all the fuss about?" As I headed toward the river Mishahua to visit him, I thought: He won't be there. If it's really true that he did that, he'll have taken off somewhere far away, where the Yaminahuas won't find him. Or maybe they've already killed him; him and his kinfolk as well. But there he was, and his family too, and the woman he stole. "Are you there, Tasurinchi?" "Ehé, ehé, here I am."

She's learning to speak. "Say something so the hablador sees you can speak, too," he ordered her. You could hardly understand what the Yaminahua woman was saying, and the other women made fun of her: "What are those noises we keep hearing?" Pretending to search about: "What animal can have gotten into the house?" Looking under the mats. They make her work and they treat her badly. Saying: "When she opens her legs, fish are going to come out of her, like they did out of Pareni." And worse things still. But it's quite true, she's learning to speak. I understood some of the things she said. "Man walks," I understood.

"So it's true, you stole yourself a Yaminahua woman," I remarked to Tasurinchi. He says he didn't steal her. He traded a sachavaca, a sack of maize, and one of cassava, for her. "The Yaminahuas should be pleased. What I gave them is worth more than she is," he assured me.

"Isn't that so?" he asked the Yaminahua woman in front of me, and she agreed. "Yes, it is," she said. I understood that, too.

Since the mischievous kamagarini stung the tip of his penis, Tasurinchi feels obliged to do certain things, suddenly, without his knowing how or why. "It's an order I hear and I have to obey it," he says. "I expect it comes from a little god or a little devil, from something that's gotten deep down inside me through my penis, whatever it may be." Stealing that woman was one of those orders, it seems.

His penis is now the same as it was before. But a spirit has stayed on, there in his soul, which tells him to be different and do things that the others don't understand. He showed me where he was urinating when the kamagarini stung him. Ay! Ay! it made him squeal, made him leap about, and he wasn't able to go on urinating. He chased the wasp away with a smack of his hand, and he heard it laugh, perhaps. A while later his penis started getting bigger. Every night it swelled up, and every morning more still. Everybody laughed at him. He was so ashamed he had them weave him a bigger cushma. He hid his penis in its pouch. But it went on growing, growing, and he could no longer hide it. It got in his way when he moved. He dragged it along the way an animal drags its tail. Sometimes people stepped on it just to hear him yelp. Ay! Atatau! He had to roll it up and perch it on his shoulder, the way I do with my little parrot. That's how they went along on their travels, heads together, keeping each other company. Tasurinchi talked to it to keep himself amused. The other listened to him, silent, attentive, just the way all of you listen to me, looking at him with its big eye. One-Eye—Little One-Eye!—just stared at him. It had grown a whole lot. The birds perched on it to sing, thinking it was a tree. When Tasurinchi urinated, a cataract of warm water, foamy as the rapids of the Gran Pongo, came out of its big mouth. Tasurinchi could have bathed in it, and his family too, maybe. He used it as a seat when he stopped to rest. And at night it was his pallet. When he went hunting, it was both sling and spear. He could shoot it to the very top of a tree to knock down the shimbillo monkeys, and using it as a club, he could kill a puma.

To purify him, the seripigari wrapped his penis in fern fronds that had been heated over live coals. He made him sip their juice and sing, for a whole night, while he himself drank tobacco brew and ayahuasca. He danced, he disappeared through the roof and came back changed into a saankarite. After that, he was able to suck the evil from him and spit it out. It was thick and yellow and smelled like drunkard's vomit. By morning his penis started shrinking, and a few moons later it was the little dwarf it had been before. But since then Tasurinchi hears those orders. "In some of my souls there's a capricious mother," he says. "That's why I got myself the Yaminahua woman."

It seems she's become used to her new husband. There she

is, by the Mishahua, settled down nicely, as though she'd always been Tasurinchi's wife. But the other women are furious, insulting her and finding any excuse to hit her. I saw them and heard them. "She's not like us" is what they say. "She's not people, whatever she may be. A monkey, perhaps, the fish perhaps that stuck in Kashiri's gullet." She went on slowly chewing at her cassava as though she didn't hear them.

Another time she was carrying a pitcher full of water, and without noticing she bumped into a child, knocking him over. Whereupon the women all set upon her. "You did it on purpose, you wanted to kill him" was what they said. It wasn't true, but that was what they said to her. She picked up a stick and confronted them, without anger. "One day they're going to kill her," I said to Tasurinchi. "She knows how to look after herself," he answered. "She hunts animals. Something I've never known women to do. And she's the one who carries the heaviest load on her back when we bring cassavas in from the field. What I'm afraid of, and what's more likely, is that she'll kill the other women. The Yaminahuas are fighting people, just like the Mashcos. Their women too, maybe."

I said that, for that very reason, he ought to be worried. And go off somewhere else right away. The Yaminahuas must be furious at what he'd done to them. What if they came to take revenge? Tasurinchi burst out laughing. The whole matter had been settled, it seems. The husband of the Yaminahua woman, along with two others, had come to see him. They'd drunk masato together and talked. And eventually come to an agreement. What they were after wasn't the woman but a shotgun, on top of the sachavaca, the maize, and the cassava he gave them. The White Fathers had told them he had a shotgun. "Look around for it," he offered. "If you can find it, take it." Finally they left. Satisfied, it seems. Tasurinchi isn't going to give the

Yaminahua woman back to her kinfolk. Because she's already learning to speak. "The others will get used to her when she has a child," Tasurinchi says. The children are already used to her. They treat her as though she were people, a woman who walks. "Mother," they call her.

That, anyway, is what I have learned.

Who knows whether this woman will make Tasurinchi, the one from the Mishahua, happy? She may just as well bring him unhappiness. Coming down to this world to marry a Machiguenga brought misfortune to Kashiri, the moon. So they say, anyway. But maybe we ought not to lament what befell him. Kashiri's mischance brings us food and allows us to warm ourselves. Isn't the moon the father of the sun by a Machiguenga woman?

That was before.

A strong, serene youth, Kashiri was bored in the sky above, Inkite, where there were no stars yet. Instead of cassava and plantain, men ate earth. It was their only food. Kashiri came down the river Meshiareni, paddling with his arms, without a pole. His canoe skirted the rocks and the whirlpools. Down it came, floating. The world was still dark and the wind blew fiercely. The rain came down in buckets. Kashiri jumped ashore on the Oskiaje, where this earth meets the worlds of the sky, where monsters live and all the rivers go to die. He looked around him. He didn't know where he was, but he was content. He started walking. Not long thereafter, he spied the Machiguenga girl who was to bring him happiness and unhappiness, sitting weaving a mat and softly singing a song to keep away the vipers. Her cheeks and forehead were painted; two red lines went up from her mouth to her temples. So, then, she was unmarried: she would learn to cook food and make masato.

To please her, Kashiri, the moon, taught her what cassava

and plantain were. He showed her how they were planted, harvested, and eaten. Since then there has been food and masato in the world. That is when after began, it seems. Then Kashiri presented himself at her father's hut. His arms were laden with the animals he had hunted and fished for him. Finally he offered to clear a field for him in the highest part of the forest and to work for him, sowing cassava and pulling out weeds till it grew. Tasurinchi agreed to let him take his daughter. They had to wait for the girl's first blood. It was a long time coming, and meanwhile the moon cleared and burned and weeded the forest patch and sowed plantain, maize, and cassava for his future family. Everything was going very well.

The girl, then, started to bleed. She stayed locked up, not speaking a word to her kinfolk. The old woman who watched over her never left her, by day or by night. The girl ceaselessly spun cotton thread, never resting. Not once did she go near the fire or eat chili peppers, so as not to bring misfortune upon herself or her kinfolk. Not once did she look at the man who was to be her husband, nor did she speak to him. She went on in that way until she stopped bleeding. Then she cut her hair and the old woman helped her to bathe herself, wetting her body with warm water poured from a pitcher. At last the girl could go live with Kashiri. At last she could be his wife.

Everything followed its course. The world was peaceful. Flocks of parrots flew overhead, noisy and content. But there was another girl in the hamlet, who may not have been a woman but an itoni, that wicked little devil. It disguises itself as a pigeon now, but then it dressed as a woman. She waxed furious, it seems, seeing all the presents Kashiri brought his new family. She would have liked to have him as her husband; she would have liked, in a word, to give birth to the sun. Because the moon's wife had given birth to the healthy child whose fire would give light and heat to our world when he grew up. So everyone would know how angry she was, she painted her face red with annatto dye. She went and posted herself at a bend in the path where Kashiri had to pass on his way back from the cassava patch. Squatting down, she emptied her body. She pushed hard, swelling herself up. Then she dug her hands into the filth and waited, storing up fury. When she saw him coming, she threw herself at him from among the trees. And before the moon could escape, she'd rubbed his face with the shit she'd just shat.

Kashiri knew at once that those stains could never be washed away. Marked by such shame, what was he going to do in this world? Sadly, he went back to Inkite, the sky above. There he has remained. Because of the stains, his light was dimmed. Yet his son is resplendent. Doesn't the sun shine? Doesn't he warm us? We help him by walking. Rise, we say to him each night as he sinks. His mother was a Machiguenga, after all.

That, anyway, is what I have learned.

But the seripigari of Segakiato tells the story differently.

Kashiri came down to the earth and spied the girl in the river, bathing and singing. He approached and threw a handful of dirt at her that hit her in the belly. She was angry and started throwing stones at him. It had started raining all of a sudden. Kientibakori must have been in the forest, dancing, having drunk his fill of masato. "Stupid woman," said the moon to the girl. "I threw mud at you so you'd have a son." All the little devils were happily farting at each other under the trees. And that's what happened. The girl got pregnant. But when her time came to give birth, she died. And her son died, too. The Machiguengas were furious. They seized their arrows and their knives. They went to Kashiri and surrounded him, saying:

"You must eat that corpse." They threatened him with their bows. They thrust their stones under his nose. The moon resisted, trembling. But they said: "Eat her up. You must eat up the dead woman."

At last, weeping bitter tears, he slit open his wife's belly. There was the baby, twinkling. He pulled it out and it came to life, it seems. It moved and whimpered in thanks. It was alive. Kashiri, on his knees, began swallowing his wife's body, starting with the feet. "That's all right, you can go now," the Machiguengas said when he'd reached her stomach. Then the moon, hoisting the remains onto his shoulder, went on his way, back to the sky above. There he is still, looking at us. Listening to me. The stains that show on him are the pieces he didn't eat.

Furious at what they'd done to Kashiri, his father, the sun stayed put, burning us. He dried up the rivers, parched the fields and the woods. Made the animals die of thirst. "He's never going to move again," said the Machiguengas, tearing their hair. They were frightened. "We're doomed to die," they sang sadly. So then the seripigari went up to Inkite. He spoke to the sun. He persuaded him, it seems. He would move again. "We'll walk together," they say he said. That's the way life was from then on, the way it is now. That's where before ended and after began. That's why we go on walking.

"Is that why Kashiri's light is so weak?" I asked the seripigari of the Segakiato. "Yes," he answered. "The moon is only half a man. Others say that a bone got stuck in his throat while he was eating a fish. And that, ever since, his light has been dim."

That, anyway, is what I have learned.

As I was coming here, even though I knew the way, I got lost. It must have been Kientibakori's fault, or his little devils', or a very powerful machikanari's. Without any warning, it suddenly started raining; the sky hadn't darkened or the air turned briny. I was fording a river and the rain was coming down so hard I couldn't climb up the bank. After two or three steps I slipped back, the earth gave way beneath my feet, and I found myself at the bottom of the channel. My little parrot was frightened, flapped his wings, and flew away squawking. The bank became a gully. Mud and water, stones, branches, bushes, trees split in two by the storm, bodies of birds and insects. All rolling down on top of me. The sky turned black; bolts of lightning flashed and crashed. The peals of thunder sounded like all the animals of the forest roaring at once. When the lord of thunder rages like that, something grave is happening. I went on trying to climb up the gully. Would I succeed? If I don't clamber up a really tall tree, I'll be carried away, I thought. Any moment now, all this is going to be a boiling caldron of water pouring down from heaven. I had no strength left to struggle; my arms and legs were badly injured from my many hard falls. I was swallowing water through my nose and my mouth. Even my eyes and my anus seemed to be taking in water. This is going to be the end of you, Tasurinchi. Your soul will take off to goodness knows where. And I touched the top of my head to feel it leaving.

I don't know how long I kept on, climbing up, rolling down, climbing up again. The channel had become a wide river after swallowing its banks. At last I was so tired out I let myself sink beneath the water. "I'm going to rest," I said. "Enough of this useless struggle." But do the ones who go like that rest? Isn't drowning the worst way to go? In a moment I'd be floating on the Kamabiría, the river of the dead, headed for the abyss with no sunlight and no fish: the lowest world, the dark land of Kientibakori. Meanwhile, without my noticing, my hands had grabbed hold of a tree trunk that the storm had cast into the river, perhaps. I don't know how I managed to climb onto it. Nor whether I fell asleep at once. The sun had set. It was dark and cold. The raindrops falling on my back felt like stones.

In my sleep I discovered the trap. What I'd taken for a tree trunk was an alligator. What sort of bark could those hard, prickly scales be? It's a caiman's back, Tasurinchi. Had the alligator noticed that I was on its back? If so, it would have been flicking its tail. Or it would have dived under to make me let go, and then bitten me underwater, the way caimans always do. Could it be dead, perhaps? If it were, it would be floating feet up. What are you going to do, Tasurinchi? Slip into the water very slowly and swim to the shore? I'd never have gotten there in that storm. You couldn't even see the trees. And, anyway, there might not be any land left in the world. Try to kill the alligator? I had no weapon. Back at the channel, while I was struggling up the bank, I'd lost my pouch, my knife, and my arrows. I'd best stay still, sitting tight on the alligator. Best wait till something or someone decided.

We were floating along, borne by the swift current. I was shivering with cold and my teeth were chattering. Thinking: Where can the little parrot be? The alligator didn't paddle with its feet or its tail, but just went where the river took it. Little by little it was getting light. Muddy water, dead animals, jumbled islets of roofs, huts, branches, and canoes. Here and there, men half eaten by piranhas and other river creatures. There were great clouds of mosquitoes, and water spiders crawling over my body. I felt them biting me. I was very hungry and perhaps I could have grabbed one of the dead fish the water was bearing along, but what if I attracted the alligator's notice? All I could do was drink. I didn't have to move to quench my thirst. I just opened my mouth and the rain filled it with fresh cold water.

At that point a little bird landed on my shoulder. From its

red-and-yellow crest, its feathers, its gold breast, and its sharp-pointed beak, I took it to be a kirigueti. But it could have been a kamagarini or even a saankarite. For whoever heard of birds talking? "You're in a bad fix," it chirped. "If you let go, the alligator's going to spot you. Its squinty eyes see a long way. It'll knock you out with one slap of its tail, grab you by the belly with its great toothy mouth, and eat you up. It'll eat you up bones and hair and all. Because it's as hungry as you are. But can you go on clinging to that caiman for the rest of your life?"

"What's the use of telling me what I know all too well?" I said. "Why don't you give me some advice, instead? What to do to get out of the water."

"Fly," it cheeped, fluttering its yellow crest. "There's no other way, Tasurinchi. Like your little parrot did when you were on the steep bank, or this way, like me." It gave a little hop, flew about in little circles, and disappeared from sight.

Can flying be that easy? Seripigaris and machikanaris fly, when they're in a trance. But they have wisdom: brews, little gods, or little devils help them. But what do I have? The things I'm told and the things I tell, that's all. And as far as I know, that never yet made anyone fly. I was cursing the kamagarini disguised as a kirigueti, when I felt something scratching the soles of my feet.

A stork had landed on the alligator's tail. I could see its long pink legs and its curved beak. It scratched my feet, looking for worms, or perhaps thinking they were edible. It was hungry, too. Frightened though I was, it made me laugh. I couldn't help myself. I burst out laughing. Just the way all of you are laughing now. Doubling over, whooping with laughter. Just like you, Tasurinchi. And the alligator woke up, of course. It realized at once that things were happening on its back that it couldn't see or understand. It opened its mouth and roared, it flicked its tail furiously, and without knowing what I was doing, there I was, all of a sudden, clinging to the stork. The way a baby monkey clings to the she-monkey, the way a newborn suckling babe clings to its mother. Frightened by the flicking tail, the stork tried to fly away. But since it couldn't, because I was clinging to it, it started squawking. Its squawks frightened the alligator even more, and me, too. We all squawked. There we were, the three of us, seeing who could squawk the loudest.

And suddenly, down below, getting farther and farther away, I saw the alligator, the river, the mud. The wind was so strong I could hardly breathe. There I was, in the air, way up high. There was Tasurinchi, the storyteller, flying. The stork was flying, and clinging to its neck, my legs twined around its legs, I was flying, too. Down below was the earth, getting smaller. There was gleaming water everywhere. Those little dark stains must be trees; those snakes, rivers. It was colder than ever. Had we left the earth? If so, this must be Menkoripatsa, the world of the clouds. There was no sign of its river. Where was the Manaironchaari, with its waters made of cotton? Was I really flying? The stork must have grown to be able to carry me. Or maybe I'd shrunk to the size of a mouse. Who knows which? It flew calmly on, with steady sweeps of its wings, letting itself be carried by the wind. Untroubled by my weight, perhaps. I shut my eyes so as not to see how far away the earth was now. Such a drop, such a long way down. Feeling sad at leaving it, maybe. When I opened them again I saw the stork's white wings, their pink edges, the regular wingbeat. The warmth of its down sheltered me from the cold. Now and then it gurgled, stretching out its neck, lifting its beak, as though talking to itself. So this was the Menkoripatsa. The seripigaris rose to this world in their trances; among these clouds they held counsel with the little saankarite gods about the evils and the mischief of the bad spirits. How I would have liked to see a seripigari floating there. "Help me," I'd say to him. "Get me out of this fix, Tasurinchi." Because wasn't I even worse off way up there, flying in the clouds, than when I was perched on the back of the caiman?

Who knows how long I flew with the stork? What to do now, Tasurinchi? You won't be able to hang on much longer. Your arms and legs are getting tired. You'll let go, your body will dissolve in the air, and by the time you reach the earth, you'll be nothing but water. It had stopped raining. The sun was rising. This cheered me up. Courage, Tasurinchi! I kicked the stork, I yanked at it, I butted it, I even bit it to make it descend. It didn't understand. It was frightened and stopped gurgling; it started squawking, pecking here and there, flying first this way, then that, like this, to get rid of me. It nearly won the tussle. Several times I was just about to slip off. Suddenly I realized that every time I squeezed its wing, we fell, as though it had stumbled in the air. That's what saved me, perhaps. With the little strength I had left, I wound my feet around one of its wings, pinning it down so that the stork could hardly move it. Courage, Tasurinchi! What I hoped for happened. Flying on only one wing now, the other one, it flapped with all its might, but even so, it couldn't fly as well as before. It tired and started descending. Down, down, squawking; despairing, perhaps. I was happy, though. The earth was getting closer. Closer, closer. How lucky you are, Tasurinchi. Here you are already. When I grazed the tops of the trees, I let go. As I fell, down and down, I could see the stork, burbling for joy, flying on both wings again, rising. Down I went, getting badly scratched and battered. Bouncing from branch to branch, breaking them, scraping the bark from the trunks, feeling that

I, too, was falling to bits. I tried to catch hold with my hands, with my feet. How lucky monkeys are, or any other creature that has a tail to hang by, I thought. The leaves and small branches, the vines and twining plants, the spiders' webs and lianas would check my fall, perhaps. When I landed, the shock didn't kill me, it seems. What joy feeling the earth beneath my body. It was soft and warm. Damp, too. Ehé, here I am. I've arrived. This is my world. This is my home. The best thing that ever happened to me is living here, on this earth, not in the water, not in the air.

When I opened my eyes, there was Tasurinchi, the seripigari, looking at me. "Your little parrot's been waiting a long time for you," he said. And there it was, clearing its throat. "How do you know it's mine?" I joked. "There are lots of parrots in the forest." "Well, this one looks like you," he answered. Yes, it was my little parrot. It jabbered, pleased to see me. "You've slept for I don't know how many moons," the seripigari told me.

Many things have happened to me on this journey, coming to see you, Tasurinchi. It's been hard getting here. I'd never have made it if it hadn't been for an alligator, a kirigueti, and a stork. Let's see if you can explain to me how that was possible.

"What saved you was your never once losing your temper from the beginning to the end of your adventure" was his comment after I'd told him what I've just told you. That's most likely so. Anger is a disorder of the world, it seems. If men didn't get angry, life would be better than it is. "Anger is what's to blame for there being comets—kachiborérine—in the sky," he assured me. "With their fiery tails and their wild careering, they threaten to throw the four worlds of the Universe into confusion."

This is the story of Kachiborérine.

That was before.

In the beginning the comet was a Machiguenga. He was young and peaceable. Walking. Content, most likely. His wife died, leaving a son, who grew up healthy and strong. He brought him up and took a new wife, a younger sister of the one he'd lost. One day, coming back from fishing for boquichicos, he found the lad mounted on his second wife. They were both panting, well satisfied. Kachiborérine went away from the hut, perturbed. Thinking: I must get a woman for my son. He needs a wife.

He went to consult the seripigari, who went and spoke to the saankarite and came back: "The one place you can get a wife for your son is in Chonchoite country," he said. "But be careful. You know why."

Kachiborérine went there, knowing full well that the Chonchoites chip their teeth to sharp points with knives and eat human flesh. He'd hardly entered their territory, just crossed the lake where it began, when he felt the earth swallow him. Everything went dark. I've fallen into a tseibarintsi, he thought. Yes, there he was, in a hole in the ground hidden by leaves and branches, with spears to impale peccaries and tapirs. The Chonchoites pulled him out, bruised and terrified. They wore devil masks that left their starving gullets showing. They were pleased, smelling him and licking him. They sniffed and licked him all over. And without further ado they ripped out his intestines, the way you clean a fish. There and then, they put the intestines to bake on hot stones. And as the Chonchoites, giddy, beside themselves with joy, were eating his entrails, Kachiborérine's gutted skin escaped and crossed the lake.

On the way back home he made a brew of tobacco. He was a seripagari too, maybe. In his trance, he learned that his wife was heating a potion with cumo poison in it, so as to kill him. Still not giving way to anger, Kachiborérine sent her a message, counseling her. Saying: "Why do you want to kill your husband? Don't do it. He has suffered a great deal. Instead, prepare a brew that will put back the intestines the Chonchoites ate." She listened without saying anything, looking out of the corner of her eye at the youth who was now her husband. The two of them were living together, happy as could be.

Soon after, Kachiborérine reached his hut. Tired out from so much journeying; sad because of his failure. The woman handed him a bowl. The yellow liquid looked like masato, but it was maize beer. Blowing the foam from the surface, he eagerly drank it down. But the liquid, mixed with a stream of blood, came pouring out of his body that was nothing but a skin. Weeping, Kachiborérine realized that he was empty inside; weeping, that he was a man without guts or heart.

Then he became angry.

It rained. Lightning flashed. All the little devils must have come out to dance in the woods. The woman was frightened and started to run. She ran, up through the woods, to the field, stumbling as she ran. There she hid in the trunk of a tree that her husband had hollowed out to make a canoe. Kachiborérine searched for her, screaming in fury: "I'm going to tear her to pieces." He asked the cassavas in the cassava field where she was hidden, and since they couldn't answer, he ripped them out by the handful. He asked the maguna and the datura: we don't know. Neither the plants nor the trees told him where she was hidden. So he slashed them with his machete and then stamped on them. Deep in the forest, Kientibakori drank masato and danced for joy.

At last, his head reeling from searching, blind with rage, Kachiborérine returned to his hut. He grabbed a bamboo cane, pounded one end, smeared it thickly with resin from the ojeé tree, and lighted it. When the flame leaped up, he grabbed the cane by the other end and shoved it up his anus, a good way up. Leaping about and roaring, he looked at the ground, looked at the forest. At last, choking with anger, pointing at the sky, he cried: "Where can I go, then, that's not this cursed world? I'll go up there above; I'll be better off there, perhaps." He'd already changed into a devil and he started rising, higher and higher. Since then, that's where he's been, up there. Since then, that's who we see, now and again, in Inkite, Kachiborérine, the comet. You don't see his face. You don't see his body. Only the flaming cane he carries around in his anus. He'll go on his way in a fury forever, maybe.

"Lucky for you that you didn't meet him when you were flying up there clutching the stork," Tasurinchi the seripigari said to me mockingly. "You'd have gotten burned by his tail." According to him, Kachiborérine comes down to earth every so often to collect Machiguenga corpses from the riverbanks. He slings them over his shoulder and carries them up yonder. He changes them into secret stars, they say.

That, anyway, is what I have learned.

We sat chatting there in that country where there are so many fireflies. Night had come on as I talked with Tasurinchi, the seripigari. The forest lighted up here, fell dark there, lighted up farther on. It seemed to be winking at us. "I don't know how you can live in this place, Tasurinchi. I wouldn't live here. Going from one place to another, I've seen all sorts of things among the men who walk. But nowhere have I seen so many fireflies, I swear. All the trees have begun to give off sparks. Isn't that a sign of some misfortune to come? I tremble every time I come to visit you, thinking of those fireflies. It's as though they're looking at us, listening to what I tell you."

"Of course they're looking at us," the seripigari assured

me. "Of course they listen carefully to what you say. Just as I do, they look forward to your coming. They're happy seeing you come, happy listening to your stories. They have a good memory, unlike what's happening to me. I'm losing my wisdom along with my strength. They stay young, it seems. Once you've gone, they entertain me, reminding me of what they heard you telling."

"Are you making fun of me, Tasurinchi? I've visited many seripigaris and I've heard something extraordinary from each one. But I never knew before that any of them could talk with fireflies."

"Well, you're seeing one right here who can," Tasurinchi said to me, laughing at my surprise. "If you want to hear, you have to know how to listen. I've learned how. If I hadn't, I'd have given up walking some time ago. I used to have a family, remember. They all went, killed by the evil, the river, lightning, a jaguar. How do you think I was able to bear so many misfortunes? By listening, storyteller. Nobody ever comes here to this part of the forest. Once in a great while, some Machiguenga from the river valleys farther down, seeking help. He comes, he goes, and I'm alone again. Nobody's going to come kill me here; no Viracocha, Mashco, Punaruna, or devil is going to climb all the way up here to this forest. But the life of a man so completely alone soon ends.

"What could I do? Rage? Despair? Go to the riverbank and stick a chambira thorn into myself? I started thinking and remembered the fireflies. They more or less preyed on my mind, just as they do you. Why were there so many of them? Why didn't they congregate in any other part of the forest the way they did here? In one of my trances, I learned why. I asked the spirit of a saankarite, back in the roof of my house. 'Isn't it on your account?' he answered. 'Couldn't they have come to keep you company? A man needs his family, if he's going to walk.' That made me think. And that was when I first spoke to them. I felt odd, talking to some little lights that kept going on and off without answering me. 'I've learned you're here to keep me company. The little god explained it to me. It was stupid of me not to have guessed before. Thank you for coming, for being everywhere around me.' One night went by, then another and another. Each time, the forest first darkened and then filled with little lights. I purified myself with water, prepared tobacco and brews, talked to them by singing to them. All night long I sang to them. And even though they didn't answer, I listened to them. Carefully. Respectfully. Very soon I was certain they heard me. 'I understand, I understand. You're testing Tasurinchi's patience.' Silent, motionless, serene, my eyes shut, waiting. I listened but heard nothing. At last, one night, after many nights, it happened. Over there, now. Sounds different from the sounds of the forest when night falls. Do you hear them? Murmurs, whispers, laments. A cascade of soft voices. Whirlpools of voices, voices colliding, intermingling, voices you can barely hear. Listen, listen, storyteller. It's always like that in the beginning. A sort of confusion of voices. Later on, you can understand them. I had earned their trust, perhaps. Very soon, we could converse. And now they're my kinfolk."

That's how it's come about, it seems. Tasurinchi and the fireflies have gotten used to each other. They now spend their nights talking together. The seripigari tells them about the men who walk and they tell him their eternal story. They, for their part, aren't happy. Before, yes, they were, it seems. They lost their happiness many moons ago, though they go on glowing nonetheless. Because all the fireflies here are males. That is the misfortune that has befallen them. Their females are the lights in the sky above. That's right, the stars of Inkite. And what are the females doing in the world up above and the males in this one? That's the story they keep telling, according to Tasurinchi. Look at them, just look at them. Little lights blinking on and off. The same as words to them, perhaps. Right here, right now, all around us, they're telling each other how they lost their women. They never tire of talking about it, he says. They spend their lives remembering their misfortune and cursing Kashiri, the moon.

This is the story of the fireflies.

That was before.

In that time, they were all one family. The males had their females and the females their males. There was peace and food, and those who went came back, breathed out by Tasurinchi.

We Machiguengas had not yet started walking. The moon lived among us, married to a Machiguenga. He was insatiable; all he wanted was to be on top of her. He got her pregnant and the sun was born. Kashiri kept mounting her more and more often. The seripigari warned him: "Some evil will happen, in this world and in the ones above, if you go on like this. Let your wife alone, don't be so greedy." Kashiri paid no attention, but the Machiguengas were alarmed. The sun might lose its light. The earth would be in darkness, cold; life would slowly disappear, perhaps. And that was what happened. There were sudden terrible upheavals. The world shook, the rivers overflowed, monstrous beings emerged from the Gran Pongo and devastated the countryside. The men who walked, dismayed, ill-counseled, lived by night, fleeing the day, to please Kashiri. Because the moon was jealous of his child and hated the sun. Were we all going to die? So it seemed. Then Tasurinchi breathed out. He blew once again. He went on blowing. He didn't kill Kashiri, but he nearly snuffed him out, leaving him only the dim light he now has. And he sent him back to Inkite, back to where he'd been before he came down seeking a wife. That's how after must have started.

So that the moon wouldn't feel lonely, Tasurinchi said to him: "Take company with you, whatever company you like." So Kashiri pointed at the females of those fireflies. Because they shone with their own light? They reminded him of the light he'd lost, perhaps. That region of Inkite to which the father of the sun was exiled must be night. And the stars up there must be the females of those fireflies. Letting themselves be mounted by the moon, that insatiable male. And the males here, without their women, waiting for them. Is that why fireflies go mad when they see a shooting star falling, down and down in a bright ball? Is that why they bump into each other, crash into the trees, flying wildly about? It's one of our women, they must be thinking. She's escaped from Kashiri. All the males dreaming: It's my wife who's escaped, my wife who's coming.

That's how after began, perhaps. The sun lives alone too, giving light and heat. It was Kashiri's fault that there was night. Sometimes the sun would like to have a family. To be near his father, however wicked he's been. He must go looking for him. And that's why he goes down, over and over again. That's what sunsets are, it seems. That's why we began walking. To put the world in order and avoid confusion. Tasurinchi the seripigari is well. Content. Walking. With fireflies all around him.

That, anyway, is what I have learned.

On each of my journeys I learn a lot, just listening. Why can men plant and harvest cassavas in the cassava patch and not women? Why can women plant and pick cotton in the field and not men? Then, one day, over by the Poguintinari, listening to the Machiguengas, I understood. "Because cassava is male and cotton female, Tasurinchi. Plants like dealing with their own kind." Females with females and males with males. That's wisdom, it seems. Right, little parrot?

Why can a woman who's lost her husband go fishing, though she can't go hunting without endangering the world? If she shoots an arrow into an animal, the mother of things suffers, they say. That may be so. I was thinking about taboos and dangers as I came. "Aren't you frightened journeying alone, storyteller?" they ask me. "You ought to take someone along with you." Sometimes I do travel in company. If someone is going my way, we walk together. If I see a family walking, I walk with them. But it's not always easy to find company. "Aren't you frightened, storyteller?" I wasn't before, because I didn't know. Now I am. I know now I might meet a kamagarini or one of Kientibakori's monsters in a ravine or a gorge. What would I do? I don't know. Sometimes when I've put up my shelter, driven the poles into the riverbank, roofed it over with palm leaves, it starts raining. And I think: What'll you do if the little devil appears? And I lie awake all night. It hasn't ever appeared so far. Perhaps the herbs in my pouch scare it away; perhaps the necklace the seripigari hung around my neck, saying: "It'll protect you against demons and the wiles of the machikanari." I haven't taken it off since. Anyone who sees a kamagarini lost in the woods dies on the spot, people assure you. I haven't seen one yet. Perhaps.

Traveling through the forest alone isn't a good thing either, because of the hunting taboos, the seripigari explained. "What will you do when you've gotten yourself a monkey or downed a pavita with your bow and arrow?" he said. "Who's going to pick up the dead body? If you touch an animal you've killed, you'll make yourself impure." That's dangerous, it seems. By listening, I learned what you have to do. Clean the blood off first, with grass or water. "Clean all the blood off and then you can touch it. Because the impurity isn't in the flesh or in the bones, but in the blood of whatever has died." That's what I do, and here I am. Talking, walking.

Thanks to Tasurinchi, the firefly seripigari, I'm never bored when I'm traveling. Nor sad, thinking: How many moons still before I meet the first man who walks? Instead, I start listening. And I learn. I listen closely, the way he did. Go on listening, carefully, respectfully. After a while the earth feels free to speak. It's the way it is in a trance, when everything and everyone speaks freely. The things you'd least expect speak. There they are: speaking. Bones, thorns. Pebbles, lianas. Little bushes and budding leaves. The scorpion. The line of ants dragging a botfly back to the anthill. The butterfly with rainbow wings. The hummingbird. The mouse up a branch speaks, and circles in the water. Lying quietly, with closed eyes, the storyteller is listening. Thinking: Let everyone forget me. Then one of my souls leaves me. And the Mother of something that is all around me comes to visit me. I hear, I am beginning to hear. Now I can hear. One and all have something to tell. That is, perhaps, what I have learned by listening. The beetle, as well. The little stone you can hardly see, it's so small, sticking out of the mud. Even the louse you crack in two with your fingernail has a story to tell. If only I could remember everything I've been hearing. You'd never tire of listening to me, perhaps.

Some things know their own story and the stories of other things, too; some know only their own. Whoever knows all the stories has wisdom, no doubt. I learned the story of some of the animals from them. They had all been men, before. They were born speaking, or, to put it a better way, they were born from speaking. Words existed before they did. And then, after that, what the words said. Man spoke and what he said appeared. That was before. Now a man who speaks speaks, and that's all. Animals and things already exist. That was after.

The first man to speak must have been Pachakamue. Tasurinchi had breathed out Pareni. She was the first woman. She bathed in the Gran Pongo and put on a white cushma. There she was: Pareni. Existing. Then Tasurinchi breathed out Pareni's brother: Pachakamue. He bathed in the Gran Pongo and put on a clay-colored cushma. There he was: Pachakamue. The one who, by speaking, would give birth to so many animals. He gave them their name, spoke the word, and men and women became what Pachakamue said. He didn't do it intentionally. But he had that power.

This is the story of Pachakamue, whose words were born animals, trees, and rocks.

That was before.

One day he went to visit his sister, Pareni. They were sitting on mats, drinking masato, when he asked after her children. "They're playing over there, up in a tree," she said. "Be careful they don't turn into little monkeys." Pachakamue laughed. The words were barely out of his mouth when the children they'd been, with hair and tails all of a sudden, deafened the day with their screeching. Hanging by their tails from the branches, swinging happily to and fro.

On another visit to his sister, Pachakamue asked Pareni: "How is your daughter?" The girl had just had her first blood and was purifying herself in a shelter behind the hut. "You're keeping her shut up like a sachavaca," Pachakamue remarked. "Whatever does 'sachavaca' mean?" Pareni exclaimed. At that moment they heard a bellowing and a scraping of hoofs on the ground. And there came the terrified sachavaca, sniffing the air, heading for the forest. "Well then, that's what it means," Pachakamue murmured, pointing at it.

Thereupon, Pareni and her husband, Yagontoro, became alarmed. Wasn't Pachakamue upsetting the order of the world with the words he uttered? The prudent thing to do was to kill him. What evils might come about if he went on speaking? They offered him masato. Once he'd gotten drunk, they lured him to the edge of a precipice. "Look, look," they said. He looked and then they pushed him off. Pachakamue rolled and rolled. By the time he got to the bottom, he hadn't even waked up. He went on sleeping and belching, his cushma covered with masato vomit.

When he opened his eyes, he was amazed. Pareni was watching him from the edge. "Help me out of here!" he begged her. "Change yourself into an animal and climb up the precipice yourself," she mocked him. "Isn't that what you do to Machiguengas?" Following her advice, Pachakamue spoke the word "sankori." And there and then he changed himself into a sankori ant, the one that builds a hanging nest in a tree trunk or on a cliff. But this time the little ant's constructions behaved oddly; they fell apart each time they had nearly reached the edge of the precipice. "What do I do now?" moaned the speaker-of-words in despair. Pareni counseled him: "Make something grow between the stones, with words, and climb up it." Pachakamue said, "Reed," and a reed sprouted and grew. But every time he hoisted himself up it, the reed broke in two and he rolled to the bottom of the ravine.

So then Pachakamue set off in the opposite direction, following the curve of the precipice. He was furious, saying, "I'll wreak havoc." Yagontoro took off after him to kill him. It was a long, hard chase. Moons went by and Pachakamue's trail grew faint. One morning, Yagontoro came across a maize plant. In a trance, he learned that the plant had grown from toasted maize seeds that Pachakamue was carrying in his pouch; they had fallen to the ground without his noticing. He was catching up with him at last. And not long after, he spied him. Pachakamue was damming a river, blocking its flow by rolling trees and boulders down into the water. He was trying to change its course so as to flood a cluster of huts and drown the Machiguengas. He was still in a rage, farting furiously. There in the forest, Kientibakori and his kamagarinis must have been dancing, drunk with joy.

Then Yagontoro spoke to him. He made him think things over, and persuaded him, it seems. He suggested they go back to Pareni together. But soon after they had set out, he killed him. A storm arose that made the rivers boil and uprooted many trees. The rain came down in torrents; the thunder rolled. Unperturbed, Yagontoro went on cutting the head off Pachakamue's corpse. Then he drove two chonta thorns through the head, a vertical one and a horizontal one, and buried it in a secret place. But he neglected to cut off the tongue, a mistake we're still paying for. As long as we don't cut it off, we'll go on being in danger, it seems. Because sometimes that tongue speaks, putting things all out of kilter. It is not known where the head is buried. The place stinks of rotten fish, they say. And the ferns around it give off smoke continually, like a fire that's going out.

After cutting Pachakamue's head off, Yagontoro set out to return to Pareni. He was pleased, believing he had saved this world from disorder. Now everyone will be able to live in peace, he was no doubt thinking. But he hadn't walked far when he started feeling sluggish. And why was it such slow going? Horrified, he saw that his legs were insect legs, his hands antennae, his arms now wings. Instead of being a man who walks, he was now a carachupa, just what his name says he is. Beneath the forest, choking on earth, through the two darts piercing it,

Pachakamue's tongue had said: "Yagontoro." And so Yagontoro had become a yagontoro.

Dead and decapitated, Pachakamue went on transforming things so they would be like his words. What was going to happen to the world? By then, Pareni had another husband and was walking, content. One morning, as she was weaving a cushma, crossing and uncrossing the cotton threads, her husband came to lick the sweat running down her back. "You look like a little bee that sucks flowers," said a voice from deep within the earth. He heard no more, for he was flying about, a happy buzzing bee borne lightly on the air.

Shortly thereafter, Pareni married Tzonkiri, who was still a man. He noticed that every time he came back from weeding the cassava patch, his wife gave him unknown fish to eat: boquichicos. What river or lake did they come from? Pareni never ate a single mouthful of them. Tzonkiri suspected that something unusual was happening. Instead of going to his cassava patch, he hid in the underbrush and watched. What he saw gave him a terrible scare: the fish were coming out from between Pareni's legs. She was giving birth to them, like children. Tzonkiri was enraged. He threw himself upon her to kill her. But before he could do so, a distant voice, from out of the earth, spoke his name. Who ever heard of a hummingbird killing a woman? "You'll never eat boquichicos again," Pareni mocked. "You'll go from flower to flower now, sipping pollen." And since then, Tzonkiri has been what he is.

By now, Pareni didn't want another husband. Together with her daughter, she started walking. She climbed into a canoe and went up the rivers; she clambered up ravines, made her way through tangled forests. After many moons, the two of them reached the Cerro de la Sal. Where both of them heard, from far, far away, words of the buried head that turned them into stone. They are now two great gray rocks, covered with moss. They are still there, perhaps. The Machiguengas used to sit in the shadow of them, drinking masato and talking together, it seems. When they went up to collect salt.

That, anyway, is what I have learned.

Tasurinchi, the herb doctor, the one who lived by the Tikompinía, is walking. He gave me the herbs I carry in my pouch and explained what each little leaf and each handful is for. This leaf, the one with burned edges, is for stopping up the jaguar's nostrils, so it can't catch the scent of the man who walks. This other one, the yellow one, wards off vipers. There are so many of them I get them all mixed up. Each one has a different use. Against evil and strangers. So the fish in the lake will swim into the net. So the arrow doesn't stray from the target. And, this one, so as not to trip or fall into a ravine.

I went to visit the herb doctor, knowing he lived in country swarming with Viracochas. It's true; they're still there. There are lots of them. As I came along the trail, I saw boats on the river, roaring, full of Viracochas. On the sandbanks, where the turtles used to come at night to hatch their young, and where men used to go to turn them over on their backs, Viracochas are now living. They're where the herb doctor used to live, too. These Viracochas haven't gone there because of the turtles, or to farm, or to fell trees, it seems. But to carry off the sand and the pebbles of the river. Searching for gold, it seems. I didn't go close; I hid from sight. But even from afar I could see that there were lots of them. They've built cabins. They're here to stay, perhaps.

I found no sign anywhere of Tasurinchi, the herb doctor, or of his kinfolk, or of any man who walks. I've come for nothing, I thought. I felt uneasy with so many Viracochas around. What would happen if I met up with one? I hid out waiting for darkness to fall so I could get a little way away from the Tikompinía. I climbed a tree, and hidden among the branches, I watched them. On both banks of the river they were digging up earth and stones, with their hands, poles, picks. And putting the stones in big sieves, the way you sift cassava for masato. And pounding the pebbles to pieces in troughs. Some went into the forest to hunt, and you could hear them shooting off their guns. The sound shook the trees, and the birds took fright and started squawking. With all that noise, there soon won't be one animal left around there. They'll go off, like Tasurinchi, the herb doctor. As soon as night had fallen, I climbed down from the tree and walked off as fast as my legs could carry me. When I was far enough away, I made myself a shelter of ungurabi leaves and went to sleep.

When I awakened, I saw one of the herb doctor's sons squatting beside me. "What are you doing here?" I asked him. "Waiting for you to wake up," he said. He'd been following me since the day before, when he'd seen me on the trail leading to the river where the Viracochas are. His family had moved three moons' journey away, upstream on a branch of the Tikompinía. We traveled slowly, so as not to run into the strangers. Getting through the forest is difficult up there. There are no trails. The trees grow very close together, intertwining, fighting with each other. Your arms get tired, hacking at the branches and the bushes that close around you, as if to say, "You shall not pass." There was mud everywhere. We sank and slid down the slopes slippery with rain. Laughing at the sight of ourselves, scratched and filthy. At last we arrived. And there Tasurinchi was. "Are you there?" "Ehé, here I am." His wife brought mats for us to sit on. We ate cassava and drank masato.

"You've gone so far in the Viracochas will surely never come here," I said. "They'll come," he answered. "It may take a while, but they'll turn up here, too. You must learn that, Tasurinchi. They always get to where we are in the end. It's been that way from the beginning. How many times have I had to leave where I was because they were coming? Since before I was born, it seems. And that's how it will be as I go and come, if my soul doesn't stay in the worlds beyond, that is. We've always been leaving because someone was coming. How many places have I lived in? Who knows, but there have been any number of them. Saying: 'We're going to look for a place so hard to reach, amid such a tangle, that they'll never come. And if they do, they'll never want to stay there.' But they've always come and they've always wanted to stay. That's just how it is. No mistake about it. They'll come and I'll go. Is that a bad thing? No, that's a good thing. It must be our destiny, Tasurinchi. Aren't we the ones who walk? So, then, we should thank the Mashcos and the Punarunas. The Viracochas too. Do they invade the places where we live? They force us to fulfill our obligation. Without them, we'd become corrupt. The sun would fall, perhaps. The world would be darkness, the earth belong to Kashiri. There would be no men, and surely much cold."

Tasurinchi, the herb doctor, speaks with the voice of an hablador.

According to him, the worst time was the tree-bleeding. He hadn't lived through it himself, but his father and mothers had. And he'd heard so many stories that it was as though he had. "So many that I sometimes think I, too, wounded the tree trunks to drain off their milk, and I, too, was hunted down, like a peccary, to be taken off to the camps." When things like that happen, they don't disappear. They linger on in one of the four worlds, and the seripigari can go see them in his trance. Those who see them come back heart-stricken, it seems, their teeth chattering with sickened disgust. The fear was so great and the confusion such that there was no trust left. Nobody believed anybody, the sons suspecting that their fathers would hunt them, and the fathers thinking the sons would cast them in chains and take them off to the camps if they ever once let their guard down. "They didn't need magic to steal the people they needed. They got as many as they wanted, through sheer cunning. The Viracochas must be wise," Tasurinchi said in awe.

In the beginning they scoured the countryside, hunting people. They went into the settlements, shooting off their guns. Their dogs barked and bit; they, too, were hunters. Overwhelmed by the noise, the men who walk took fright, like the birds I saw by the river. But they couldn't take wing. They trapped them in their huts. They trapped them on the trails, and in their canoes if they took to the river. Get a move on, damn you! Move along there, Machiguenga! They carried off the ones who had hands to bleed the trees. They didn't take the newborn or old people. "They're of no use," they said. But they carried off the women too, to look after the fields and prepare food. Get along there! Get along there! They entered the camps with a rope around their necks. All those who had been caught were there. Get along there, Machiguenga! Get along there, Piro! Get along there, Yaminahua! Get along there, Ashaninka! And there they stayed, all mixed together. They were of great use to the Viracochas, it seems; they were pleased. Few left the camps. They would go quickly, so enraged or so sad their souls wouldn't come back, perhaps.

The worst, says Tasurinchi, the herb doctor, was when the camps began to be short of men because so many went. Get on with it, damn you! But they couldn't. They had no strength left. Too weak to lift their arms, they were slowly dying. The Viracochas were furious. "What will we do without workmen?" they said. "What are we going to do?" Then they told the ones who were tied up to go out and hunt people. "Buy your freedom," they said. "And presents as well. Here's food. And clothes. And here's a gun, too. Does that suit you?" It suited all of them, it seems. They said to each of the Piros: "Catch three Machiguengas and you can go forever. Here's a gun for you." And to each Mashco: "Catch a few Piros and you can go home, taking your wife and these gifts with you. Take the dog to help you." They were happy, perhaps. So as to leave the camp, they became hunters of men. Families began to bleed, just like the trees. Everyone hunted everyone. With guns, with bows and arrows, with traps, with lassos, with knives. Get along, damn you! And they turned up back in the camps, saying: "There you are, I've caught them for you. Give me my wife," they said. "Give me my gun. Give me gifts. I'm going now."

So trust was lost. Everyone was the enemy of everyone then. Was Kientibakori dancing for joy? Did the earth tremble? Did the rivers carry away the dwelling places? Who knows? "All of us must go," they said fearfully. They had lost knowledge, too. "What was it we did to have become so corrupt?" they wept. There were killings every day. The rivers must have run red with blood, and the trees been spattered. Women gave birth to dead children; they went before they were born, not wanting to live where everything was evil and confusion. Before, there were many men who walk; after, very few. That was the tree-bleeding. "The world has fallen into chaos," they raged. "The sun has fallen."

Can things that once happened happen again? The herb doctor says yes: "They're there, in one of the worlds, and like souls, they can come back. It'll be our fault if that happens, perhaps." Best to be prudent and to keep memory alive.

Three of the sons of Tasurinchi, the herb doctor, have gone since he's been living up there. Seeing them go one after the other, he thought: Can the evil that carried off whole families be back? He hasn't been able to find out whether their souls came back. "Maybe so, maybe not," he said to me. He's not yet thoroughly acquainted with the place where he's living and doesn't know why certain things happen. Everything there is still mysterious to him. But there are a great many herbs there. Some he already knew; others not. He's learning to know them. He gathers them, spends a long time looking at them, comparing them, smelling them, and sometimes he puts them in his mouth. He chews them and spits them out, or else swallows them. Saying: "This one is useful."

His three sons all went the same way. They woke up dizzy in the head, shivering and sweating. And tottering as though they'd been drunk. They couldn't stand up. They tried to walk, to dance, and fell down. They couldn't even talk, it seems. When it happened to the eldest, Tasurinchi thought it was a warning that he should leave. It wasn't a good place to live, perhaps. "I couldn't tell," he says. "This evil was different from the others. There were no herbs against it." Kamagarini evils, maybe. Those little devils always come out to do harm when it's raining. Kientibakori watches them from the edge of the forest, laughing. It had thundered and torrents of rain had fallen the evening before, and it's well known that when that happens, a kamagarini is drawing near.

When that son went, Tasurinchi's family moved a little higher up in the forest. Shortly thereafter, the second son started feeling dizzy and falling down. Just like the first one. When that one died, they went somewhere else. Then the same thing happened to the third one. Tasurinchi decided not to move again. "The ones who have gone will see to it that we're protected against the kamagarini that's trying to throw us out of here," he said. That must have been how it was. No one else has had a dizzy spell and fallen down since then.

"There's an explanation for that," the herb doctor says. "There's one for everything. Even the manhunts during the tree-bleeding. But it's not easy to learn what it is. Even the seripigari doesn't always succeed. It may be that the three of them went to talk with the mothers of this place. With three dead here, the mothers aren't likely to look on us as intruders. We belong here now. Don't these trees and birds know us? The water and the air here? That may be the explanation. Since they went, we haven't felt any enmity. As though we're accepted here."

I spent many moons with him. I very nearly stayed on to live there, near the herb doctor. I helped him set traps for pavitas and went to the lake with him to fish for boquichicos. I worked with Tasurinchi clearing the forest, where he's going to make his new field when the one he has now needs to rest. During the afternoons we used to talk. As the women killed each other's lice, spun, wove mats and cushmas, or chewed and spat out cassava for masato, we talked together.

The herb doctor had me tell him stories of men who walk. Ones he'd known, and ones he'd never seen as well. I told him about all of you, the way I tell all of you about him. Moons went by and I had no desire to leave. Something was happening that had never happened to me before. "Are you getting tired of walking?" he asked me. "It happens to a lot of people. Don't worry, storyteller. If that's how it is, change your ways. Stay in one place and have a family. Build your hut, clear the forest, take care of your field. You'll have children. Give up walking, and give up being a storyteller. You can't stay here; there are a great many of us in my family. But you can go farther up, cutting a path through the forest, a two or three moons' journey. There's a ravine with a stream at the bottom waiting for you, I think. I can go with you that far. Do you want a family? I can help you there too, if that's what you want. Take that woman, she's old and quiet and she'll help you because she knows how to cook and spin far better than most. Or here's my youngest daughter, if she's more to your liking. You won't be able to touch her yet because she hasn't bled. If you mounted her now, some misfortune would happen, perhaps. But wait a little, and meanwhile she'll be learning how to be your wife. Her mothers will teach her. Once she bleeds, you'll bring me a peccary, fish, fruits of the earth, showing me gratitude and respect. Is that what you want, Tasurinchi?"

I thought his proposal over for quite some time. I felt like accepting it. I even dreamed I'd accepted it and was leading a different life. It's a good life I'm living, that I know. The men who walk receive me gladly, give me food, pay me compliments. But my days are spent journeying, and how much longer will I be able to keep that up? Distances between families grow greater and greater. Lately, I often think as I'm walking that one day my strength will give out. Isn't that so, little parrot? And there I'll lie, exhausted, on one forest trail or another. No Machiguenga will pass that way, perhaps. My soul will go and my empty body begin to rot as birds peck at it and ants crawl over it. The grass will grow between my bones, perhaps. And the capybara will gnaw away the garment of my soul. When such fear comes to a man, shouldn't he change his habits? So it seemed to Tasurinchi, the herb doctor.

"I accept your proposal, then," I said to him. He went

with me to the place that was waiting for me. It took us two moons to get there. We had to go up and down through stretches of forest where the path disappeared altogether, and as we climbed up a slope, shimbillo monkeys, with earsplitting screams, hurled bits of bark down at us from the branches overhead. In the ravine we found a jaguar cub caught in a thornbush. "This little jaguar means something," the herb doctor fretted. But he couldn't discover what. And so, instead of killing it and skinning it, he let it loose in the forest. "Isn't this a good place to live?" he asked me, pointing. "You can make your cassava patch up there in that high forest. It will never be flooded. There are lots of trees and not much grass, so the earth should be good and the cassava grow well." Yes, it was a place that was livable. Though the nights were the coldest I'd ever felt anywhere. "Before making up your mind, we'll see if there's game to hunt," said Tasurinchi. We set traps. We caught a capybara and a majaz. Later, we shot a pavita kanari from a shelter at the top of a tree. I decided to stay there and put up my hut.

But before we'd begun felling the trees, the herb doctor's son appeared, the one who had guided me to his new hut. Saying: "Something's happened." We went back. The old woman Tasurinchi was going to give me as a wife was dead. She'd pounded barbasco and made a brew, muttering: "I don't want them to rage at me, saying: 'Because of her we've been left without a storyteller.' They'll say I tricked him, that I gave him a potion so he'd take me as his wife. I'd rather go."

I helped the herb doctor burn the hut, the cushma, the pots, the necklaces, and all the other things that belonged to the woman. We wrapped her in several straw mats and placed her on a raft of tucuma palm planks. We pushed it out into the river till the current carried her away downstream.

"It's a warning that you must either pay heed to or ignore," Tasurinchi said to me. "If I were you, I wouldn't ignore it. Because each man has his obligation. Why is it we walk? So there will be light and warmth, so that everything will be peaceful. That is the order of the world. The man who talks to fireflies does what he's obliged to do. I move on when Viracochas appear. That's my destiny, perhaps. And yours? To visit people, speak to them, tell them stories. It is dangerous to disobey fate. Look, the woman who was to be your wife has gone. If I were you, I'd start walking at once. What's your decision?"

I decided to do what Tasurinchi, the herb doctor, advised. And the next morning, as the eye of the sun began to gaze down at this world from Inkite, I was already walking. I am thinking now of that Machiguenga woman who went so as not to be my wife. I am talking now to all of you. Tomorrow will be as it will be.

That, anyway, is what I have learned.

FOR SIX MONTHS in 1981, I was responsible for a program on Peruvian television called the Tower of Babel. The owner of the channel, Genaro Delgado, had lured me into this venture by flashing before my eyes three shiny glass beads: the need to raise the standard of the channel's programs, which had fallen to an absolute low of stupidity and vulgarity during the preceding twelve years of state ownership imposed by the military dictatorship; the excitement of experimenting with a means of communication which, in a country such as Peru, was the only one able to reach, simultaneously, a number of very different audiences; and a good salary.

It really was an extraordinary experience, though also the most tiring and most exasperating one that has ever come my way. "If you organize your time well and devote just half your day to the program, that'll be enough," Genaro had predicted. "And you'll be able to go on with your writing in the afternoon." But in this case, as in so many others, theory was one thing and practice another. The truth was that I devoted every single morning, afternoon, and evening of those months to the Tower of Babel, and most important, the many hours when I didn't seem to be actually working but was nonetheless busy worrying about what had gone wrong on the previous program and trying to anticipate what would go worse still on the next one.

There were four of us who got out the Tower of Babel programs: Luis Llosa, the producer and director of photography; Moshé dan Furgang, the editor; Alejandro Pérez, the cameraman; and myself. I had brought Lucho and Moshé to the channel. They both had film experience—they had each made shorts—but neither they nor I had worked in television before. The title of the program was indicative of its intent: to show something of everything, to create a kaleidoscope of subjects. We naïvely hoped to prove that a cultural program need not be soporific, esoteric, or pedantic, but could be entertaining and not over any viewer's head, since "culture" was not synonymous with science, literature, or any other specialized field, but a way of looking at things, an approach capable of tackling anything of human interest. The idea was that during our hour-long program each week—which often stretched to an hour and a half—we would touch on two or three themes as different as possible, so that the audience would see that a cultural program had as much to offer as, let us say, soccer or boxing, or salsa and humor, and that political reporting or a documentary on the Indian tribes of Amazonia could be entertaining as well as instructive.

When Lucho and Moshé and I drew up lists of subjects, people, and locales that the Tower of Babel could use and planned the most lively way of presenting them, everything went like a charm. We were full of ideas and eager to discover the creative possibilities of the most popular medium of communication of our time.

What we discovered in practice, however, was our dependence on material factors in an underdeveloped country, the subtle way in which they subvert the best intentions and thwart the most diligent efforts. I can say, without exaggeration, that most of the time that Lucho, Moshé, and I put in on the Tower of Babel was spent not on creative work, on trying to improve the program intellectually and artistically, but was wasted in an attempt to solve problems that at first sight seemed trivial and unworthy of our notice. What to do, for instance, to get the channel's vans to pick us up at the agreed time so as not to miss appointments, planes, interviews? The answer was for us to go personally to the drivers' homes and wake them up, go with them to the channel's offices to collect the recording equipment and from there to the airport or wherever. But as a solution it cost us hours of sleep and didn't always work. It could turn out that, on top of everything else, the blessed van's battery had gone dead, or higher-ups had neglected to authorize the replacement of an oil pan, an exhaust pipe, a tire ripped to shreds the day before on the murderous potholes along the Avenida Arequipa.

From the very first program, I noticed that the images on the screen were marred by strange smudges. What were those dirty half-moons anyway? Alejandro Pérez explained that they were due to defective camera filters. They were worn out and needed replacing. Okay then, replace them. But how to go about getting this done? We tried everything short of murder, and nothing worked. We sent memos to Maintenance, we begged, we got on the phone, we argued face-to-face with engineers, technicians, department heads, and I believe we even took the problem to the owner-director of the channel. They all agreed with us, they were all indignant, they all issued strict orders that the filters be replaced. They may well have been. But the grayish half-moons disfigured all our programs, from first to last. Sometimes, when I tune in on a television program, I can still see those intrusive shadows and think—with a touch of melancholy: Ah, Alejandro's camera.

I don't know who it was who decided that Alejandro Pérez would work with us. It turned out to be a good idea, for when allowances have been made for the "underdevelopment handicap"—which he accepted philosophically, never turning a hair—Alejandro is a very skillful cameraman. His talent is purely intuitive, an innate sense of composition, movement, angle, distance. Alejandro became a cameraman by accident. He'd started out as a house painter, come to Lima from Huánuco, and someone had given him the idea that he might earn himself a little extra money by helping to load the cameras in the stadium on days when a soccer match was being televised. From having to load them so often he learned how to handle them. One day he stood in for an absent cameraman, then another day for another, and almost before he knew it, he turned out to be the channel's star cameraman.

At first his habitual silence made me nervous. Lucho was the only one who managed to talk to him. Or, at any rate, they understood each other subliminally, for in all those six months I can't remember ever hearing Alejandro utter a complete sentence, with subject, verb, and predicate. Only short grunts of approval or dismay, and an exclamation that I feared like the plague, because it meant that, once again, we had been defeated by all-powerful, omnipresent imponderables: "It's fucked up again!" How many times did the sound equipment, the film, the reflector, the monitor "fuck up"? Everything could "fuck up" innumerable times: every one of the things we worked with possessed that fundamental property, perhaps the only one toward which all of them, always, gave proof of a dog-like loyalty. How often did minutely planned projects, interviews obtained after exhausting negotiations, go all to hell because close-mouthed Alejandro came out with his fateful grunt: "It's fucked up again!"

I remember especially well what happened to us in Puerto Maldonado, a town in Amazonia where we had gone to make a documentary short on the death of the poet and guerrilla fighter Javier Heraud. Alaín Elías, Heraud's comrade and the leader of the guerrilla detachment that had been scattered or captured the day Heraud was killed, had agreed to recount, in front of the camera, everything that had happened on that occasion. His testimony was interesting and moving—Alaín had been in the canoe with Javier Heraud when the latter had been shot to death, and he himself had been wounded in the shoot-out. We had decided to round the documentary out with views of the locale where the incident had taken place and, if possible, with accounts from the inhabitants of Puerto Maldonado who could recall the events of twenty years before.

Even Moshé—who ordinarily stayed behind in Lima to keep up with the editing of the programs—went off to the jungle with Lucho, Alejandro Pérez, and me. In Puerto Maldonado several witnesses agreed to be interviewed. Our great find was a member of the police force who had participated, first off, in the initial incident in the center of town that had revealed the presence of the guerrilleros in Puerto Maldonado to the authorities—an encounter in which a civil guard had been killed—and then later, in the manhunt for Javier Heraud and the shoot-out. The man had since retired from the police force and was working on a farm. Persuading the ex-policeman to allow himself to be interviewed had been extremely difficult, since he was filled with apprehension and reluctant to talk. We finally convinced him and even managed to get permission to interview him in the police station from which the patrols had set out on that day long ago.

At the very moment we started interviewing the ex-policeman, Alejandro's reflectors began to burst like carnival balloons. And when they had all exploded—so that there would be no doubt that the household gods of Amazonia were against the Tower of Babel—the battery of our portable generator quit and the recording equipment went dead. Fucked up again. And one of the first fruits of the program as well. We returned to Lima empty-handed.

Am I exaggerating things so that they stand out more clearly? Perhaps. But I don't think I'm stretching things much. I could tell dozens of stories like this one. And many others to illustrate what is perhaps the very symbol of underdevelopment: the divorce between theory and practice, decisions and facts. During those six months we suffered from this irreducible distance at every stage of our work. There were schedules that gave each of the various producers their fair share of time in the cutting rooms and the sound studios. But in point of fact it was not the schedules but the cunning and the clever maneuvering of each producer or technician that determined who would have more or less time for editing and recording, and who could count on the best equipment.

Of course we very soon caught on to the stratagems, ruses, wiles, or charm that had to be used, not to obtain special privileges, but merely to do a more or less decent job of what we were being paid to do. We were not above such tricks ourselves, but all of them had the disadvantage of taking up precious time that we ought to have devoted to purely creative work. Since

I've been through this experience, my admiration is boundless whenever I happen to see a program on television that is well edited and recorded, lively and original. For I know that behind it there is much more than talent and determination: there is witchcraft, miracle. Some weeks, after viewing the program on the monitor one last time, looking for the perfect finishing touch, we would say to each other: "Good, it came out exactly right in the end." But despite that, on the television screen that Sunday, the sound would fade away altogether, the image leap out of focus, and completely blank frames appear . . . What had "fucked up" this time? The technician on duty was drunk or asleep, he'd pressed the wrong button or run the film backward . . . Television is a risky business for perfectionists; it is responsible for countless cases of insomnia, tachycardia, ulcers, heart attacks . . .

In spite of all this, and by and large, those six months were exciting and intense. I remember how moved I was interviewing Borges in his apartment in downtown Buenos Aires, where his mother's room was kept exactly the way she left it the day she died (an old lady's purple dress laid out on the bed); he apparently never forgave me for having said that his home was a modest one, with a leaky roof. I remember being moved, too, by the portraits of writers painted by Ernesto Sábato, which he allowed us to film in his little house in Santos Lugares, where we went to visit him. Ever since I'd lived in Spain in the early seventies, I had wanted to interview Corín Tellado, whose sentimental romances, radio soap operas, photo-novels, and television melodramas are devoured by countless thousands in Spain and Hispano-America. She agreed to appear on the Tower of Babel and I spent an afternoon with her, on the outskirts of Gijón, in Asturias—she showed me the basement of the house she was occupying, with thousands of novelettes stowed away on bookshelves: she finishes one every two days, each exactly a hundred pages long. She was living there in seclusion because at the time she had been the victim of attempted extortion, though whether a political group or common criminals were behind it was not clear.

From the houses of writers we took our cameras to the stadiums—we did a program on one of the best Brazilian soccer clubs, the Flamengo, and interviewed Zico, the star of the moment, in Rio de Janeiro. We went to Panama, where we visited amateur and professional boxing rings, trying to discover how and why this small Central American country had been the cradle of so many Latin American and world champions in nearly every weight class. In Brazil, we managed to get our cameras into the exclusive clinic of trim, athletic Dr. Pitanguí, whose scalpels made all the women in the world who could pay for his services young and beautiful; and in Santiago de Chili we spoke with Pinochet's Chicago Boys and with his Christian Democratic opponents, who, in the midst of extreme repression, were resisting dictatorship.

We went to Nicaragua on the second anniversary of the revolution, to report on the Sandinistas and their adversaries; and to the University of California at Berkeley, where the great poet, Czeslaw Milosz, a recent winner of the Nobel Prize for Literature, worked in a tiny office in the Department of Slavonic Languages. We went to Coclecito, Panama, where we visited General Omar Torrijos at his home there; though theoretically no longer active in government, he was still the lord and master of the country. We spent the entire day with him, and although he was most affable with me, I was not left as agreeably impressed by him as were other writers who had been his guests. He struck me as the typical Latin American caudillo of unhappy memory, the providential "strongman," authoritative and macho, adulated by civil and military courtiers, who filed through the place all day, flattering him with sickening servility. The most exciting person in the general's Coclecito house was one of his mistresses, a curvaceous blonde we came upon reclining in a hammock. She was just another piece of furniture, for the general neither spoke to her nor introduced her to the guests who came and went . . .

Two days after our return to Lima from Panama, Lucho Llosa, Alejandro Pérez, and I felt a cold shiver run down our spines. Torrijos had just died in a fatal crash of the little plane in which he had sent us back to Panama City from Coclecito. The pilot was the same one we had flown with.

I fainted in Puerto Rico, just a day after recording a short program on the marvelous restoration of old San Juan, guided by Ricardo Alegría, who had been the moving spirit of the project. I was suffering from dehydration as a result of stomach poisoning, contracted in the chicha bars of a north Peruvian village, Catacaos, where we had gone to do a program on straw-hat weaving, a craft the inhabitants have been practicing for centuries; on the secrets of the tondero, a regional dance; and on its picanterías, where fine chicha and highly spiced stews are served (these latter responsible, naturally, for my case of poisoning). Words cannot express my thanks to all the Puerto Rican friends who virtually terrorized the kind doctors of San Jorge Hospital into curing me in time for the Tower of Babel to appear on the air at the usual hour that Sunday.

The program ran regularly every week, and considering the conditions under which we worked, this was quite a feat. I wrote the scripts in vans or planes, went from airport to sound studio to cutting room, and from there to catch another plane to travel hundreds of miles to be in another town or country, often for less time than it had taken me to get there. During those six months, I skipped sleeping, eating, reading, and, naturally, writing. As the channel's budget was limited, I arranged for several of my trips abroad to coincide with invitations to attend literary congresses or give lectures, thus relieving the channel of having to pay my travel and per-diem expenses. The trouble with this arrangement was that it forced me to become a psychic quick-change artist, shifting within seconds from a lecturer to a journalist, from an author with a microphone placed before him to an interviewer who took his revenge by interviewing his interviewers.

Though we did a fair number of programs on the current scene in other countries, most of them dealt with Peruvian subjects. Popular dances and fiestas, university problems, pre-Hispanic archaeological sites, an old ice-cream vendor whose tricycle had cruised the streets of Miraflores for half a century, the story of a Piura bordello, the sub-world of prisons. We discovered how wide an audience the Tower of Babel was reaching when we started getting requests and considerable pressure from various personalities and institutions who wanted us to take notice of them. The most unexpected was perhaps the PIP, the Peruvian Secret Police. A colonel appeared in my office one day, suggesting that I devote a Tower of Babel broadcast to the PIP to celebrate some anniversary or other; to make the program more exciting, the PIP would stage a mock arrest of cocaine smugglers, complete with a shoot-out . . .

One of the calls I received, when the six-month period I had agreed to work for the channel was nearly over, came from a friend I hadn't seen for ages: Rosita Corpancho. There was her warm voice with its drawling Loretano accent, just as in my university years. There, too, intact or perhaps even increased, was her enthusiastic devotion to the Summer Institute of Linguistics. Surely I remembered the Institute? Of course,

Rosita . . . Well, the Institute was about to celebrate its I-don't-know-how-many-years in Peru, and what was more, it would soon be packing its bags, having decided that its mission in Amazonia had ended. Would it be possible, perhaps, for the Tower of Babel . . . ? I interrupted her to say that, yes, I would be pleased to do a documentary on the work of the linguist-missionaries. And would take advantage of the trip to the jungle to do a program on some of the lesser-known tribes, something we'd had in mind from the beginning. Rosita was delighted and told me she would coordinate everything with the Institute so that we could get about readily in the jungle. Had I any particular tribe in mind? Without hesitation I answered: "The Machiguengas."

Ever since my unsuccessful attempts in the early sixties at writing about the Machiguenga storytellers, the subject had never been far from my mind. It returned every now and then, like an old love, not quite dead coals yet, whose embers would suddenly burst into flame. I had gone on taking notes and scribbling rough drafts that I invariably tore up. And reading, every time I could lay my hands on them, the papers and articles about Machiguengas that kept appearing here and there in scientific journals. The lack of interest in the tribe was giving way to curiosity on several counts. The French anthropologist France-Marie Casevitz-Renard, and another, an American, Johnson Allen, had spent long periods among them and had described their organization, their work methods, their kinship structure, their symbolism, their sense of time. A Swiss ethnologist, Gerhard Baer, who had also lived among them, had made a thorough study of their religion, and Father Joaquín Barriales had begun publishing, in Spanish translation, his large collection of Machiguenga myths and songs. A number of Peruvian anthropologists, classmates of Mascarita's, notably Camino Díez Canseco and Víctor J. Guevara, had studied the tribe's customs and beliefs.

But never in any of these contemporary works had I found any information whatsoever about storytellers. Oddly enough, all reference to them broke off around the fifties. Had the function of storyteller been dying out and finally disappeared at the very time that the Schneils had discovered it? In the reports that the Dominican missionaries—Fathers Pío Aza, Vicente de Cenitagoya, and Andrés Ferrero—wrote about them in the thirties and forties, there were frequent allusions to storytellers. And even earlier, among nineteenth-century travelers as well. One of the first references occurs in the book written by Paul Marcoy, the explorer. On the banks of the Urubamba he came across an "orateur," whom the French traveler witnessed literally hypnotizing an audience of Antis for hours on end. "Do you think those Antis were Machiguengas?" the anthropologist Luis Román asked me, showing me the reference. I was certain they were. Why did modern anthropologists never mention storytellers? It was a question I asked myself each time one of these studies or field observations came to my attention, and I saw, once again, that no mention was made, even in passing, of those wandering tellers of tales, who seemed to me to be the most exquisite and precious exemplars of that people, numbering a mere handful, and who, in any event, had forged that curious emotional link between the Machiguengas and my own vocation (not to say, quite simply, my own life).

Why, in the course of all those years, had I been unable to write my story about storytellers? The answer I used to offer myself, each time I threw the half-finished manuscript of that elusive story into the wastebasket, was the difficulty of inventing, in Spanish and within a logically consistent intellectual framework, a literary form that would suggest, with any reasonable degree of credibility, how a primitive man with a magico-religious mentality would go about telling a story. All my attempts led each time to the impasse of a style that struck me as glaringly false, as implausible as the various ways in which philosophers and novelists of the Enlightenment had put words into the mouths of their exotic characters in the eighteenth century, when the theme of the "noble savage" was fashionable in Europe. Despite these failures, perhaps because of them, the temptation was still there, and every now and then, revived by some fortuitous circumstance, it took on new life, and the murmurous, fleeting, rude, and untamed silhouette of the storyteller invaded my house and my dreams. How could I fail to have been moved at the thought of seeing the Machiguengas face-to-face at last?

Since that trip in mid-1958 when I discovered the Peruvian jungle, I had returned to Amazonia several times: to Iquitos, to San Martín, to the Alto Marañón, to Madre de Dios, to Tingo María. But I had not been back to Pucallpa. In the twenty-three years that had gone by, that tiny, dusty village that I remembered as being full of dark, gloomy houses and evangelical churches, had been through an industrial and commercial "boom," followed by a depression, and now, as Lucho Llosa, Alejandro Pérez, and I landed there one September afternoon in 1981 to film what was to be the next-to-last program of the Tower of Babel, it was in the first stages of another "boom," though for bad reasons this time: trafficking in cocaine. The rush of heat and the burning light, in whose embrace people and things stand out so sharply (unlike Lima, where even bright sunlight has a grayish cast), are something that always has the effect on me of an emulsive draft of enthusiasm.

But that morning brought the discovery that it was the Schneils whom the Institute had sent to meet us at the Pucallpa airport, and that impressed me even more than the heat and the beautiful landscape of Amazonia. The Schneils in person. They had come to the end of their quarter of a century in the Amazon, the whole of it spent working with the Machiguengas. They were surprised that I remembered them—I have the feeling they didn't remember me at all—and could still recall so many details of what they had told me back then, during our two conversations at the Yarinacocha base. As we bounced this way and that in the jeep on our way to the Institute, they showed me photographs of their children, young people, some already through college, living in the States. Did they all speak Machiguenga? Of course, it was the family's second language, even before Spanish. I was pleased to learn that the Schneils would be our guides and interpreters in the villages we visited.

Lake Yarina was still a picture postcard, and dusk there more beautiful than ever. The bungalows of the Institute had proliferated along the lakeshore. The minute we climbed out of the jeep, Lucho, Alejandro, and I set to work. We agreed that as soon as night fell, to serve as an introduction to our trip to the forests of the Alto Urubamba, the Schneils would brief us on the places and people we would be seeing up there.

Other than the Schneils, not one of the linguists whom I had met on my previous journey was still in Yarinacocha. Some had gone back to the States; others were doing fieldwork in other jungle regions around the world; and some had died, as had Dr. Townsend, the founder of the Institute. But the linguists whom we met and interviewed, who acted as our guides as we photographed the place from various angles, appeared to be the identical twins of the ones I remembered. The men had close-cropped hair and the athletic, healthy appearance of people who exercise daily, eat according to the instructions of a dietician, don't smoke, and take neither coffee nor alcohol, and the women, encased in dresses as plain as they were decent, without a speck of makeup or a shadow of coquetry, exuded an overwhelming air of efficiency. Men and women alike had the cheerful, imperturbable look of people who believe, who are doing what they believe in, and who know for certain that the truth is on their side: the sort of people who have always fascinated and terrified me.

As long as the light and the caprices of Alejandro Pérez's equipment permitted, we went on collecting material for the program on the Institute: a seminar of bilingual teachers from various villages that was taking place at the time; the elementary readers and grammar books compiled by the linguists; their personal testimony and an overall view of the small town that the Yarinacocha base of operations had become, with its school, its hospital, its sports field, its library, its churches, its communications center, and its airport.

As darkness fell, after a combined work session and meal during which we rounded off our plans for the part of the program devoted to the Institute, we began mapping out the part we would be recording during the following days: the Machiguengas. In Lima I had unearthed and consulted all the documents concerning them that I had been accumulating over the years. But it was chiefly a conversation with the Schneils—once again at their house, once again over tea and cookies prepared by Mrs. Schneil—that provided us with firsthand information on the state of the community that they knew inside out, since it had been their home for the past twenty-five years.

Things had changed considerably for the Machiguengas of the Alto Urubamba and Madre de Dios since the day when Edwin Schneil, stark-naked, had approached that family and it had not fled. Had things changed for the better? The Schneils were firmly convinced that they had. For the moment, the dispersion that had characterized Machiguenga life had largely come to an end—and this was true of the ones on the other side of the Pongo de Mainique as well. The diaspora—little groups scattered here and there with virtually no contact between them, each one fighting desperately for survival—was over; had it continued, it would have meant, purely and simply, the disintegration of the community, the disappearance of its language, and the assimilation of its members by other groups and cultures. After many efforts on the part of the authorities, Catholic missionaries, anthropologists, ethnologists, and the Institute itself, the Machiguengas had begun to accept the idea of forming villages, of coming together in places suitable for working the soil, breeding animals, and developing trade relations with the rest of Peru. Things were evolving rapidly. There were already six settlements, some of them very recent. We would be visiting two of them, New World and New Light.

Of the five thousand surviving Machiguengas—an approximate figure—nearly half were now living in those settlements. One of them, moreover, was half Machiguenga and half Campa (Ashaninka), and thus far the cohabitation of members of the two tribes had not given rise to the slightest problem. The Schneils were optimistic and believed that the remaining Machiguengas—including the most elusive of all, the ones known as Kogapakori, would gradually abandon their refuges in the heart of the forest and form new settlements when they saw the advantages that living in community brought to their brothers: a less uncertain life and the possibility of being helped in case of emergency. With heartfelt enthusiasm the Schneils told us of the concrete steps that had already been taken in the villages to integrate them into national life. Schools and agricultural cooperatives, for instance. Both in New World and in New Light there were bilingual schools, with native teachers. We would be seeing them.

Did this mean that the Machiguengas were slowly ceasing to be that primitive people, shut in on itself, pessimistic and defeated, that they had described to me in 1958? To a certain extent, yes. They were less reluctant—the ones who lived in communities, at any rate—to try out novelties, to progress; they had more love of life, perhaps. But as far as their isolation was concerned, one couldn't talk thus far of any real change. Because, even though we could reach their villages in two or three hours in the Institute planes, a journey by river to one of these settlements from any sizable Amazonian town was a matter of days and sometimes weeks. So the idea of their becoming an integral part of Peru was perhaps a little less remote than in the past, but was certainly not a reality as yet.

Would we be able to interview any Machiguengas in Spanish? Yes, a few, though not many. The cacique or governor of New Light, for example, spoke Spanish fluently. What? Did the Machiguengas have caciques now? Hadn't one of the distinctive features of the tribe been the absence of any sort of hierarchic political organization, with leaders and subordinates? Yes, certainly. Before. But that anarchic system typical of them was explained by their dispersion: now that they were gathered together in villages, they needed authorities. The administrator or chief of New Light was a young man and a splendid community leader, a graduate of the Mazamari Bible School. A Protestant pastor, in other words? Well, yes, you might call him that. Had the Bible been translated into Machiguenga yet? Of course, and they had been the translators. In New World and New Light we would be able to film copies of the New Testament in Machiguenga.

I remembered Mascarita and our last conversation in the seedy café on the Avenida España. I heard once again his prophecies and his fulminations. From what the Schneils told us, Saúl's fears, that evening, were becoming a reality. Like other tribes, the Machiguengas were in the very midst of the process of acculturation: the Bible, bilingual schools, an evangelical leader, private property, the value of money, trade, Western clothes, no doubt . . . Was all this a good thing? Had it brought them real advantages as individuals, as people, as the Schneils so emphatically maintained? Or were they, rather, from the free and sovereign "savages" they had been, beginning to turn into "zombies," caricatures of Westerners, as Mascarita had put it? Would a visit of just a couple of days be long enough for me to find out? No, of course it wouldn't.

In the Yarinacocha bungalow that night, I lay awake for a long time thinking. Through the fly screen on the window, I could see a stretch of lake traversed by a golden wake, but the moon, which I imagined as being full and bright, was hidden from me by a clump of trees. Was it a good or a bad omen that Kashiri, that male astral body, sometimes malevolent, sometimes benevolent, of Machiguenga mythology, was concealing his stained face from me? Twenty-three years had passed since I had first slept in one of these bungalows. In all those years it was not only I who had changed, lived through a thousand experiences, grown older. Those Machiguengas, whom I knew, if at all, from only two brief accounts by this American couple, a conversation in Madrid with a Dominican, and a few ethnological studies, had also undergone great changes. Quite evidently, they no longer fitted the images of them that my imagination had invented. They were no longer that handful of tragic, indomitable beings, that society broken up into tiny families, fleeing, always fleeing, from the whites, from the mestizos, from the mountain people, and from other tribes, awaiting and stoically accepting their inevitable extinction as individuals and as a group, yet never giving up their language, their gods, their customs. An irrepressible sadness came over me at the thought that this society scattered in the depths of the damp and boundless forests, for whom a few tellers of tales acted as circulating sap, was doomed to disappear.

How many times in those twenty-three years had I thought of the Machiguengas? How many times had I tried to understand them, intuitively, to write about them; how many plans had I made to journey to their lands? Because of them, all the people or institutions everywhere in the world that might resemble or in any way be associated with the Machiguenga storytellers had held an immediate fascination for me. The wandering troubadours of the Bahia pampas, for instance, who, to the basso continuo of their guitars, weave together medieval romances of chivalry and local gossip in the dusty villages of northeastern Brazil. Seeing one of them that afternoon, in the market square of Uaúa, was enough for me to glimpse, superimposed on the figure of the caboclo, in a leather vest and hat, recounting and singing, to an amused audience, the story of Princess Magalona and the twelve peers of France, the greenish-yellow skin, decorated with symmetrical red stripes and dark spots, of the half-naked storyteller who, far, far from there, on a little beach hidden beneath the jungle foliage of Madre de Dios, was telling an attentive family squatting on their heels about the breathing contest between Tasurinchi and Kientibakori that was the origin of all the good and bad beings in the world.

But even more than the Bahian troubadour, it was the Irish *seanchaí* who had reminded me, so forcefully, of the Machiguenga storytellers. *Seanchaí*: "teller of ancient stories," "the one who knows things," as someone in a Dublin bar had offhandedly translated the word into English. How to explain, if it was not because of the Machiguengas, the rush of emotion, the sudden quickening of my heartbeat that impelled me to intrude, to ask questions, and later on to pester and infuriate Irish friends and acquaintances until they finally sat me down in front of a *seanchaí?* A living relic of the ancient bards of Hibernia, like those ancestors of his whose faint outline blends, in the night of time, with the Celtic myths and legends that are the intellectual foundations of Ireland, the *seanchaí* still recounts, in our own day, old legends, epic deeds, terrible loves, and disturbing miracles, in the smoky warmth of pubs; at festive gatherings where the magic of his words calls forth a sudden silence; in friendly houses, next to the hearth, as outside the rain falls or the storm rages. He can be a tavernkeeper, a truck driver, a parson, a beggar, someone mysteriously touched by the magic wand of wisdom and the art of reciting, of remembering, of reinventing and enriching tales told and retold down through the centuries; a messenger from the times of myth and magic, older than history, to whom Irishmen of today listen spellbound for hours on end. I always knew that the intense emotion I felt on that trip to Ireland, thanks to the *seanchaí*, was metaphorical, a way of hearing, through him, the storyteller, and of living the illusion that, sitting there squeezed in among his listeners, I was part of a Machiguenga audience.

And at last, tomorrow, in this unexpected way, guided by the Schneils themselves, I was going to meet the Machiguengas. So life has its novelistic side, does it? Indeed it does! "I've already told you I want to end with a zoom shot, Alejandro you cunt," Lucho Llosa raved in the next bed, tossing and turning under the mosquito net.

We left at dawn in two of the Institute's single-engine Cessnas, carrying three passengers each. Despite his adolescent face, the pilot of the little plane I was in had already spent several years with the linguist-missionaries, and before piloting planes for them in Amazonia, he had done the same thing in the jungles of Central America and Borneo. The morning was bright and clear and from the air we could easily make out all the meanders of the Ucayali and then of the Urubamba—the little islands, the spluttering launches with outboard motors or pequepeques, the canoes, the channels, the rapids and tributaries—and the tiny villages that at rare intervals showed up as a clearing of huts and reddish earth in the endless green plain. We flew over the penal colony of Sepa, and over the Dominican mission of Sepahua, then left the Alto Urubamba to follow the winding course of the Mipaya, a muddy snake on whose banks, around ten in the morning, we spotted our first destination: New World.

The name Mipaya has historical echoes. Beneath the tangle of vegetation, rubber camps proliferated a century ago. After the terrible death toll that the tribe suffered in the years of the tree-bleeding, the ruined rubber tappers, once the boom was over, tried to clear plantations in the region during the twenties, recruiting their labor by the old system of hunting Indians. It was then that there occurred, here on the shores of the Mipaya, the only instance of Machiguenga resistance known to history. When a planter of the region came to carry off the young men and women of the tribe, the Machiguengas received him with a rain of arrows and killed or wounded several Viracochas before being exterminated. The jungle had covered over the scene of the violence with its thick undergrowth of tree trunks, branches, and dead leaves, and not a trace remained of that infamy. Before landing, the pilot circled around the twenty or so conical-roofed huts several times, so that the Machiguengas of New World would remove their children from the one street of the settlement, which served as the landing strip. The Schneils had flown in the same Cessna as I, and the minute they climbed out of the plane, a hundred or so villagers surrounded them, showing signs of great excitement and joy, jostling each other to touch and pat them, all talking at the same time in a rhythmic tongue full of harsh sounds and extreme tonal shifts. Save for the schoolmistress dressed in a skirt and blouse and wearing sandals, all the Machiguengas were barefoot, the men in skimpy loincloths or cushmas, the women in yellow or gray cotton tunics of the sort worn by many tribes. Only a few old women wore pampanillas, a thin shawl tucked in at the waist, leaving their breasts bare. Nearly all of them, men and women, had red or black tattoos.

So there they were. Those were the Machiguengas.

I had no time to be carried away by emotion. To make the most of the light, we started work immediately, and fortunately no catastrophe kept us from filming the huts—all of them exactly the same: a simple platform of tree trunks supported on pilings, with thin walls of cane that reached only halfway up on each side, and a tuft of palm leaves for a roof; the interiors were austere, no more than a place for storing rolled-up mats, baskets, fishing nets, bows and arrows, small quantities of cassava and maize, and a few hollow gourds containing liquids—or from interviewing the schoolmistress, the only one who could express herself in Spanish, though with difficulty. She also looked after the village store, to which a motor launch brought provisions twice a month. My attempts to get any information about storytellers out of her were of no avail. Could she understand who it was I was asking her about? Apparently not. She looked at me with a surprised, slightly anxious expression, as though begging me to express myself in an intelligible way again.

Although we could not talk with them directly but only through the Schneils, the other Machiguengas were obliging enough and we were able to record some dances and songs and film an old woman delicately painting geometric designs on her face with annatto dye. We took shots of the crops sprouting in the fields, the poultry runs, the school, where the teacher insisted that we listen to the national anthem in Machiguenga. The face of one of the children was eaten away by a form of leprosy known as uta, which the Machiguengas attribute to the sting of a pink firefly whose abdomen is speckled with gleaming little dots of light. From the natural, uninhibited way in which the boy acted, running about among the other children, he did not seem, at first sight, to be the object of either discrimination or mockery because of his disfigurement.

As evening set in and we were loading our equipment for the flight to the village—New Light—where we were to spend the night, we learned that New World would probably have to change its location soon. What had happened? One of those chance geographical occurrences that are the daily bread of life in the jungle. During the last rainy season the Mipaya had radically changed its course because of heavy floods and was now so far distant from New World that when the waters were down to their winter level the inhabitants had to go a very long way to reach its shores. So they were looking for another spot, less subject to unforeseeable mischances, in order to resettle. That would not be difficult for people who had spent their lives on the move—their settlements were evidently born under an atavistic sign of eternal wandering, of a peripatetic destiny—and besides, their huts of tree trunks, cane, and palm leaves were far easier to take down and put up again than were the little houses of civilization.

They explained to us that the twenty-minute flight from

New World to New Light was misleading, since it took at least a week to go from one to the other on foot through the jungle, or a couple of days by canoe.

New Light was the oldest of the Machiguenga villages—it had just celebrated its second birthday—and had a little more than twice the number of huts and inhabitants as in New World. Here too, only Martín, the village chief and head administrator, who was the teacher of the bilingual school, was dressed in a shirt, trousers, and shoes, and wore his hair cut in Western style. He was quite young, short, deadly serious, and spoke fast, fluent, syncopated Spanish, dropping a good many word endings. The welcome the Machiguengas of New Light gave the Schneils was as exuberant and noisy as the one in the previous village; all the rest of the day and during a good part of the night we saw groups and individuals patiently waiting for others to take their leave of them so that they could approach and start a crackling conversation full of gestures and grimaces.

In New Light, too, we recorded dances, songs, drum solos, the school, the shop, seed-sowing, looms, tattoos, and an interview with the head of the village, who had been through Bible school at Mazamari; he was young and very thin, with hair cropped almost to his skull, and ceremonious gestures. He was a disciple well versed in the teachings of his masters, for he preferred talking about the Word of God, the Bible, and the Holy Spirit to talking about the Machiguengas. He had a sullen way of beating about the bush and resorting to endless vague biblical verbiage whenever he didn't care to answer a question. I tried twice to draw him out on the subject of storytellers, and each time, looking at me without understanding, he explained all over again that the book he had on his knee was the word of God and of his apostles in the Machiguenga language.

Our work finished, we went to swim in a gorge of the

Mipaya, some fifteen minutes' walk from the village, guided by the two Institute pilots. Twilight was coming on, the most mysterious and most beautiful hour of the day in Amazonia, as long as there isn't a cloudburst. The place was a real find, a branch of the Mipaya deflected by a natural barrier of rocks, forming a sort of cove where one could swim in warm, quiet waters, or, if one preferred, expose oneself to the full force of the current, protected by the portcullis of rocks. Even silent Alejandro started splashing and laughing, madly happy in this Amazonian Jacuzzi.

When we got back to New Light, young Martín (his manners were exquisite and his gestures genuinely elegant) invited me to drink lemon verbena tea with him in his hut next to the school and the village store. He had a radio transmitter, his means of communication with the headquarters of the Institute at Yarinacocha. There were just the two of us in the room, which was as meticulously neat and clean as Martín himself. Lucho Llosa and Alejandro Pérez had gone to help the pilots unload the hammocks and mosquito nets we were to sleep in. The light was failing fast and the dark shadows were deepening around us. The entire jungle had set up a rhythmical chirring, as always at this hour, reminding me that, beneath its green tangle, myriads of insects dominated the world. Soon the sky would be full of stars.

Did the Machiguengas really believe that the stars were the beams of light from the crowns of spirits? Martín nodded impassively. That shooting stars were the fiery arrows of those little child-gods, the ananeriites, and the morning dew their urine? This time Martín laughed. Yes, that was their belief. And now that the Machiguengas had stopped walking, so as to put down roots in villages, would the sun fall? Surely not: God would take care of keeping it in place. He looked at me for a moment with an amused expression: how had I found out about these beliefs? I told him that I'd been interested in the Machiguengas for nearly a quarter of a century and that from the first I'd made a point of reading everything that was written about them. I told him why. As I spoke, his face, friendly and smiling to begin with, grew stern and distrustful. He listened to me grimly, not a muscle of his face moving.

"So, you see, my questions about storytellers aren't just vulgar curiosity but something much more serious. They're very important to me. Perhaps as important as to the Machiguengas, Martín." He remained silent and motionless, with a watchful gleam in the depth of his eyes. "Why didn't you want to tell me anything about them? The schoolmistress at New World wouldn't tell me anything about them, either. Why all this mystery about the habladores, Martín?"

He assured me he didn't understand what I was talking about. What was all this business about "habladores"? He'd never heard a word about them, either in this village or in any other of the community. There might be habladores in other tribes perhaps, but not among the Machiguengas. He was telling me this when the Schneils came in. We hadn't drunk up all that lemon verbena, the most fragrant in all Amazonia, had we? Martín changed the subject, and I thought it best not to pursue the matter.

But an hour later, after we'd taken our leave of Martín and I'd put up my hammock and mosquito net in the hut they'd loaned us, I went out with the Schneils to enjoy the cool evening air, and as we walked in the open surrounded by the dwellings of New Light, the subject came irresistibly to my lips once again.

"In the few hours I've been with the Machiguengas, there are many things I haven't been able to figure out yet," I said.

"I have realized one thing, however. Something important."

The sky was a forest of stars and a dark patch of clouds hid the moon, its presence visible only as a diffuse brightness. A fire had been made at one end of New Light, and fleeting silhouettes suddenly stole around it. All the huts were dark except for the one they'd lent to us, some fifty meters away, which was lit by the greenish light of a portable kerosene lamp. The Schneils waited for me to go on. We were walking slowly over soft ground where tall grass grew. Even though I was wearing boots, I had begun to feel mosquitoes biting my ankles and insteps.

"And what is that?" Mrs. Schneil finally asked.

"That all this is quite relative," I went on impetuously. "I mean, baptizing this place New Light and calling the village chief Martín. The New Testament in Machiguenga; sending the Indians to Bible school and making pastors out of them; the violent transition from a nomadic life to a sedentary one; accelerated Westernization and Christianization. So-called modernization. I've realized that it's just outward show. Even though they've started trading and using money, the weight of their own traditions exerts a much stronger pull on them than all that."

I stopped. Was I offending them? I myself didn't know what conclusion to draw from this whole hasty process of reasoning.

"Yes, of course." Edwin Schneil coughed, somewhat disconcerted. "Naturally. Hundreds of years of beliefs and customs don't disappear overnight. It'll take time. What's important is that they've begun to change. Today's Machiguengas are no longer what they were when we arrived, I assure you."

"I've realized that there are depths in them they won't yet allow to be touched," I interrupted him. "I asked the schoolmistress in New World, and Martín as well, about habladores. And they both reacted in exactly the same way: denying that they existed, pretending they didn't even know what I was talking about. It means that even in the most Westernized Machiguengas, such as the schoolmistress and Martín, there's an inviolable inner loyalty to their own beliefs. There are certain taboos they're not prepared to give up. That's why they keep them so thoroughly hidden from outsiders."

There was a long silence in which the chirring of the invisible night insects seemed to grow deafening. Was he going to ask me who habladores were? Would the Schneils also tell me, as the schoolmistress and the village chief-pastor had, that they'd never heard of them? I thought for a moment that habladores didn't exist: that I'd invented them and then housed them in false memories so as to make them real.

"Ah, habladores!" Mrs. Schneil exclaimed at last. And the Machiguenga word or sentence crackled like dead leaves. It seemed to me that it came to greet me, across time, from the bungalow on the shores of Yarinacocha where I had heard it for the first time when I was little more than an adolescent.

"Ah," Edwin Schneil repeated, mimicking the crackling sound twice in a faintly uneasy tone of voice. "Habladores. *Speakers*. Yes, of course, that's one possible translation."

"And how is it that you know about them?" Mrs. Schneil said, turning her head just slightly in my direction.

"Through you. Through the two of you," I murmured.

I sensed that they opened their eyes wide in the darkness and exchanged a look, not understanding. I explained that since that night in their bungalow on the shores of Lake Yarina when they had told me about them, the Machiguenga habladores had lived with me, intriguing me, disturbing me, that since then I had tried a thousand times to imagine them as they wandered through the forest, collecting and repeating stories, fables, gossip, tales they'd invented, from one little Machiguenga island to another in this Amazonian sea in which they drifted, borne on the current of adversity. I told them that, for some reason I found hard to pin down, the existence of those storytellers, finding out what they were doing and what importance it had in the life of their people, had been, for twenty-three years, a great stimulus for my own work, a source of inspiration and an example I would have liked to emulate. I realized how excited my voice sounded, and fell silent.

By a sort of unspoken agreement, we had halted alongside a pile of tree trunks and branches heaped up in the center of the clearing as though ready to be set alight for a bonfire. We had sat down or leaned back against the logs. Kashiri could now be seen, a yellow-orange crescent, surrounded by his vast harem of sparkling fireflies. There were a lot of mosquitoes as well as clouds of gnats, and we waved our hands back and forth to shoo them away from our faces.

"How really odd. Who would ever have thought that you'd remember a thing like that? And, stranger still, that it would take on such importance in your life?" Edwin Schneil said at last, just to say something. He seemed perplexed and a little flustered. "I didn't even remember our having touched, back then, on the subject of—storytellers? No, speakers—is that the right word? How odd, how very odd."

"It doesn't surprise me at all that Martín and the schoolmistress of New World didn't want to tell you anything about them," Mrs. Schneil broke in after a moment. "It's a subject no Machiguenga likes to talk about. It's something very private, very secret. Not even with the two of us, who've known them for such a long time now, who've seen so many of them born.

I don't understand it. Because they tell you everything, about their beliefs, their ayahuasca rites, the witch doctors. They don't keep anything to themselves. Except anything having to do with the habladores. It's the one thing they always shy away from. Edwin and I have often wondered why there's that taboo."

"Yes, it's a strange thing," Edwin Schneil agreed. "It's hard to understand, because they're very communicative and never object to answering any question they're asked. They're the best informants in the world; ask any anthropologist who's been around here. Maybe they don't want to talk about them or have people meet them, because the habladores are the repositories of their family secrets. They know all the Machiguengas' private affairs. What's that proverb? You don't wash dirty linen in public. Perhaps the taboo about habladores has to do with some feeling of that sort."

In the darkness, Mrs. Schneil laughed. "Well, that's a theory that doesn't convince me," she said. "Because the Machiguengas aren't at all secretive about their personal concerns. If you only knew how often they've left me flabbergasted and red in the face from what they tell me . . ."

"But, in any case, I can assure you you're wrong if you think it's a religious taboo," Edwin Schneil declared. "It isn't. The habladores aren't sorcerers or priests, like the seripigari or the machikanari. They're tellers of tales, that's all."

"I know that," I said. "You explained that to me the first time. And that's precisely what moves me. That the Machiguengas consider mere storytellers so important that they have to keep their existence a secret."

Every so often a silent shadow passed by, crackled briefly, and the Schneils crackled back what must have been the equivalent of a "Good night," and the shadow disappeared into the darkness. Not a sound came from the huts. Was the whole village already fast asleep?

"And in all these years, you've never heard an hablador?" I asked.

"I've never been that lucky," Mrs. Schneil said. "Up until now they've never offered me that opportunity. But Edwin's had the chance."

"Twice, even." He laughed. "Though in a quarter of a century that's not very often, is it? I hope what I'm going to say won't disappoint you. But I do believe I wouldn't want to repeat the experience."

The first time had been by sheer happenstance, ten years or more before. The Schneils had been living in a small Machiguenga settlement on the Tikompinía for several months, when one morning, leaving his wife in the village, Edwin had gone off to visit another family of the community a few hours upriver by canoe, taking with him a young boy to help him paddle. On reaching their destination, they found that instead of the five or six Machiguengas who lived there, whom Edwin knew, there were at least twenty people gathered together, a number of them from distant hamlets. Oldsters and young children, men and women were squatting in a half circle, facing a man sitting cross-legged in front of them, declaiming. He was a storyteller. Nobody objected to Edwin Schneil and the lad sitting down to listen. And the storyteller did not interrupt his monologue when they joined the audience.

"He was a man getting on in years and spoke so fast that I had trouble following him. He must have been speaking for a good while already. But he didn't seem tired; quite the contrary. The performance went on for several hours more. Every now and then they'd hand him a gourdful of masato and he'd take a swallow to clear his throat. No, I'd never seen that storyteller before. Quite old, at first sight, but as you know, one ages quickly here in the jungle. An old man, among the Machiguengas, can mean one no more than thirty. He was a short man, with a powerful build, very expressive. You or I or anyone else who talked on and on for that many hours would be hoarse-voiced and worn out. But he wasn't. He went on and on, putting everything he had into it. It was his job, after all, and I don't doubt he did it well."

What did he talk about? It was impossible to remember. What a hodgepodge! A bit of everything, anything that came into his head. What he'd done the day before, and the four worlds of the Machiguenga cosmos; his travels, magic herbs, people he'd known; the gods, the little gods, and fabulous creatures of the tribe's pantheon. Animals he'd seen and celestial geography, a maze of rivers with names nobody could possibly remember. Edwin Schneil had had to concentrate to follow the torrent of words that leapt from a cassava crop to the armies of demons of Kientibakori, the spirit of evil, and from there to births, marriages, and deaths in different families or the iniquities of the time of the tree-bleeding, as they called the rubber boom. Very soon Edwin Schneil found himself less interested in the storyteller than in the fascinated, rapt attention with which the Machiguengas listened to him, greeting his jokes with great roars of laughter or sharing his sadness. Their eyes avid, their mouths agape, not one pause, not a single inflection of what the man said was lost on them.

I listened to the linguist the way the Machiguengas had listened to the storyteller. Yes, they did exist, and were like the ones in my dreams.

"To tell the truth, I remember very little of what he said," Edwin Schneil added. "I'm just giving you a few examples.

What a mishmash! I can remember his telling about the initiation ceremony of a young shaman, with ayahuasca, under the guidance of a seripigari. He recounted the visions he'd had. Strange, incoherent ones, like certain modern poems. He also spoke of the properties of a little bird, the chobíburiti; if you crush the small bones of its wing and bury them in the floor of the hut, that assures peace in the family."

"We tried his formula and it really didn't work all that well," Mrs. Schneil joked. "Would you say it did, Edwin?"

He laughed.

"The storytellers are their entertainment. They're their films and their television," he added after a pause, serious once more. "Their books, their circuses, all the diversions we civilized people have. They have only one diversion in the world. The storytellers are nothing more than that."

"Nothing less than that," I corrected him gently.

"What's that you say?" he put in, disconcerted. "Well, yes. But forgive me for pressing one point. I don't think there's anything religious behind it. That's why all this mystery, the secrecy they surround them with, is so odd."

"If something matters greatly to you, you surround it with mystery," it occurred to me to say.

"There's no doubt about that," Mrs. Schneil agreed. "The habladores matter a great deal to them. But we haven't discovered why."

Another silent shadow passed by and crackled, and the Schneils crackled back. I asked Edwin whether he'd talked with the old storyteller that time.

"I had practically no time to. I was exhausted when he'd finished talking. All my bones ached, and I fell asleep immediately. I'd sat for four or five hours, remember, without changing position, after having paddled against the current nearly all day. And listened to that chittering of anecdotes. I was all tuckered out. I fell asleep, and when I woke up, the storyteller had gone. And since the Machiguengas don't like to talk about them, I never heard anything more about him."

There he was. In the murmurous darkness of New Light all around me I could see him: skin somewhere between copper and greenish, gathered by the years into innumerable folds; cheekbones, nose, and forehead decorated with lines and circles meant to protect him from the claws and fangs of wild beasts, the harshness of the elements, the enemy's magic and his darts; squat of build, with short muscular legs and a small loincloth around his waist; and no doubt carrying a bow and a quiver of arrows. There he was, walking amid the bushes and the tree trunks, barely visible in the dense undergrowth, walking, walking, after speaking for ten hours, toward his next audience, to go on with his storytelling. How had he begun? Was it a hereditary occupation? Was he specially chosen? Was it something forced upon him by others?

Mrs. Schneil's voice erased the image. "Tell him about the other storyteller," she said. "The one who was so aggressive. The albino. I'm sure that will interest him."

"Well, I don't know whether he was really an albino." Edwin Schneil laughed in the darkness. "Among ourselves, we also called him the gringo."

This time it hadn't been by chance. Edwin Schneil was staying in a settlement by the Timpía with a family of old acquaintances, when other families from around about began arriving unexpectedly, in a state of great excitement. Edwin became aware of great palavers going on; they pointed at him, then went off to argue. He guessed the reason for their alarm and told them not to worry; he would leave at once. But when the family he was staying with insisted, the others all agreed that he could stay. However, when the person they were waiting for appeared, another long and violent argument ensued, because the storyteller, gesticulating wildly, rudely insisted that the stranger leave, while his hosts were determined that he should stay. Edwin Schneil decided to take his leave of them, telling them he didn't want to be the cause of dissension. He bundled up his things and left. He was on his way down the path toward another settlement when the Machiguengas he'd been staying with caught up with him. He could come back, he could stay. They'd persuaded the storyteller.

"In fact, nobody was really convinced that I should stay, least of all the storyteller," he added. "He wasn't at all pleased at my being there. He made his feeling of hostility clear to me by not looking at me even once. That's the Machiguenga way: using your hatred to make someone invisible. But we and that family on the Timpía had a very close relationship, a spiritual kinship. We called each other 'father' and 'son' . . ."

"Is the law of hospitality a very powerful one among the Machiguengas?"

"The law of kinship, rather," Mrs. Schneil answered. "If 'relatives' go to stay with their kin, they're treated like princes. It doesn't happen often, because of the great distances that separate them. That's why they called Edwin back and resigned themselves to his hearing the storyteller. They didn't want to offend a 'kinsman.' "

"They'd have done better to be less hospitable and let me leave." Edwin Schneil sighed. "My bones still ache and my mouth even more, I've yawned so much remembering that night."

It was twilight and the sun had not yet set when the storyteller began talking, and he went on with his stories all night long, without once stopping. When at last he fell silent, the light was gilding the tops of the trees and it was nearly mid-morning. Edwin Schneil's legs were so cramped, his body so full of aches and pains, that they had to help him stand up, take a few steps, learn to walk again.

"I've never felt so awful in my life," he muttered. "I was half dead from fatigue and physical discomfort. An entire night fighting off sleep and muscle cramp. If I'd gotten up, they would have been very offended. I only followed his tales for the first hour, or perhaps two. After that, all I could do was to keep trying not to fall asleep. And hard as I tried, I couldn't keep my head from nodding from one side to the other like the clapper of a bell."

He laughed softly, lost in his memories.

"Edwin still has nightmares remembering that night's vigil, swallowing his yawns and massaging his legs." Mrs. Schneil laughed.

"And the storyteller?" I asked.

"He had a huge birthmark," Edwin Schneil said. He paused, searching his memories or looking for words to describe them. "And hair redder than mine. A strange person. What the Machiguengas call a serigórompi. Meaning an eccentric; someone different from the rest. Because of that carrot-colored hair of his, we called him the albino or the gringo among ourselves."

The mosquitoes were drilling into my ankles. I could feel their bites and almost see them piercing my skin, which would now swell into horribly painful little blisters. It was the price I had to pay every time I came to the jungle. Amazonia had never failed to exact it of me.

"A huge birthmark?" I stammered, scarcely able to get the words out. "Do you mean uta? An ulcer eating his face away, like that little boy we saw this morning in New World . . ."

"No, no. A birthmark. An enormous dark birthmark,"

Edwin Schneil interrupted, raising his hand. "It covered the whole right side of his face. An impressive sight, I assure you. I'd never seen a man with one like it, never. Neither among the Machiguengas nor anywhere else. And I haven't seen its like since, either."

I could feel the mosquitoes biting me on all the parts of my body that had no protection: face, neck, arms, hands. The clouds that had hidden the moon were gone and there was Kashiri, clear and bright and not yet full, looking at us. A shiver ran down my body from head to foot.

"He had red hair?" I murmured very slowly. My mouth was dry, but my hands were sweating.

"Redder than mine." He laughed. "A real gringo, I swear. Though perhaps an albino, after all. I didn't have much time to get a close look at him. I've told you what a state I was in after that storytelling session. As though I'd been anesthetized. And when I came to, he was gone, of course. So he wouldn't have to talk to me or bear the sight of my face any longer."

"How old would you say he was?" I managed to get out, with immense fatigue, as though I'd been the one who'd been talking all night long.

Edwin Schneil shrugged. "Who knows?" He sighed. "You've doubtless realized how hard it is to tell how old they are. They themselves don't know. They don't calculate their age the same way we do, and what's more, they all reach that average age very quickly. What you might call Machiguenga age. But certainly younger than I am. About your age, or perhaps a bit younger."

I pretended to cough two or three times to conceal how unnerved I was. I suddenly felt a fierce, intolerable desire to smoke. It was as though every pore in my body had suddenly opened, demanding to inhale a thousand and one puffs of smoke. Five years before, I had smoked what I thought would be my last cigarette; I was convinced that I'd freed myself from tobacco forever; for a long time now, the very smell of cigarette smoke had irritated me, and here, out of the blue, in the darkness of New Light, an overwhelming urge to smoke had arisen from who knows what mysterious depths.

"Did he speak well?" I heard myself ask softly.

"Speak well?" Edwin Schneil asked. "He spoke on and on, without stopping, without pausing, without punctuation marks." He laughed, deliberately exaggerating. "The way storytellers talk. Spilling out all the things that ever were and ever will be. He was what he was, in a word: a teller of tales, and a real chatterbox."

"I mean Machiguenga," I said. "Did he speak it well? Couldn't he . . ."

"Go on," Schneil said.

"Nothing," I said. "A nonsensical idea. Nothing, nothing."

Though I was under the impression that my attention was concentrated on the gnats and mosquitoes biting me and my longing to smoke, I must have asked Edwin Schneil, as in a dream, with a strange ache in my jaws and tongue, as though I were exhausted from using them too much, how long ago all this had been—"Oh, it must have been three and a half years or so ago," he replied—and whether he had heard him again, or seen him, or had news of him, and listened as he answered no to all three questions, as I knew he would: it was a subject the Machiguengas didn't like to talk about.

When I said good night to the Schneils—they were sleeping at Martín's—and went off to the hut where my hammock was,

I woke up Lucho Llosa to ask him for a cigarette. "Since when have you smoked?" he said in surprise as he handed me one with hands fumbling from sleep.

I didn't light it. I held it between my fingers at my lips, going through the motions of smoking, all through that long night, while I swung gently in the hammock, listening to the quiet breathing of Lucho, Alejandro, and the pilots, hearing the chirring of the forest, feeling the seconds go by, one by one, slow, solemn, improbable, filled with wonder.

We returned to Yarinacocha very early. Halfway there, we were forced to land because we were overtaken by a storm. In the small Campa village on the banks of the Urubamba where we took refuge, there was an American missionary who might have been a character out of Faulkner—single-minded, fearlessly stubborn, and frighteningly heroic. He had lived in this remote corner of the world for years with his wife and several small children. In my memory I can still see him standing in the torrential rain, energetically leading hymns with both arms and singing in his throaty voice to set a good example, under a flimsy shelter that threatened to collapse at any moment beneath the tremendous downpour. The twenty or so Campas barely moved their lips and gave the impression that they were making no sound, yet kept their eyes riveted on him with the same rapt fascination with which the Machiguengas doubtless contemplated their storytellers.

When we resumed our flight, the Schneils asked me whether I wasn't feeling well. Yes, perfectly well, I replied, though rather tired, since I hadn't slept very much. We stayed in Yarinacocha just long enough to climb into the jeep that would take us to Pucallpa to catch the Fawcett flight to Lima. In the plane Lucho asked me: "Why the long face? What went wrong this time?" I was on the point of explaining why I wasn't saying a word and looked more or less stunned, but when I opened my mouth I realized I wouldn't be able to. It couldn't be summed up in a mere anecdote; it was too unreal and too literary to be plausible, and too serious to joke about as though it were just an amusing incident.

I now knew the reason for the taboo. Did I? Yes. Could it be possible? Yes, it could. That was why they avoided talking about them, that was why they had jealously hidden them from anthropologists, linguists, Dominican missionaries over the last twenty years. That was why they did not appear in the writings of modern ethnologists on the Machiguengas. They were not protecting the institution or the idea of the storyteller in the abstract. They were protecting him. No doubt because he had asked them to. So as not to arouse the Viracochas' curiosity about this strange graft onto the tribe. And they had gone on doing as he asked for so many years now, providing him refuge by way of a taboo which had spread to the entire institution, to the hablador in the abstract. If that was how it had been, they had a great deal of respect for him. If that was how it was, in their eyes he was one of them.

We began editing the program that same night at the channel after going home to shower and change, and I to a pharmacy for ointment and antihistamines for the insect bites. We decided that the program would be in the form of a travelogue, intercutting commentaries and recollections with the interviews we'd done in Yarinacocha and the Alto Urubamba. As he edited the material, Moshé grumbled at us as usual for not having taken certain shots some other way, or for having taken others the way we had. It was then that I remembered that he, too, was Jewish.

"How do you get along with the Chosen People here in Peru?"

"Like a monkey with a mirror, of course," he said. "Why? Do you want to get yourself circumcised?"

"I wonder if you'd do me a favor. Would you have any way of finding out where a family of the community that went to Israel is now?"

"Are we going to do a Tower of Babel on kibbutzim?" Lucho said. "In that case, we'll have to do one on the Palestinian refugees. But how can we? Doesn't the program end next week?"

"The Zuratas. The father, Don Salomón, had a little grocery store in Breña. The son, Saúl, was a friend of mine. They went to Israel in the early seventies, it seems. If you could find out their address there, you'd be doing me a favor."

"I'll see what I can do," Moshé answered. "I imagine they keep a register of such things in the community."

The program on the Institute of Linguistics and the Machiguengas turned out to be longer than we'd foreseen. When we gave it to Control they informed us that on that particular Sunday they'd sold space for a definite time slot, so that if we didn't cut the program ourselves to exactly one hour, the operator would do it any old way he pleased when he put it on the air. Thoroughly pissed off, we had to cut it in a rush, as time was running short. We were already editing the final Tower of Babel for the following Sunday. We'd decided that it would be an anthology of the twenty-four previous programs. But as usual we had to change our plans. For the very start of the program, I'd tried to persuade Doris Gibson to let herself be interviewed and help us compile a short biography of her life as a founder and director of magazines, a businesswoman, a fighter against dictatorship and also its victim—on one famous occasion she'd hauled off and slapped the policemen who had come to seize copies of *Caretas*—and above all, a woman who, in a society that in those days was far more macho and prejudiced than it is now, had been able to make a career for herself and achieve success in fields that were considered male monopolies. At the same time, Doris had been one of the most beautiful women in Lima, courted by millionaires, and the muse of famous painters and poets. The impetuous Doris, who is nonetheless very shy, had turned me down, because, she said, the cameras intimidated her. But that last week she had changed her mind and sent word that she was willing to appear on the program.

I interviewed her, and that interview, together with the anthology, saw the end of the Tower of Babel. Faithful to its destiny, the final program, which Moshé, Lucho, Alejandro, and I watched at my house, sitting around a tableful of Chinese food and ice-cold beer, fell victim to technical imponderables. For one of those mysterious reasons—celestial sabotage—which were the daily bread of the channel, unexpected jazz numbers appeared out of nowhere just as the broadcast began and provided background music to all of Doris's stories about General Odría's dictatorship, police seizures of *Caretas*, and Sérvulo Gutiérrez's paintings.

After the program was over and we were drinking to its death and non-resurrection, the phone rang. It was Doris, asking me whether it wouldn't have been more appropriate to have backed her interview with Arequipan yaravíes (she is, among other things, a fiercely loyal Arequipeña) rather than that outlandish jazz. After Lucho, Moshé, and Alejandro had had a good laugh at the explanations I had invented to justify the use of jazz on the program, Moshé said: "By the way, before I forget, I found out what you asked me to."

More than a week had gone by and I hadn't reminded him, because I could guess the answer and was a little unnerved at the prospect of having my suspicions confirmed.

"It seems they never did go to Israel," he said. "Where did you get the idea they'd left the country?"

"You mean the Zuratas?" I asked, knowing very well what he was talking about.

"Don Salomón, at least, didn't go. He died here. He's buried in the Jewish cemetery in Lima, the one on the Avenida Colonial." Moshé took a scrap of paper out of his pocket and read: "October 23, 1960. That's the day they buried him, if you need further details. My grandfather knew him and attended his funeral. As for his son, your friend, he may have gone to Israel, but I couldn't find out for sure. None of the people I asked knew anything about him."

But I do, I thought. I know everything.

"Did he have a big birthmark on his face?" Moshé asked. "My grandfather even remembers that. Did they call him the Phantom of the Opera?"

"An enormous one. We called him Mascarita."

GOOD THINGS happen and bad things happen. It's bad that wisdom should be getting lost. Before, there were any number of seripigaris, and if the man who walks had any doubts about what to eat, how to cure the evil, or which stones protect against Kientibakori and his little devils, he went and asked. There was always a seripigari close by. Smoking, drinking brew, thinking, talking with the saankarites in the worlds up above, he could find the answer. But now there are few of them and some of them shouldn't call themselves seripigaris. Can they counsel you? Their wisdom has dried up on them like a worm-eaten root, it seems. This brings much confusion. Wherever I go, that's what the men who walk say. Could it be because we don't keep on the move enough? they say. Can it be that we've grown lazy? We're not fulfilling our obligation, perhaps.

That, anyway, is what I have learned.

The wisest seripigari I ever knew has gone. Maybe he's come back; maybe not. He lived on the other side of the Gran

Pongo, by the Kompiroshiato. His name was Tasurinchi. Nothing held any secrets for him, in this world or in the others. He could tell which worms you can eat by the color of their rings and the way they crawled. He looked at them like this, wrinkling up his eyes, with his deep gaze. He would study them for a good while. And there it came; he knew. Everything I know about worms I learned from him. The one that lives on giant reeds, the chakokieni, is good; the one that lives on lupana is bad. The one that lives on rotten tree trunks, the shigopi, is good, and also the one that lives on cassava fibers. The one that lodges in the shells of tortoises is extremely bad. The best and the tastiest is the one that lives on the pulp left after maize or cassava go through a sieve to make masato. This worm, the kororo, sweetens the mouth, relieves hunger, and brings untroubled sleep. But the worm that lives on the corpses of caimans washed up on the shores of a lake does the body harm and brings on the same visions as a bad trance.

Tasurinchi, the one from the Kompiroshiato, made people's lives better. He had recipes for everything. Using everything. He taught me many of them. Here's one I still remember. If someone dies from snakebite, his body must be burned immediately; otherwise, it will breed reptiles and the forest all around will teem with poisonous beings. And here's another. It's not enough just to burn the house of someone who's gone; you have to do it with your back turned. Looking at the flames brings misfortune. It was frightening talking with that seripigari. You realized how much you didn't know. Ignorance has its dangers, perhaps. "How have you learned so many things?" I asked him. And I said: "It's as though you'd been living since before we started walking, and you'd seen everything and tried everything."

"The most important thing is not to be impatient and allow

what must happen to happen," he answered. Saying: "If a man lives calmly, without getting impatient, he has time to think and to remember." That way, he'll meet his destiny, perhaps. He'll live content, maybe. He won't forget what he's learned. If he gets impatient, rushing to outstrip time, the world gets out of order, it seems. And the soul falls into a spiderweb of mud. That is confusion. The worst thing that can happen, let's say. In this world and in the soul of the man who walks. Then he doesn't know what to do, where to go. He doesn't know how to protect himself either, saying: What shall I do? What must I do? Then the devils and the little devils creep into his life and play with it. The way, perhaps, that children play with frogs, making them jump. Mistakes are always the result of confusion, it seems."

"What should one do so as not to lose one's serenity, Tasurinchi?" "Eat what's permitted and respect the taboos, storyteller." Otherwise, what happened to Tasurinchi that time could happen to anyone.

What happened to him?

This happened to him. That was before.

He was a great hunter. He knew how big the trap should be for the sajino, or the noose for the paujil. He knew how to hide a cage so that the ronsoco would walk into it. But, above all, he knew how to shoot a bow. The very first arrow he loosed always hit the mark.

One day when he'd gone out to hunt, after fasting and painting his face in the proper way, he felt the leaves moving not far from where he was. He sensed a shape and halted, saying: A big animal! He approached slowly, heedlessly. Not taking the time to make sure what it was, he boldly shot his arrow. He ran to see. There it was, lying on the ground, dead. What had fallen? A deer. He was very frightened, of course. Some evil would befall him now. What happens to someone who kills a forbidden animal? There was no seripigari close by to put that question to. Would his body be covered with blisters? Would he be racked by horrible pains? Would the kamagarinis snatch one of his souls and carry it off to the top of a tree for the buzzards to peck at? Many moons passed and nothing happened. Then Tasurinchi swelled with pride. "That story about not killing deer is all humbug," his family heard him say. "Just coward's talk." "How dare you say that!" they scolded him, looking about in all directions, and above and below, in fright. "I killed one and I feel quite peaceful and happy," he answered.

That's what Tasurinchi kept saying, and finally all the saying led to doing. He started hunting deer. He followed their trail to the collpa where they went to lick the salty earth. He followed them to the pool where they gathered to drink. He sought out the caves where the females went to give birth. He lay in wait in a hiding place, and when he saw the deer he shot his arrows at them. They lay there dying, looking at him with their big eyes. Sorrowful, as though asking: What have you done to me? He slung them across his back. He was pleased, perhaps. He didn't mind being stained with the blood of what he had hunted. Nothing mattered to him now. He wasn't afraid of anything, it seems. He brought the kill to his hut. "Cook it. Like sachavaca, the very same way," he ordered his wife. She obeyed, trembling with fear. Sometimes she tried to warn him. "This food is going to bring evil upon us," she whimpered. "Upon you and me and everybody, perhaps. It's as though you ate your children or your mothers, Tasurinchi. We're not Chonchoites, are we? When have Machiguengas ever eaten human flesh?" Chewing and choking on great mouthfuls of meat, he would say: "If deer are people who have turned into something else, the Chonchoites are quite right. It's food, and it's delicious.

Look what a feast I'm having; look how I'm enjoying this food." And he farted and farted. In the forest Kientibakori drank masato, dancing and feasting. His farts were like thunder; his belches like the jaguar's roar.

And it was true; despite the deer he shot and ate, nothing happened to Tasurinchi. Some families took fright; others, persuaded by his example, started eating forbidden flesh. The world was thrown into confusion, then.

One day, Tasurinchi found tracks in the forest. That made him very happy. The trail was wide and easy to follow and his experience told him it was a herd of deer. He followed it for many moons, full of hope, his heart pounding. How many shall I kill? he dreamed. If I'm lucky, as many as I have arrows. I'll drag them home one at a time, cut them up, salt them, and we'll have food for a long time.

The trail came to an end in the dark waters of a small lake; in one corner was a waterfall, half hidden by the branches and leaves of the trees. The vegetation muffled the sound of the water and the place did not seem to be this world but Inkite. Just as peaceful, perhaps. Here the herd came to drink. Here the deer gathered to chew the cud. Here they slept, keeping each other warm. Excited by his discovery, Tasurinchi looked all around. There it was; that was the best tree. He would have a clear view from there; from there he could shoot off his arrows. He climbed up, made his hiding place with branches and leaves. Quietly, quietly, as though his souls had leaked away and his body were an empty skin, he waited.

Not for long. Soon his sharp hunter's ears caught the sound, troc, troc, far away, the drumbeat of deer hoofs in the forest: troc, troc, troc. Suddenly he saw it: a stag, tall and proud, with the sad look of one who has been a man. Tasurinchi's eyes shone. His mouth watered perhaps. Thinking: How tender, how tasty! He aimed and shot. But the arrow whistled past the stag, as though curving so as to miss it, and flew on, lost in the depths of the forest. How many times can a man die? Many times, it seems. This stag did not die. Nor was it frightened. What was happening? Instead of fleeing, it began drinking. Stretching its neck from the shore of the lake, plunging its muzzle into the water, lifting it out, clacking its tongue, it drank, shh, shh. Shh, shh, content. As though unaware of danger. Calm. Could it be deaf? Could it be a deer with no sense of smell? Tasurinchi now had a second arrow ready. Troc, troc. Then he saw another stag arriving, pushing through the branches, making the leaves rustle. It took its place next to the first one and began drinking. They seemed content, both of them, drinking water. Shh, shh, shh. Tasurinchi loosed his arrow. It missed this time, too. What was happening? The two stags went on drinking, not taking fright, not fleeing. What's happening to you, Tasurinchi? Is your hand trembling? Have you lost your eyesight? Can you no longer judge distance? What was he going to do? He was utterly bewildered; he couldn't believe it. His world had gone dark. And there he was, shooting. He shot all his arrows. Troc, troc. Troc, troc. The deer kept on coming. More and more, so many, so very many. The drumbeat of their hoofs echoed and reechoed in Tasurinchi's ears. Troc, troc. They didn't seem to be coming from this world, but from the one below or above. Troc, troc. He understood then. Perhaps. Was it you or they who'd fallen into the trap, Tasurinchi?

There were the deer, calm, not angry. Drinking, eating, moving about, mating. Twining their necks together, butting each other. As though nothing had happened, as though nothing were going to happen. But Tasurinchi knew that they knew that he was there. Could they be avenging their dead in this way? By making him endure this painfully long wait? No, this was only the beginning. What had to happen would not happen while the sun was in Inkite, but later, when Kashiri rose. Kashiri the resentful, the stained one. Darkness fell. The sky filled with stars. Kashiri sent his pale light. Tasurinchi could see the eyes of the deer, glistening with regret at no longer being men, with sadness at not walking. Then suddenly, as though at a command, the animals started moving. All at the same time, it seems. They all came to Tasurinchi's tree. There they were, at his feet. A great many of them. A forest of deer, you might say. One after another, in an orderly way, not hurrying, not getting in each other's way, they butted the tree. Playfully at first, then harder. Harder still. He was sad. Saying: "I'm going to fall." He never would have believed that before going he'd be like a shimbillo monkey, clinging to a branch, trying not to drown in that dark mass of deer. But he held out the whole night. Sweating and moaning, he resisted, hoping his arms and legs would not give out. At dawn, his strength gone, he let himself fall. Saying: "I must accept my fate."

Now he, too, is a deer, like the others. There he is, I hear, wandering up and down the forest, troc, troc. Fleeing the jaguar, frightened of the snake. Troc, troc. Hiding from the puma and from the arrows of the hunter who, through ignorance or wickedness, kills and eats his brothers.

When I come upon a deer, I remember the story the seripigari of the Kompiroshiato told me. What if this one were Tasurinchi the hunter? Who can tell? I for my part have no way of telling whether a deer was or wasn't a man who walks, before. I just step back a little way and look at it. Perhaps it recognizes me; perhaps when it sees me it thinks: I was like him. Who knows?

In a bad trance a machikanari of the rainbow river, the

Yoguieto, turned into a jaguar. How did he know? Because of the terrible urge he felt to kill deer and eat them. "I grew blind with rage," he said. And roaring with hunger, he began running through the forest, tracking them. Until he came upon one and killed it. When he changed back into a machikanari, he had shreds of flesh between his teeth and his nails were bloody from all the ripping and tearing he'd done. "Kientibakori must have been pleased," he said. He may well have been.

That, anyway, is what I have learned.

Like the deer, every animal in the forest has its story. Whether little, middle-sized, or big. The one that flies, like the hummingbird. The one that swims, like the boquichico. The one that lives in a herd, like the huangana. Before, they were all something different from what they are now. Something happened to all of them that you could tell a story about. Would you like to know their stories? So would I. Many of the ones I know I heard from the seripigari of the Kompiroshiato. If I'd had my way, I'd still be there listening to him, the way all of you are listening, here, now. But, one day, he threw me out of his hut. "How long are you going to stay here, Tasurinchi?" he scolded me. "You have to be on your way. You're a storyteller, I'm a seripigari, and now, with all your questions and your making me talk so much, you're turning me into what you are. Would you like to become a seripigari? If so, you'd have to be born again. Pass all the tests. Purify yourself. Have many trances, bad ones and good ones, and, above all, suffer. Attaining wisdom is difficult. You're already old; I don't think you'll get that far. And besides, who knows whether that's your destiny? Be off with you; start walking. Talk; keep talking. Don't disturb the order of the world, storyteller."

It's true; I was always asking him questions. He knew everything, and that made me all the more curious. "Why do the men who walk paint their bodies with annatto?" I once asked him. "Because of the moritoni," he replied. "You mean that little bird?" "The very same." And with that, he started me thinking. Why do you suppose the Machiguengas avoid killing the moritoni? Why do they make a point of not stepping on it when they come upon it in the tall grass? Why do you feel grateful when you see it perching on a branch and notice its little white legs and its black breast? It's thanks to the achiote bush that gives us annatto and to the moritoni bird that we're walking, Tasurinchi. Without the two of them, the men who walk would have disappeared. They'd have boiled to death, burning with blisters till they burst like bubbles.

That was before.

In those days, the moritoni was a child who walks. One of its mothers is said to be Inaenka. Yes, the evil that destroys flesh was a woman then. The evil that burns the face, leaving it full of holes. Inaenka. She was that evil and she was the mother of the moritoni, too. She looked like a woman, like any other, except that she had a limp. Do all devils limp? It seems they do. They say that Kientibakori does, too. Her limp made Inaenka furious; she wore a long cushma, so long that no one ever saw her feet. It wasn't easy to recognize her, to know that she wasn't a woman but what she was.

Tasurinchi was fishing from the riverbank. Suddenly an enormous súngaro fell into his net. He was very pleased. He'd get a tubful of oil out of it, maybe. Just then he saw a canoe in front of him, cleaving the water. He could make out a woman paddling, and several children. A seripigari sitting in Tasurinchi's hut breathing in tobacco immediately saw the danger. "Don't call to her," he warned. "Can't you see it's Inaenka?" But Tasurinchi, being impatient, had already whistled, had already waved to her. The paddles propelling the canoe were raised. Tasurinchi saw the craft come into shore. The woman jumped out onto the bank; she was pleased.

"That's a fine fish you've caught, Tasurinchi," she said as she approached. She walked slowly and he didn't notice her limp. "Come on, carry it to your hut, and I'll cook it for you. Just for you."

Tasurinchi, puffed up with vanity, obeyed. He hoisted the fish onto his back and set off for his hut, unaware that he had met his fate. Knowing what was going to happen, the seripigari looked at him sadly. When he was a few steps from his hut, the fish slipped off his back, drawn by the power of an invisible kamagarini. Tasurinchi saw that when it touched the ground the creature's skin started coming off, as though it had had boiling water sprinkled on it. He was so astonished he wasn't able to call out to the seripigari or even move. That was fear. I expect his teeth chattered. He was so overcome he didn't realize that the same thing was happening to him as to the súngaro. Only when he felt the heat and smelled scorched flesh did he look at his body: his skin, too, was peeling off. He could see his bloody guts in places. He fell to the ground, terrified, screaming. Kicking and weeping, Tasurinchi was. Then Inaenka came over and looked at him with her real face, a blister of boiling water. She wet him thoroughly, from head to foot, enjoying seeing Tasurinchi losing his skin like the fish, bubbling and dying from her evil.

Inaenka began dancing for joy. "I'm the mistress of the sickness that kills swiftly," she goaded men, shrieking so loudly the whole forest would hear. "I've killed them and now I'm going to stew them and season them with annatto and eat them!" she shouted. Kientibakori and his little devils danced merrily, pushing and biting each other in the forest. Singing: "Ehé, ehé, she's Inaenka."

It was only then that the woman whose face was a boiling blister noticed that the seripigari was there, too. He was quietly watching what was going on, without anger, without fear, breathing in tobacco through his nose. He sneezed calmly, as though she weren't there and nothing had happened. Inaenka decided to kill him. She went over to him and was about to sprinkle a little boiling water on him when the seripigari imperturbably showed her two white stones dangling from around his neck.

"You can't do anything to me while I have these stones," he reminded her. "They protect me from you and from all the evils in the world. Perhaps you didn't know?"

"What you say is true," said Inaenka. "I'll wait here near you till you fall asleep. Then I'll remove the stones, throw them in the river, and sprinkle you as much as I like. Nothing will save you. Your skin will come off, the way the fish's did, and you'll blister, the way Tasurinchi did."

And that's what must have happened. However hard he fought against sleep, the seripigari couldn't resist. During the night, dazed by the false light of Kashiri, the stained one, he fell asleep. Inaenka limped to his side. Very carefully, she removed his two stones and threw them into the river. After that, she was able to sprinkle water on him from her great blister of a face, and gloated as the seripigari's body boiled, swelled with innumerable blisters, and started peeling and bursting.

"What a feast I'm going to have myself now," you could hear her shouting as she leapt and danced. From the canoe beached on the shore, Inaenka's children had seen her misdeeds. Perhaps they were disturbed. Perhaps sad.

There was an achiote close by. One of the children of the evil-bringing woman noticed that the little bush was stretching out its branches and waving its leaves in his direction. Could it be trying to tell him something? The boy drew near and took shelter beneath the burning breath of its fruit. "I'm Potsotiki," he heard it say in a tremulous voice. "Inaenka, your mother, will be the end of the people who walk if we don't do something." "What can we do?" said the boy sadly. "She has this power, she is the sickness that kills swiftly." "If you'll help me, we can save the men who walk. If they disappear, the sun will fall. It will no longer warm this world. Or would you rather that everything turned dark and Kientibakori's demons became masters of everything?" "I'll help you," the boy said. "What must I do?"

"Eat me," the annatto bush instructed him. "Your face will change and your mother won't recognize you. You're to go up to her and say to her: 'I know a place where what's imperfect becomes perfect, where monsters become men. There, your feet will be like those of other women.' And then you're to lead her to this place." Sagely waving its leaves and branches and making its fruit dance gaily, Potsotiki gave him directions as to the path he must follow.

Inaenka, busy rending the last remains of her kill, watching the guts and the hearts appearing, took no notice of their plotting. Once she had hacked the bodies into pieces, she roasted them, flavored with the annatto she was so fond of. In the meantime, the boy had eaten Potsotiki. He'd changed into a red boy, clay-red, annatto-red. He went up to his mother and she did not recognize him. "Who are you?" she asked. "How can you come near me without trembling? Don't you know who I am?"

"Of course I do," said the annatto-boy. "I've come to get you, because I know a place where you can be happy. If anyone sets foot there and bathes in the rivers, it's enough to straighten anything that's crooked, and any limbs that anyone has lost grow back again. I'll take you there. You'll lose your limp. You'll be happy, Inaenka. Follow me."

Their journey was endless. They crossed forests, rivers, lakes, gorges; they went up and down wooded slopes and through more forests still. Rain poured down on them many times. Lightning flashed above their heads and tempests roared at them, deafening them. After crossing a steaming bog with whistling butterflies, they were there. The Oskiaje. There all the rivers of this world and the other worlds meet; the Meshiareni comes down from the starlit sky; the Kamabiría, whose waters carry the souls of the dead to the worlds of the deep, also runs through it. There were monsters of every shape and size, beckoning to Inaenka with their trunks and claws. "Come, come, you're one of us," they grunted at her.

"Why have you brought me here?" Inaenka whispered. Alarmed, enraged, smelling the trap at last. "I've trod this earth, and my feet are still crooked."

"Potsotiki, the annatto bush, counseled me to bring you here," her son revealed. "So you wouldn't go on destroying the people who walk, that's why. The sun mustn't fall through your fault."

"Very well," Inaenka said, accepting her fate. "You've saved them, perhaps. But I'll follow you day and night. Day and night, till I've sprinkled you with my fiery water. I'll cover you with blisters. I'll watch you peeling, kicking the ground. I'll laugh at your suffering. You cannot free yourself of me."

But he did free himself. To escape from Inaenka, his soul had to give up its human wrapping; that was what it had to do, and that is what it did. It left his body and started wandering, wandering in search of a refuge, it made its home in that little black bird with white legs. He is now a moritoni. He now lives by the river and sleeps nestled in the grass. Thanks to him and to Potsotiki, the men who walk were saved from the evil that makes the skin peel off, that burns and kills swiftly. That's why we paint our skin with annatto dye, it seems. Seeking Potsotiki's protection. Nobody steps on the moritoni he comes upon sleeping in the grass; instead, he walks away. When a moritoni gets caught on the twigs sticky with resin that the hunters set out in the drinking places, he frees it and breathes on it to take away the cold and the fear it feels; the women cradle it between their breasts until it can fly. And that must be the reason why.

Nothing that happens happens just because, said Tasurinchi, the seripigari of the Kompiroshiato. There's a reason for everything; everything is a cause or a result of something. Perhaps that's so. There are more little gods and little devils than drops of water in the biggest lake and the biggest river, he used to say. They're involved with everything that exists. The sons of Kientibakori so as to perturb the world, the sons of Tasurinchi so as to preserve its order. One who knows causes and consequences has wisdom, perhaps. I haven't attained it yet, he said, even though I'm fairly wise and can do certain things that others can't. What can you do, Tasurinchi? Fly, talk with the souls of the dead, visit the worlds of below and above, enter the bodies of the living, foresee the future, understand the language of some of the animals. That's a lot. But there are so many other things I don't know.

That, anyway, is what I have learned.

It's true; he guessed rightly: if I weren't a storyteller I would have liked to be a seripigari. To be able to control trances through wisdom so that they'd always be good ones. Once, over there by the tapir-river, the Kimariato, I had a bad trance, and in it I lived through a story I'd rather not remember. Nonetheless, I still remember it.

Here is the story.

That was after, by the tapir-river.

I was people. I had a family. I was asleep. Then I woke up. I'd barely opened my eyes when I understood. Alas, poor Tasurinchi! I'd changed into an insect, that's what. A buzz-buzz bug, perhaps. A Gregor-Tasurinchi. I was lying on my back. The world had grown bigger, it seemed to me. I was aware of everything. Those hairy, ringed legs were my legs. Those transparent mud-colored wings, which creaked when I moved and hurt me so much, had once been my arms. The stench that surrounded me: was that my odor? I saw the world differently: I could see the underside and the top, the back and the front, at the same time. Because now, being an insect, I had several eyes. What's happened to you, Gregor-Tasurinchi? Did a bad witch eat a lock of your hair and change you? Did a little kamagarini devil get into you through your ass-eye and turn you into this? I was covered with shame at seeing myself the way I was. What would my family say? Because I had a family, like the other men who walk, it seemed. What would they think, seeing me changed into a repulsive insect? All you can do with buzz-buzz bugs is squash them. Can you eat them? Can you cure evil with them? You can't even make filthy machikanari potions with them, perhaps.

But my family didn't say anything. They pretended. They came and went in the hut or down by the river, as though they hadn't noticed the misfortune that had befallen me. They must have felt ashamed, too. Saying: Look how he's been changed! That might have been the reason they avoided mentioning me by name. Who knows? And in the meantime, I saw everything. The world seemed content, the same as before. I could see the children lifting stones off anthills and happily eating the soft-shelled ants, squabbling over them. The men, going to clear the weeds from the cassava patches or painting themselves with annatto and huito before going off to hunt. The women, cutting up the cassava, chewing it, spitting it out, leaving it to rest in the masato tubs; unraveling cotton to weave cushmas. When night fell, the old men got the fires ready, cutting two reeds and making a hole near the tip of the smaller one, planting it firmly in the dirt, holding it fast with their feet, placing the other reed in the hole and turning it, turning it, patiently, till a thread of smoke started rising. Then they'd collect the dust in a banana leaf, wrap the leaf in cotton, and shake it till the fire caught. Then they lighted the fires for the families to sleep around. The men and women came and went, getting on with life, content perhaps. Without mentioning the change I'd suffered, showing neither anger nor surprise. Who asked after the storyteller? Nobody. Did anybody take a sack of cassava and another of maize to the seripigari, saying: "Change him back into a man who walks?" Nobody. Many people bustled about, their eyes avoiding the corner where I was. Poor Gregor-Tasurinchi! Furiously fluttering my wings and wriggling my legs; trying to turn over, fighting to get up. Ay, ay!

How could I ask for help without talking? I didn't know. That was the worst torment, perhaps. Bound to suffer, knowing that nobody would come and put me right side up. Would I never walk again? I remembered the tortoises. When I went to hunt them on the little beach where they come out of the water to bury their young; how I turned them over, catching hold of their shell. That's the way I was now, frantically waving my legs in the air, unable to right myself, just like them. I was a buzz-buzz bug, and I felt like a tortoise. Like them, I would be thirsty and hungry, and then my soul would go. Does the soul of a buzz-buzz bug come back? Perhaps it does.

Suddenly I noticed. They'd shut me up. Who was it who had done that, who were they? My family, yes, that was who.

They'd closed off the hut, sealed up all the holes I might be able to escape through. They'd shut me up like a girl with her first blood. But who would come bathe Gregor-Tasurinchi and bring him back to the land of the living, pure and clean now? Nobody would come, perhaps. Why had they done this to me? Out of shame, most likely. So that nobody visiting them would see me and feel repelled by me or make fun of them. Had my kinfolk pulled a lock of hair from my head and taken it to the machikanari so he'd change me into Gregor-Tasurinchi? No, it must have been a little devil or even Kientibakori. I had done something wrong, perhaps, for them to shut me up like an enemy, on top of the evil I'd suffered. Why didn't they fetch a seripigari who'd give me back my own bodily wrapping, instead? Maybe they've gone to the seripigari and have shut you up so you don't hurt yourself by going outside.

That gave me hope. Don't give up, Gregor-Tasurinchi, not yet; it was a little ray of sunshine in the storm. Meanwhile, I went on trying to turn over. My legs hurt from waving them about so much and my wings creaked with my efforts as though they were splitting apart. How much time went by? Who knows? But suddenly I succeeded. Courage, Gregor-Tasurinchi! Perhaps I moved more energetically; perhaps I stretched one of my legs out farther. I don't know. But my body contracted, moved sideways, flipped over, and there it was, I could feel it underneath me, hard. Firm, solid: the ground. I shut my eyes, intoxicated. But the joy of having righted myself disappeared immediately. What was that horrible pain in my back? As though I'd been burned. I'd torn my right wing on a splinter as I took those sudden leaps, or before, while I was struggling so violently. There it was, dangling down, split in two, dragging along. That was perhaps my wing. I was beginning to feel hungry as well. I was frightened. The world had turned into an unknown one. Dangerous, perhaps. At any moment someone might squash me. Crush me. Eat me. Poor Gregor-Tasurinchi! Lizards! Trembling, trembling all over. Had I ever seen them eating cockroaches or beetles or any of the insects they chase? My broken wing hurt more and more, so much I could hardly move. And hunger-thorns still piercing my belly. I tried to eat the dry straw stuffed into the wall, but it tore my mouth without getting any softer, so I spat it out. I started scratching around here and there in the damp earth till I came across a nest of larvae. They were very small, squirming about, trying to escape. They were pocos, wood-worm larvae. I swallowed them slowly, shutting my eyes, happy. Feeling that the pieces of my soul that had been leaving were returning to my body. Yes, happy.

I hadn't finished swallowing the larvae when a distinctly unpleasant smell made me leap into the air, trying to fly. I felt something panting, very close by. The heat of its breath went up my nose. It smelled—it was—dangerous, perhaps. The lizard! So it had appeared. There was its triangular head between two worm-eaten partitions. There were its gummy eyes looking at me. Gleaming with hunger. Despite the pain, I flapped my wings, but trying, trying my best, I couldn't get off the ground. I took a few feeble hops, it seems. Losing my balance, hobbling. The pain of my wound was more severe now. There it came, there it was. Contracting like a snake, wriggling from side to side, it slid its body between the partitions and was inside. So there was the lizard. It crept closer and closer, quite slowly, never taking its eyes off me. How big it looked! Then, swiftly, swiftly, it came at me on its two legs. I saw it open its enormous mouth. I saw its two rows of teeth, curved and white; its steamy breath blinded me. I felt it bite, I felt it pulling off the damaged wing. I was so frightened I felt no pain. I was falling into a deeper trance, as though I were dropping off to sleep. I could see its crumpled green skin, its maw palpitating as it digested, and how it half closed its great eyes as it swallowed that mouthful of me. I would resign myself to my destiny, then. Better that way. Feeling sad, perhaps. Waiting for it to finish eating me. Then, once I'd been eaten, I could see through its insides, through its soul, through its bulging eyes—everything was green—that my family was coming back.

They entered the hut, as apprehensive as before. I wasn't there anymore! Saying: Where could he have gone? They went over to the corner where the buzz-buzz bug had been, they looked, they searched. Gone! They sighed with relief, as though they'd been rescued from some great danger. They might have smiled; they were pleased. Thinking: We're free of that shameful thing. They'd have nothing to hide from their visitors now. They could now go on with their everyday lives, perhaps.

And that's the end of the story of Gregor-Tasurinchi, over by the Kimariato, the tapir-river.

I asked Tasurinchi, the seripigari, the meaning of what I'd been through in that bad trance. He pondered my question for a while, then made a gesture with his hand as though to chase something invisible away. "Yes, it was a bad trance," he agreed at last, thoughtfully. "Gregor-Tasurinchi! I wonder why. Something bad behind it, doubtless. Being changed into a buzz-buzz bug must be the work of a kamagarini. I can't really tell you for certain. I'd have to go up the pole of my hut and ask the saankarite in the world of clouds. He'd know, I expect. You'd best forget it. Don't talk about it anymore. What's remembered goes on living and can happen again." But I haven't been able to forget and I go on telling about it.

I wasn't always the way all of you see me now. I don't mean my face. I've always had this stain the color of dark-purple maize. Don't laugh. I'm telling you the truth. I was born with it. It's true; you needn't laugh. I know what you're thinking. "If you'd been born that way, Tasurinchi, your mothers would have thrown you into the river. If you're here, walking, you were born pure. It was only later that something or someone made you the way you are." Is that what you're thinking? You see: I saw it even though I'm not a seer, and it didn't take smoke or a trance.

I've asked the seripigari many times: "What does it mean, having a face like mine?" No saankarite has been able to explain it, it seems. Why did Tasurinchi breathe me out this way? Shh, shh, don't get angry. What are you shouting about? All right, it wasn't Tasurinchi. Kientibakori, then? No? All right, it wasn't him either. Doesn't the seripigari say that everything has its cause? I haven't found one for my face yet. So some things may not have one. They just happen, that's all. I know you don't agree. I can see it just by looking at your eyes. Yes, I grant you, not knowing the cause doesn't mean there isn't one.

Before, this stain used to matter a lot to me. I didn't say so. Only to myself, to my souls. I kept it to myself, and this secret was eating me alive. Bit by bit it was eating me up, here inside. I was sad, it seems. Now I don't mind. At least I think I don't. That could be because of all of you. That's the way it's been, perhaps. Because I realized that it didn't matter to the people I went to visit, to talk to. Many moons ago, the first time, I asked a family I was living with along the Koshireni. "Does it matter to you, seeing what I look like? Does it matter to you that I'm the way I am?" "What people do and what they don't do matters," Tasurinchi, the oldest one, explained to me. Saying: "Walking, fulfilling their destiny, matters. The hunter not touching what he's killed, or the fisherman what he's caught; respecting the taboos matters. It matters if they're capable of walking so that the sun won't fall. So that the world remains orderly. So that darkness and evils don't return. That's what matters. Stains on a face don't, I expect." That's wisdom, they say.

What I really wanted to say is that, before, I wasn't what I am now. I became a storyteller after being what you are at this moment: listeners. That's what I was, a listener. It happened without my willing it, little by little. Without even realizing it, I began finding my destiny. Slowly, calmly. It appeared bit by bit. Not with tobacco juice, or with ayahuasca brews. Or with the help of the seripigari. I discovered it all by myself.

I went from one place to another seeking out the men who walk. Are you there? Ehé, here I am. I stayed in their huts and helped them clear the weeds from the cassava patch and set traps. As soon as I found out by what river, in what gorge there was a family of men who walk, I went to visit them. Even if I had to go a very long way and cross the Gran Pongo, I went. At last I arrived. There they were. Have you come? Ehé, I've come. Some of them knew me; others got to know me. They asked me in; they gave me food and drink. They lent me a mat to sleep on. I stayed with them for many moons. I felt like one of the family. "Why have you come this far?" they asked me. "To learn how you prepare tobacco before sniffing it up your nostrils," I answered. "To learn how you glue the long bones of the pavita kanari together with resin to use for breathing in tobacco," I said. They let me listen to what they said, to learn what they were. I wanted to know how they lived, that is to say. To hear it from their mouths. What they are, what they do, where they come from, how they're born, how they go, how they come back. The men who walk. "Very well," they said to me. "Let us walk together then."

I marveled at what they said. I remembered everything.

About this world and the others. About what was before and what was after. I remembered the explanations and the causes. At first the seripigaris didn't trust me. Later on, they did. They let me listen to them, too. The stories about Tasurinchi. The evil deeds of Kientibakori. The secrets of rain, lightning, the rainbow, of the colors and lines men paint on themselves before they set out to hunt. Of all the things I heard, I didn't forget a one. Sometimes, when I went to visit a family, I told them what I'd seen and learned. They didn't all know the whole of it, and even if they did, they liked hearing it again. Me, too. The first time I heard the story of Morenanchiite, the lord of thunder, it made a great impression on me. I asked everyone about it. I made them tell it once, many times. Does the lord of thunder have a bow? Yes, he has a bow. But instead of loosing arrows he looses thunder. And does he go about accompanied by jaguars? Yes. By pumas too, it seems. And though he's not a Viracocha, does he have a beard? Yes, he has a beard. So I repeated the story of Morenanchiite everywhere I went. They listened to me and were pleased, perhaps. Saying: "Tell us that one again. Tell us, tell us." Little by little, without knowing what was happening, I started doing what I'm doing now.

One day, as I arrived to visit a family, I heard them saying behind my back: "Here comes the storyteller. Let's go listen to him." It surprised me a lot. "Are you talking about me?" I asked. They all nodded their heads. "Ehé, ehé, it's you we're talking about." So there I was—the storyteller. I was thunderstruck. There I was. My heart was like a drum. Banging away in my chest: boom, boom. Had I met my destiny? Perhaps. That's how it was that time, it seems. It was in a little ravine by the Timpshía where there were Machiguengas. There aren't any there now. But every time I pass by that ravine my heart starts dancing again. Thinking: Here I was born a second time.

Here I came back without having gone. That's how I began to be what I am. It was the best thing that ever happened to me, I expect. Nothing better will ever happen, I believe. Since then I've been talking. Walking. And I shall keep on till I go, it seems. Because I'm the storyteller.

That, anyway, is what I have learned.

Is a face like mine an evil? Is being born with more or fewer fingers than the right number an evil? Is it a misfortune to look like a monster without being one? A misfortune and an evil at the same time, it must be. To look like one of those twisted, crookbacked, misshapen beings with claws and fangs that Kientibakori breathed out on the day of creation, over there in the Gran Pongo, and not be one. To look like a demon or a little devil, and be only a man breathed out by Tasurinchi, must be both the work of evil and a misfortune. And that's just what it is, I'd say.

When I started walking, I heard that a woman had drowned her newborn girl in the river because she lacked a foot or a nose, because she had stains, or because two children had been born instead of one. I didn't understand, it seems. "Why did you do that? Why did you kill it?" "It wasn't perfect, so it had to go." I didn't understand. "Tasurinchi only breathed out perfect men and women," they explained. "Monsters were breathed out by Kientibakori." I'll never be able to understand that, perhaps. Being what I am, having the face I have, I'll doubtless find it difficult. When I hear: "I threw her into the river because she was born a little devil, I killed him because he was born a demon," I don't understand all over again. What are you laughing about?

If imperfect people were impure, if they were children of Kientibakori, why were there men who had a limp, who had marks on their skin, who had deformed hands or were blind?

How come they were still here, walking? Why hadn't they been killed? Why didn't they kill me, with this face of mine, I asked them. They, too, laughed. How could they be children of Kientibakori, devils or monsters! Were they born that way? They were pure; they were born perfect. They'd become that way later. It was their own doing, or that of a kamagarini or some other demon of Kientibakori's. Who knows why they changed them. Only their outside is that of a monster; inside, they're still pure, no doubt about it.

Even if you don't believe me, it wasn't Kientibakori's little devils who changed me like this. I was born a monster. My mother didn't throw me into the river; she let me live. And what used to seem cruel to me, before, now seems fortunate. Every time I go visit a family I don't know yet, I think maybe they'll be frightened and say: "He's a monster, he's a devil," when they see me. There, you're laughing again. All of you laugh like that when I ask you: "Do you think I'm a devil? Is that what my face means?" "No, no, no, and you're not a monster. You're Tasurinchi, the storyteller." You make me feel at peace. Content, even.

The souls of the children that the mothers drown in the rivers and the lakes go down to the bottom of the Gran Pongo. That's what they say. Down to the depths. Deeper than the whirlpools and the falls of muddy water, to caves full of crabs. There they must be, amid enormous rocks, deafened by the din, suffering. There the souls of those children will meet the monsters that Kientibakori breathed out when he fought with Tasurinchi. That was the beginning, it seems. Before, the world we walk in was empty. Does someone who drowns in the Gran Pongo come back? He sinks, deeper and deeper, in the roaring waters, a whirlpool traps his soul and spins it around and around, taking it lower and lower. All the way down to the dark muddy bottom, where monsters live. So then it settles there among the souls of other drowned children. Listening to the devils and the monsters lamenting the day that Tasurinchi first breathed out. The day when so many Machiguengas appeared.

This is the story of creation.

This is the fight between Tasurinchi and Kientibakori.

That was before.

It happened over yonder, in the Gran Pongo. That was where the beginning began. Tasurinchi came down from Inkite along the river Meshiareni with an idea in his head. Puffing out his chest. Good lands, rivers full of fish, forests teeming with game, all the many animals to eat began appearing. The sun was in its place in the sky, warming the world. Content, looking at things as they appeared. Kientibakori threw one of his terrible temper tantrums. Seeing what was happening up above, he spewed toads and vipers. Tasurinchi was breathing out and Machiguengas had begun appearing, too. Then Kientibakori abandoned Gamaironi, the world of black clouds and waters, and went up a river of piss and shit. In a fury, steaming with rage he was, saying: "I can do it better!" He began breathing out as soon as he reached the Gran Pongo. But it wasn't Machiguengas he breathed out: rotten lands, rather, where nothing grew; swamps where only vampires could live, the air was so foul. Snakes appeared. Vipers, caimans, mice, mosquitoes, bats. Ants, turkey buzzards. All the plants that give fever, that burn the skin, that are not good to eat appeared, and only those. Kientibakori went on breathing out, and instead of Machiguengas, kamagarinis and little devils on pointed, twisted feet with spurs appeared. She-devils with donkey faces, eating earth and moss. And squat, four-footed men, the hairy, bloodthirsty achaporo. Kientibakori raged. He raged in such fury that the beings he breathed out, the evils and the predators, came out even more impure, even more malevolent. When the two of them had had done with breathing out and gone back—Tasurinchi to Inkite and Kientibakori to Gamaironi—this world was what it is now.

That's how after began, it seems.

That's how we started walking. In the Gran Pongo. And we've been walking ever since. And ever since, we've been resisting evils, suffering the cruel misdeeds of Kientibakori's devils and little devils. Before, the Gran Pongo was forbidden. Only the dead returned there, souls that went and didn't come back. Now many go there: Viracochas and Punarunas go. Machiguengas, too. They must go with fear and respect. Thinking, no doubt: Is that loud noise only the sound of water striking against rocks as it falls? Only a river as it narrows between cliffs? It doesn't sound like that. The noise comes from below as well. It must be the moans and cries of drowned children rising from the caverns at the bottom. You can hear them on moonlit nights. They're sad; they're moaning. Kientibakori's monsters are abusing them, perhaps. Making them pay with torments for being there. Not because they're impure, but because they're Machiguengas, perhaps.

That, anyway, is what I have learned.

A seripigari said to me: "Being born with a face like yours isn't the worst evil; it's not knowing one's obligation." Not being at one with one's destiny, then? That happened to me before I became what I am now. I was no more than a wrapping, a shell, the body of one whose soul has left through the top of his head. For a family and for a people too, the worst evil would be not knowing their obligation. A monster-family, a monster-people, that's what it would be, with not enough hands or feet, or too many. We are walking, and the sun is up above. That must be our obligation. We're fulfilling it, it seems. Why do we survive the evils of countless devils and little devils? That must be the reason. That must be why we're here now. I talking, you listening. Who knows?

The people who walk are my people now. Before, I walked with another people and I believed it was mine. I hadn't been born yet. I was really born once I began walking as a Machiguenga. That other people stayed behind. It, too, had its story. It was a small people and lived very far from here, in a place that had been its own and no longer was, belonging now to others. Because it had been occupied by strong, cunning Viracochas. Like the tree-bleeding time? Exactly. Despite the presence of the enemy in their forests, they spent their days hunting tapir, sowing cassava, brewing masato, dancing, and singing. A powerful spirit had breathed them out. He had neither face nor body. Jehovah-Tasurinchi, that was who he was. He protected them, it seems. He had taught them what they must do and also taught them the taboos. So they knew their obligation. They lived quietly, it's said. Content and without anger, perhaps.

Until one day, in a remote little ravine, a child was born. He was different. A serigórompi? Yes, perhaps. He started saying: "I am the breath of Tasurinchi, I am the son of Tasurinchi, I am Tasurinchi. I am all three things at once." That's what he said. And that he'd come down from Inkite to this world, sent by his father, who was himself, to change the customs because the people had become corrupt and no longer knew how to walk. They must have listened to him in astonishment. Saying: "He must be an hablador." Saying: "Those must be stories he's telling." He went from one place to another, the way I do. Talking and talking. Raveling things and unraveling them, giving advice. He had a different wisdom, it seems. He wanted to impose new customs, because—so he said—the ones people were practicing were impure. They were evil. They brought misfortune. And he kept saying to everyone: "I'm Tasurinchi." So he should be obeyed, be respected. He alone, only he. The others weren't gods, but devils and little devils breathed out by Kientibakori.

He was good at convincing people, they say. A seripigari with many powers. He had his own magic, too. Could he have been a bad sorcerer, a machikanari? Or a good one, a seripigari? Who knows? He had the power to change a few cassavas and a few catfish into a whole lot, into enough cassavas and enough catfish so that everybody had something to eat. He could make an arm grow back on those who had lost one, and give the blind their eyes back; he could even make the souls of those who had gone come back to their very same body as before. Some people were impressed and began following him and doing what he told them to. They gave up their customs; they no longer obeyed the age-old taboos. They became different, perhaps.

The seripigaris grew alarmed. They journeyed; they met together in the hut of the oldest. They drank masato, sitting in a circle on mats. "Our people will disappear," they said. It would melt away like a cloud, perhaps. Be nothing but wind in the end. "What will make us any different from the others?" they asked fearfully. Would they be like Mashcos? Would they be like Ashaninkas or Yaminahuas? Nobody would know who was who; neither they nor the others. "Aren't we what we believe, the stripes we paint on ourselves, the way we set our traps?" they argued. If they listened to this storyteller and did everything differently, did everything backward, wouldn't the sun fall? What would keep them together if they became the same as everybody else? Nothing, nobody. Would everything be confusion? And so, because he'd come to dim the brightness of the world, the seripigaris condemned him. Saying: "He's an impostor and a liar; he must be a machikanari."

The Viracochas, the powerful ones, were also worried. There was much disorder, people were restless, full of doubts because of the clever talk of that storyteller. "Is what he's telling us true or false? Ought we to obey him?" And they pondered what he meant by the stories he told them. So then the ones whose word was law killed him, believing they'd be free of him that way. In accordance with their custom, when someone did wrong, stole or violated the taboo, the Viracochas flogged him and put a crown of chambira thorns on his head. After that—the way they do with big river paiche so the water inside them will drain out—they nailed him to two crossed tree trunks and left him to bleed. They did the wrong thing. Because, after he'd gone, that storyteller came back. He might have come back so as to go on throwing this world into even worse confusion than before. They began saying among themselves: "It was true. He's the son of Tasurinchi, the breath of Tasurinchi, Tasurinchi himself. All three things together, in a word. He came. He went and has come back again." And then they began doing what he taught them to do and respecting his taboos.

Since that seripigari or that god died, if he really did die, terrible misfortunes befell the people into which he had been born. The one breathed out by Jehovah-Tasurinchi. The Viracochas drove that people out of the forest where they'd lived up until then. Out, out! Like the Machiguengas, that people had to start walking through the jungle. The rivers, the lakes, the ravines of this world saw them arrive and depart. Never sure they'd be able to stay in the place they'd arrived at, they, too, had to become accustomed to living on the move. Life had become dangerous, as though at any moment a jaguar might attack them or a Mashco arrow fell them. They must have lived in fear, expecting evil. Expecting the spells of machikanaris. Lamenting their fate each day of their lives, perhaps.

They were driven out of all the places where they camped. They would put up their huts and there would come the Viracochas to do them in. There would come the Punarunas and the Yaminahuas, blaming them for every wrong and every misfortune; even accusing them of having killed Tasurinchi. "He made himself man and came to this world and you betrayed him," they said as they seized them. If Inaenka passed by somewhere, sprinkling her scalding water on people and their skin peeled off and they died, nobody said: "It's the blister that's come to a head that brings on these calamities, it's Inaenka sneezing and farting." What they said was: "It's the fault of those accursed foreigners who killed Tasurinchi. They've now cast spells so as to fulfill their obligations to their master Kientibakori." The belief had spread everywhere: that they helped the little devils, dancing and drinking masato with them, perhaps. So then they went to the huts of those whom Jehovah-Tasurinchi had breathed out. They beat them and took everything they had; they pierced them with arrows and burned them alive. So they were always on the run. Making their escape, hiding. In scattered bands, they wandered through all the forests of the world. When will they come to kill us? they'd think. Who will kill us this time? The Viracochas? The Mashcos? Nobody would take them in. When they came by and asked the master of the house: "Are you there?" the answer always was: "No, no, I'm not." Just as with the people who walk, families had to separate so as to be accepted. If they weren't too big a family, if they cast no shadow, other peoples allowed them a place to sow, to hunt, to fish. Sometimes they gave orders:

"You can stay but you can't sow. Or hunt. That's the custom." So there they would stay for a few moons; many, perhaps. But it always ended badly. If it rained a lot or there was a drought, if some catastrophe occurred, people started hating them. Saying: "It's your fault. Out!" They were driven out again, and it seemed that they were going to disappear.

Because this story happened again and again in many places. Always the same, like a seripigari who can't get back from a bad trance, who has lost his way and keeps going around and around in the clouds. Yet, despite so many misfortunes, that people didn't disappear. In spite of its sufferings, it survived. It wasn't warlike, it never won wars, yet it's still here. It lived dispersed, its families scattered through the forests of the world, and yet it endured. Greater peoples, warriors, strong peoples, Mashcos and Viracochas with wise seripigaris, peoples who seemed indestructible, all went. Disappeared, that is to say. No trace of them remained in the world, nobody remembered them, after. Those survivors, however, are still about. Journeying, coming and going, escaping. Alive and walking. Down through time, and through all this wide world, too.

Could it be that despite everything that happened to it, Jehovah-Tasurinchi's people never was at odds with its destiny? Always fulfilled its obligation; always respected the prohibitions, too. Was it hated because it was different? Was that why, wherever it went, peoples would not accept it? Who knows? People don't like living with people who are different. They don't trust them, perhaps. Other customs, another way of speaking would frighten them, as though the world had suddenly become confused and dark. People would like everyone to be the same, would like others to forget their own customs, kill their seripigaris, violate their own taboos, and imitate theirs.

If it had done that, Jehovah-Tasurinchi's people would have disappeared. Not one storyteller would have survived to tell their story. I wouldn't be here talking, perhaps.

"It is a good thing for the man who walks to walk," the seripigari says. That is wisdom, I believe. It is most likely a good thing. For a man to be what he is. Aren't we Machiguengas now the way we were a long time ago? The way we were that day in the Gran Pongo when Tasurinchi began breathing us out: that's how we are. And that's why we haven't disappeared. That's why we keep on walking, perhaps.

I learned that from all of you. Before I was born, I used to think: A people must change. Adopt the customs, the taboos, the magic of strong peoples. Take over the gods and the little gods, the devils and the little devils of the wise peoples. That way everyone will become more pure, I thought. Happier, too. It wasn't true. I know now that that's not so. I learned it from you. Who is purer or happier because he's renounced his destiny, I ask you? Nobody. We'd best be what we are. The one who gives up fulfilling his own obligation so as to fulfill that of another will lose his soul. And his outer wrapping too, perhaps, like Gregor-Tasurinchi, who was changed into a buzz-buzz bug in that bad trance. It may be that when a person loses his soul the most repulsive beings, the most harmful predators, come and make their lair in the empty body. The botfly devours the fly; the bird, the botfly; the snake, the bird. Do we want to be devoured? No. Do we want to disappear without a trace? No, again. If we come to an end, the world will come to an end, too. It seems we'd best go on walking. Keeping the sun in its place in the sky, the river in its bed, the tree rooted in the ground and the forest on the earth.

That, anyway, is what I have learned.

Tasurinchi is well. Walking. I was on my way to visit him

there where he lives, by the Timpanía, when I met him on the trail. He and two of his sons were returning from a visit to the White Fathers, the ones who live on the banks of the Sepahua. He'd brought them his maize harvest. He'd been doing so for some time now, he told me. The White Fathers give him seed, machetes to clear the forest, spades to work the ground and grow potatoes, yams, maize, tobacco, coffee, and cotton. Later on, he sells them what he doesn't need, and that way he can buy more things. He showed me what he's already acquired: clothes, food, an oil lamp, fishhooks, a knife. "Maybe next time I can buy myself a shotgun as well," he said. Then he'd be able to hunt anything in the forest, he told me. But he wasn't happy, Tasurinchi wasn't. Worried, rather; his forehead wrinkled and his eyes hard. "In the ground here by the Timpanía you can only sow a crop a couple of times in the same place, never more," he lamented. "And in some places only once. It's bad earth, it seems. My last sowing of cassavas and yams produced a miserable yield." It's land that tires quickly, it appears. "It wants me to leave it in peace," Tasurinchi said. "This earth here along the Timpanía is lazy," he complained bitterly. "You barely put it to work and it starts asking for a rest. That's its nature."

Talking of this and that, we reached his hut. His wife ran out to meet us, all upset. She'd painted her face in mourning, and waving her hands and pointing, she said the river was a thief. It had stolen one of her three hens, it seemed. She was holding it in her arms to warm it, since it appeared to be sick, as she filled her water jar. And then, all of a sudden, everything started shaking. The earth, the forest, the hut, everything started shaking. "Like when you have the evil," she said. It shook as though it were dancing. In her fright she let go of the hen and saw the current carry it away and devour it before she could rescue it. It's true that the current is very swift there in that gorge of the Timpanía. Even close into shore, there is whitewater.

Tasurinchi was furious and began beating her. Saying: "I'm not beating you because you let it fall into the river. That could happen to anyone. I'm beating you because you lied. Instead of making up a story about the earth shaking, why don't you say you fell asleep? It slipped out of your arms, didn't it? Or maybe you left it on the bank and it fell in. Or you threw it into the river in a fit of temper. Don't talk of things that didn't happen. Are you a storyteller, may I ask? Don't lies bring harm to a family? Who's going to believe you when you say the earth began dancing? If it had, I'd have felt it, too."

And as Tasurinchi scolded her, raging and beating her, the earth began shaking. Don't laugh. I'm not making it up; I didn't dream it. It happened. It started dancing. First we heard a deep growling, as though the lord of thunder were down below, making his jaguars roar. A sound of war, many drums beating all together, down in the earth's entrails. A deep, threatening sound. We suddenly felt that the world was restless. The earth was moving about, dancing, leaping as though it were drunk. The trees moved, and Tasurinchi's hut; the waters of the river bubbled and seethed, like cassava boiling in a tub. There was anger in the air, it seemed. The sky filled with terrified birds; parrots squawked in the trees; from the forest came the grunts, whistles, and croaks of frightened animals. "Again!" Tasurinchi's wife screamed. We looked all about, confused, not knowing whether to run or to stay where we were. The children were crying; clinging to Tasurinchi, they howled. He, too, was frightened, and so was I. "Is this world coming to an end?" he said. "Is darkness returning, is chaos coming?"

When the shaking stopped at last, the sky turned black, as

though the sun had begun to fall. Then all at once, very suddenly, it was dark. A great dust storm arose, from everywhere, blanketing this world in an ashen color. I could hardly see Tasurinchi and his family with all the dust blowing in the strong wind. Everything was gray. "Something very grave is happening and we don't know what it is," said Tasurinchi fearfully. "Can it be the end of us men who walk? The time has come for us to go, perhaps. The sun has fallen. It may not rise again."

I know now that it didn't fall. I know now that if it had fallen, we wouldn't be here. The dust storm moved on, the sky cleared, and the earth was still at last. A smell of brine and rotted plants lingered in the air, a sickening stench. The world wasn't pleased, it seemed. "You see, I didn't lie; it did shake. That's why the river swallowed up the hen," said Tasurinchi's wife. But he was hardheaded, insisting: "That's not certain." He was enraged. "You lied," he screamed at his wife. "Perhaps that's why the earth shook just now." He began beating her again, thrusting his chest out, roaring from the sheer effort he was expending. Tasurinchi, the one from the Timpanía, is a very stubborn man. It's not the first time he's fallen into a fury. I've seen him have fits of rage at other times. That may be why few people visit him. He refused to admit he'd been wrong, but I could see, as anyone could have, that his wife had spoken the truth.

We ate; we lay down for a night's rest on the mats; in just a little while, long before dawn, I heard him get up. I saw him go out and sit down on a stone a few paces away from the hut. There was Tasurinchi, sitting brooding in the moonlight. I got up in the semi-darkness and went out to talk to him. He was grinding up tobacco to inhale. I saw him tamp down the powder in the hollow turkey bone, and then he asked me to blow it up his nose for him. I placed it in one nostril and blew; he breathed it in deeply, anxiously, closing his eyes. Then I placed it in his other nostril and blew. And after that he breathed the powder that was left into my nose. He was worried, Tasurinchi was. Tormented, even. Saying: "I can't sleep," in the voice of a man who is very tired. "Two things have happened that make a person think. The river stole one of my hens and the earth started shaking. And, what's more, the sky grew dark. What must I do?" I didn't know; I was as bewildered as he was. Why are you asking me that, Tasurinchi? "These things happening, one right after the other, almost at the same time, mean that I must do something," he said to me. "But I don't know what. There's no one I can ask hereabouts. The seripigari is many moons' walk away, up the Sepahua."

Tasurinchi spent the whole day sitting on that stone, not speaking to anyone. Neither drinking nor eating. When his wife came out to bring him some mashed bananas, he wouldn't even let her come near; he made a threatening gesture with his hand as though he were about to hit her again. That night he didn't come inside his hut. Kashiri shone brightly up in the sky and I could see Tasurinchi, not moving, his head buried in his chest, trying his best to understand these misfortunes. What were they telling him to do? Who knows? The whole family was silent, worried, even the little ones. Watching him anxiously, not daring to move. Wondering: What's going to happen?

Around midday, Tasurinchi, the one by the Timpanía, got up from the stone. He approached the hut with a lively step; we saw him coming, beckoning to us with open arms. A determined expression on his face, it seemed.

"We start walking," he said, his voice earnest, commanding. "Get moving. This minute. We must go far from here. That's what it means. If we stay, evils will come, catastrophes will occur. That's the message. I've understood it at last. This place has had enough of us. So we must go."

It must have been hard for him to make up his mind. The faces of the women and of the men too, the sadness of the family showed how painful it was for them to leave. They'd been by the Timpanía for a good while. With the crops they sold to the White Fathers of the Sepahua they'd been buying things. They seemed happy, perhaps. Had they perhaps met their destiny? They hadn't, it seems. Were they becoming corrupt staying in the same place such a long time? Who knows? Leaving everything like that, all of a sudden, without knowing where they were going, without knowing whether they would ever again have what they had left behind, must have been a great sacrifice. It must have meant sorrow for one and all.

But nobody in the family protested; neither the wife, nor the children, nor the lad who was living close by because he wanted to marry Tasurinchi's eldest daughter. Not one of them protested. Old and young began getting ready, there and then. "Quickly, quickly, we must get away from here; this place has become an enemy," Tasurinchi said, hurrying them along. He was bursting with energy again, impatient to leave. Saying: "Yes, quickly, quickly, we must go, we must escape," bustling about, spurring himself on.

I helped them get ready and left with them. Before leaving, we burned down the two huts and anything that couldn't be carried, as though someone had died. "All the impure things we have remain here," Tasurinchi assured his family. We walked for several moons. There was little food. No animals fell into the traps. At last we caught some catfish in a pond. We ate. When night came, we sat and talked. I talked to them all night long, perhaps.

"I feel more at peace now," Tasurinchi said to me when I left them several moons later. "I don't believe I'll fall into such a rage again. I've done so very often of late. Perhaps that's over and done with. I did the right thing by starting to walk, it seems. I feel it here, in my breast." "How did you know you had to leave that place?" I asked him. "I remembered something I knew when I was born," he answered. "Or perhaps I learned it in a trance. If an evil occurs on the earth, it's because people have stopped paying attention to the earth, because they don't look after it the way it ought to be looked after. Can it talk the way we do? To say what it wants to say, it has to do something. Shake, perhaps. To say: Don't forget me. To say: I'm alive, too. I don't want to be ill-treated. That's what it could have been complaining of when it jiggled around. Perhaps I made it sweat too much. Perhaps the White Fathers aren't what they seem, but kamagarinis, allies of Kientibakori, advising me to go on living there where I was, just because they want to harm the earth. Who knows? But if it complained, then I had to do something, you see. How do we help the sun, the rivers? How do we help this world, everything that's alive? By walking. I've fulfilled the obligation, I believe. Look, it already shows. Listen to the ground beneath your feet; walk on it, storyteller. How still and firm it is! It must be pleased, now that it can feel us walking on it once again."

Where can Tasurinchi be now? I don't know. Can he have stayed on in that region where we parted? Who knows? Someday I'll know. He is well, most likely. Content. Walking, perhaps.

That, anyway, is what I have learned.

When I left Tasurinchi, I turned around and started walking toward the Timpanía. I hadn't been to visit the Machiguengas there for some time. But before I got there, various unexpected things happened and I had to take off in another direction. That's why I'm here with you, perhaps.

As I was trying to jump over a bed of nettles, I got a thorn in my foot. Here, in this foot. I sucked and spat the thorn out. Some evil must have remained inside my foot because, very soon, it started hurting. It hurt a lot. I stopped walking and sat down. Why had this happened to me? I searched in my pouch. That's where I keep the herbs the seripigari gave me against snakebite, against sickness, against strange things. And in the strap of my knapsack was the iserepito that wards off bad spells. I still carry that little stone about with me. Why didn't the herbs or the iserepito protect me from the little devil in the nettles? My foot was so swollen it looked as if it were somebody else's. Was I changing into a monster? I made a fire and put my foot close to the flames so the evil would come out from inside with the sweat. It hurt terribly; I roared, trying to frighten away the pain. I must have fallen asleep from all that sweating and roaring. And in my sleep I kept hearing parrots chattering and laughing.

I had to stay in that place for many moons while the swelling in my foot went down. I tried to walk, but ay, ay, it hurt dreadfully. I wasn't short of food, happily; I had cassava and maize and some bananas in my knapsack. And what's more, luck was with me, it seems. Right there, without having to get up, by crawling just a little way, I managed to break off a small green branch and pin it down with a knotted cord that I hid in the dirt. Very soon a partridge got caught in the trap. That gave me food for several days. But they were days of torment, not because of the thorn, but because of the parrots. Why were there so many of them? Why were they watching me so closely? There were any number of flocks; they settled on all the branches and bushes around. More and more kept arriving. They had all begun looking at me. Was something happening? Why were they squawking so much? Did all that chattering have anything to do with me? Were they talking about me? Now and then they would come out with one of those odd parrot laughs that sound so human. Were they making mock of me? Saying: You'll never leave here, storyteller. I threw stones at them to scare them off. Useless. They flapped about for a moment and settled on their perches again. There they were, myriads of them, above my head. What is it they want? What's going to happen?

The second day, all of a sudden, they left. The parrots flew off in terror. All at the same time, squawking, shedding feathers, flying into each other, as though an enemy were approaching. They'd smelled danger, it seems. Because just then, right over my head, leaping from branch to branch, there came a talking monkey, a yaniri. Yes, the very same, the big red howling monkey, the yaniri. Enormous, noisy, surrounded by his band of females. Leaping and swinging all around him, happy at being with him. Happy to be his females, perhaps. "Yaniri, yaniri," I shouted. "Help me! Weren't you a seripigari once? Come down and cure this foot of mine; I want to continue my journey." But the talking monkey paid no attention to me. Can it be true that it was once, before, a seripigari who walked? That's why it must not be hunted or eaten, perhaps. When you cook a talking monkey, the air is filled with the smell of tobacco, they say. The tobacco that the seripigari he once was used to inhale and drink in his trances.

The yaniri and his band of females had barely disappeared when the parrots came back. In even greater numbers. I began observing them. They were of every sort. Large, small, tiny; with long curved beaks or stubby ones; there were parakeets and toucans and macaws, but mostly cockatoos. All chattering loudly at the same time, without a letup, a thundering of parrots in my ears. I felt uneasy, looking at them. Slowly I looked at each and every one of them. What were they doing there? Something was going to happen, that was certain, in spite of my herbs against strange things. "What do you want, what are you saying?" I started screaming at them. "What are you talking about, what are you laughing at?" I was frightened, but also curious. I'd never seen so many all together. It couldn't be by chance. It couldn't be for no reason at all. So what was the explanation? Who had sent them to me?

Remembering Tasurinchi, the friend of fireflies, I tried to understand their chattering. Since they were all around me, talking so insistently, could they have come on my account? Were they trying, perhaps, to tell me something? I shut my eyes, listening closely, concentrating on their chatter. Trying to feel that I was a parrot. It wasn't easy. But the effort made me forget the pain in my foot. I imitated their cries, their gurgles; I imitated their cooing. All the sounds they made. Then, between one pause and another, little by little, I began to hear single words, little lights in the darkness. "Calm down, Tasurinchi." "Don't be scared, storyteller." "Nobody's going to hurt you." Understanding what they were saying, perhaps. Don't laugh; I wasn't dreaming. I could understand what they were saying more and more clearly. I felt at peace. My body stopped trembling. The cold went away. So they hadn't been sent here by Kientibakori. Or by a machikanari's spell. Could they have come out of curiosity, rather? To keep me company?

"That's exactly the reason, Tasurinchi," a voice murmured, standing out clearly from the others. Now there was no doubt. It spoke and I understood it. "We're here to keep you company and keep your spirits up while you get well. We'll stay here till you can walk again. Why were you frightened of us? Your teeth were chattering, storyteller. Have you ever seen a parrot eat a Machiguenga? We, on the other hand, have seen lots of Machiguengas eat parrots. Go ahead and laugh, Tasurinchi: it's better that way. We've been following you for a long time. Wherever you go, we're there. Haven't you ever noticed before?"

I never had. In a trembling voice I asked: "Are you making fun of me?" "I'm telling the truth," the parrot insisted, beating the leaves with its wings. "You've had to get a thorn stuck in you to discover your companions, storyteller."

We had a long conversation, it seems. We talked together all the time I was there waiting for the pain to go away. While I held my foot to the fire to make it sweat, we talked. With that parrot; with others, too. They kept interrupting each other as we chatted. At times I couldn't understand what they said. "Be quiet, be quiet. Speak a little more slowly, and one at a time." They didn't obey me. They were like all of you. Exactly like you. Why are you laughing so hard? You sound like parrots, you know. They never waited for one to finish speaking before they all started talking at once. They were pleased that we were able to understand each other at last. They nudged each other, flapping their wings. I felt relieved. Content. What's happening is very strange, I thought.

"Luckily, you've realized we're talkers," one of them suddenly said. All the others were silent. There was a great stillness in the forest. "Now you doubtless understand why we're here, accompanying you. Now you realize why we've been following you ever since you were born again and started walking and talking. Day and night; through forests, across rivers. You're a talker too, aren't you, Tasurinchi? We're alike, don't you think?"

Then I remembered. Each man who walks has his animal which follows him. Isn't that so? Even if he doesn't see it and never guesses which animal it is. According to what he is, according to what he does, the mother of the animal chooses him and says to her little one: "This man is for you, look after him." The animal becomes his shadow, it seems. Was mine a parrot? Yes, it was. Isn't it a talking animal? I knew it and felt that I'd known it from before. If not, why was it that I had always been particularly fond of parrots? Many times in my travels I've stopped to listen to their chattering and laughed at the uproar and all the flapping of wings. We were kinfolk, perhaps.

It's been a good thing knowing that my animal is the parrot. I'm more confident now when I'm traveling. I'll never feel alone again, perhaps. If I'm tired or frightened, if I feel angry about something, I know what to do now. Look up at the trees and wait. I don't think I'll be disappointed. Like gentle rain after heat, the chattering will come. The parrots will be there. Saying: "Yes, here we are, we haven't abandoned you." That's doubtless why I've been able to journey alone for such a long time. Because I wasn't journeying alone, you see.

When I first started wearing a cushma and painting myself with huito and annatto, breathing in tobacco through my nose and walking, many people thought it strange that I should travel alone. "It's foolhardy," they warned me. "Don't you know the forest is full of horrible demons and obscene devils breathed out by Kientibakori? What will you do if they come out to meet you? Travel the way the Machiguengas do, with a youngster and at least one woman. They'll carry the animals you kill and remove those that fall into your traps. You won't become unclean from touching the dead bodies of the animals you've killed. And what's more, you'll have someone to talk to. Several people together are better able to deal with any kamagarinis that might appear. Who's ever seen a Machiguenga entirely on his own in the forest!" I paid no attention, for in my wanderings I'd never felt lonely. There, among the branches, hidden in the leaves of the trees, looking at me with their green eyes, my companions were following me, most likely. I felt they were there, even if I didn't know it, perhaps.

But that's not the reason why I have this little parrot. Because that's a different story. Now that he's asleep, I can tell it to you. If I suddenly stop and start talking nonsense, don't think I've gone out of my head. It will just mean that the little parrot has woken up. It's a story he doesn't like to hear, one which must hurt him as much as that nettle hurt me.

That was after.

I was headed toward the Cashiriari to visit Tasurinchi and I'd caught a cashew bird in a trap. I cooked it and started eating it, when suddenly I heard a lot of chattering just above my head. There was a nest in the branches, half hidden by a large spiderweb. This little parrot had just hatched. It hadn't yet opened its eyes and was still covered with white mucus, like all chicks when they break out of the shell. I was watching, not moving, keeping very quiet, so as not to upset the mother parrot, so as not to make her angry by coming too near her newborn chick. But she was paying no attention to me. She was examining it closely, gravely. She seemed displeased. And suddenly she started pecking at it. Yes, pecking at it with her curved beak. Was she trying to remove the white mucus? No. She was trying to kill it. Was she hungry? I grabbed her by the wings, keeping her from pecking me, and took her out of the nest. And to calm her I gave her some leftovers of the cashew bird. She ate with gusto; chattering and flapping her wings, she ate and ate. But her big eyes were still furious. Once she'd finished her meal, she flew back to the nest. I went to look and she was pecking at the chick again. You haven't woken up, my little parrot?

Don't, then; let me finish your story first. Why did she want to kill her chick? It wasn't out of hunger. I caught the mother parrot by the wings and flung her as high in the air as I could. After flapping around a bit, she came back. Facing up to me, furious, pecking and squawking, she came back. She was determined to kill the chick, it seems.

It was only then that I realized why. It wasn't the chick she'd hoped it would be, perhaps. Its leg was twisted, and its three claws were just a stump. Back then I hadn't yet learned what all of you know: that animals kill their young when they're born different. Why do pumas claw their cubs that are lame or one-eyed? Who do sparrow hawks tear their young to pieces if they have a broken wing? They must sense, since the life of young such as that is not perfect, it will be difficult, with much suffering. They won't know how to defend themselves, to fly, or hunt, or flee, or how to fulfill their obligation. They must sense that they won't live long, for other animals will soon eat them. "That's why I'll eat it myself, so that it feeds me at least," they perhaps tell themselves. Or could it be that, like Machiguengas, they refuse to accept imperfection? Do they, too, believe that imperfect offspring were breathed out by Kientibakori? Who knows?

That's the story of the little parrot. He's always curled up on my shoulder, like this. What do I care if he's not pure, if he's got a game leg and limps, if he flies even this high he'll fall? Because, besides his stump of a foot, his wings turned out to be too short, it seems. Am I perfect? Since we're alike, we get on well together and keep each other company. He travels on this shoulder, and every now and then, to amuse himself, he climbs up over my head and settles on the other shoulder. He goes and comes, comes and goes. He clings to my hair when he's climbing, pulling it as though to warn me: "Be careful or

I'll fall; be careful or you'll have to pick me up off the ground." He weighs nothing; I don't feel him. He sleeps here, inside my cushma. Since I can't call him father or kinsman or Tasurinchi, I call him by a name I invented for him. A parrot noise. Let's hear you imitate it. Let's wake him up; let's call him. He's learned it and repeats it very well: Mas-ca-ri-ta, Mas-ca-ri-ta, Mas-ca-ri-ta . . .

FLORENTINES are famous, in Italy, for their arrogance and for their hatred of the tourists that inundate them, each summer, like an Amazonian river. At the moment, it is hard to determine whether this is true, since there are virtually no natives left in Firenze. They have been leaving, little by little, as the temperature rose, the evening breeze stopped blowing, the waters of the Arno dwindled to a trickle, and mosquitoes took over the city. They are veritable flying hordes that successfully resist repellents and insecticides and gorge on their victims' blood day and night, particularly in museums. Are the zanzare of Firenze the totem animals, the guardian angels of Leonardos, Cellinis, Botticellis, Filippo Lippis, Fra Angelicos? It would seem so. Because it is while contemplating their statues, frescoes, and paintings that I have gotten most of the bites that have raised lumps on my arms and legs neither more nor less ugly than the ones I've gotten every time I've visited the Peruvian jungle.

Or are mosquitoes the weapon that the absent Florentines

resort to in an attempt to put their detested invaders to flight? In any case, it's a hopeless battle. Neither insects nor heat nor anything else in this world would serve to stave off the invasion of the multitudes. Is it merely its paintings, its palaces, the stones of its labyrinthine old quarter that draw us myriads of foreigners to Firenze like a magnet, despite the discomforts of the summer season? Or is it the odd combination of fanaticism and license, piety and cruelty, spirituality and sensual refinement, political corruption and intellectual daring, of its past that holds us in its sway in this stifling city deserted by its inhabitants?

Over the last two months, everything has gradually been closing: the shops, the laundries, the uncomfortable Bibliotèca Nazionale alongside the river, the movie theaters that were my refuge at night, and, finally, the cafés where I went to read Dante and Machiavelli and think about Mascarita and the Machiguengas of the headwaters of the Alto Urubamba and the Madre de Dios. The first to close was the charming Caffè Strozzi, with its Art Deco furniture and interior, and air-conditioning besides, making it a marvelous oasis on scorching afternoons; then the next to close was the Caffè Paszkowski, where, though drenched with sweat, one could be by oneself, on its time-hallowed, démodé upstairs floor, with its leather easy chairs and blood-red velvet drapes; then after that the Caffè Gillio; and last of all, the one that was in all the guidebooks and always jammed, the Caffè Rivoire, in the Piazza della Signoria, where a caffè macchiato cost me as much as an entire meal in a neighborhood trattoria. Since it is not even remotely possible to read or write in a gelateria or a pizzeria (the few hospitable enclaves still open), I have had to resign myself to reading in my pensione in the Borgo dei Santi Apostoli, sweating profusely in the sickly light of a lamp seemingly designed to make reading arduous or to condemn the stubborn reader to premature blindness. These are inconveniences which, as the terrible little monk of San Marcos would have said (the unexpected consequence of my stay in Firenze has been the discovery, thanks to his biographer Rodolfo Ridolfi, that the much maligned Savonarola was, all in all, an interesting figure, one better, perhaps, than those who burned him at the stake), favorably predispose the spirit toward understanding better, to the point of virtually experiencing them personally, the Dantesque tortures of the infernal pilgrimage; or to reflecting, with due calm, upon the terrifying conclusions concerning the cities of men and the government of their affairs drawn by Machiavelli, the icy analyst of the history of this republic, from his experiences as one of its functionaries.

The little gallery in the Via Santa Margherita, between an optician's shop and a grocery store and directly opposite the so-called Church of Dante, where Gabriele Malfatti's Machiguenga photographs were being shown, has also shut, of course. But I managed to see them several times more before its chiusura estivale. The third time she saw me come in, the thin girl in glasses who was in charge of the gallery informed me that she had a fidanzato. I was obliged to assure her in my bad Italian that my interest in the exhibition had no ulterior personal motives, that it was more or less patriotic; it had nothing to do with her beauty, only with Malfatti's photographs. She never quite believed that I spent such a long time peering at them out of sheer homesickness for my native land. And why especially the one of the group of Indians sitting in a sort of lotus position, listening, enthralled, to that gesticulating man? I am sure she never took my assertions seriously when I declared that the photograph was a consummate masterpiece, something to be savored slowly, the way one contemplates *The Allegory of Spring* or *The Battle of San Remo* in the Uffizi. But at last, after seeing me four or five times in the deserted gallery, she was a little less mistrustful of me, and one day she even permitted herself a friendly overture, informing me that an "Inca combo" played Peruvian music on traditional instruments every night in front of the Church of San Lorenzo: why didn't I go see them; they would bring back memories of my homeland. (I obeyed, I went, and I discovered that the Incas were two Bolivians and two Portuguese from Rome who were trying out an incompatible synthesis of Portuguese fados and Santa Cruz carnival music.) The Santa Margherita gallery closed a week ago and the thin girl in glasses is now spending her vacation in Ancona, with her parents.

No matter: I don't need to see that photograph again. I know it by heart, millimeter by millimeter. And I've thought about it so much that, curiously enough, I know that the naked seated figures with their long locks of straight hair, the silhouette of the storyteller, the background of thick tree trunks, tangled branches, and feathery fronds outlined against the horizon beneath a mass of great potbellied gray clouds will be the most lasting memory of this Florentine summer. More enduring and more moving, perhaps, than the artistic and architectonic marvels of the Renaissance, the harmonious murmur of Dante's terza rima, or the rustic ritornellos (in his case unfailingly compatible with diabolical intelligence) of Machiavelli's prose.

I am certain that the photograph shows a Machiguenga storyteller. It is the only thing about which I have no doubts. Who could that man, declaiming before that enraptured audience, be, except that figure ancestrally entrusted with the task of arousing the curiosity, the fantasy, the memory, the appetite for dreams and fabrication of the Machiguenga people? How did Gabriele Malfatti manage to be present on that occasion, to be allowed to take photographs? Perhaps the reason for the secrecy that surrounded the storyteller of recent years—the stranger who had turned into a Machiguenga—no longer existed when the Italian visited that region. Or perhaps in these last years the situation in the Alto Urubamba had evolved so rapidly that the storytellers no longer fulfill their age-old function, have lost their authenticity and become a pantomime put on for tourists, like the ceremonies with annatto or the healings by shamans of other tribes.

But I don't think that's the case. Life has admittedly changed in that region, but not in any way likely to increase tourism. First came the oil wells, and with them, camps for those who were taken on as workers: many Campas, Yaminahuas, Piros, and, surely, Machiguengas. Later on, or at the same time, the drug traffic began and, like a biblical plague, spread its network of coca plantations, laboratories, and secret landing strips, with—as a logical consequence—periodic killings and vendettas between rival gangs of Colombians and Peruvians; the burning of coca crops, the police searches and wholesale roundups. And finally—or perhaps at the same time, closing the triangle of horror—terrorism and counterterrorism. Detachments of the revolutionary Sendero Luminoso movement, severely repressed in the Andes, have come down to the jungle and operate in this part of Amazonia, now periodically reconnoitered by the Army and even, it is said, bombarded by the Air Force.

What effect has all this had on the Machiguenga people? Has it hastened its dismemberment and disintegration? Do the villages that had begun to bring them together some five or six years ago still exist? These villages will, of course, have been exposed to the irreversible disruptive mechanism of this contradictory civilization, represented by the high wages paid by Shell and Petro Perú, the coffers stuffed full of dollars from the drug trade, and the risks of being drawn into the bloody wars of smugglers, guerrilleros, police, and soldiers, without having the faintest idea of what the deadly game is all about. As happened when they were invaded by the Inca armies, the explorers, the Spanish conquistadors and missionaries, the rubber and wood traders in the days of the Republic, the gold prospectors and the twentieth-century immigrants. For the Machiguengas, history marches neither forward nor backward: it goes around and around in circles, repeats itself. But even though the damage to the community has been considerable because of all this, it is likely that many of them, faced with the upheavals of the last few years, will have opted for the traditional response ensuring their survival: diaspora. Start walking. Once again. As in the most persistent of their myths.

Does my ex-friend, ex-Jew, ex-white man, and ex-Westerner, Saúl Zuratas, walk with them, taking those short steps with the whole foot planted flat on the ground, like palmipeds, so typical of all the Amazonian tribes? I have decided that it is he who is the storyteller in Malfatti's photograph. A personal decision, since objectively I have no way of knowing. It's true that the face of the figure standing is the most heavily shadowed—on the right side, where his birthmark was. This might be a key to identifying him. But at that distance the impression could be misleading; it might be no more than the sun's shadow (his face is tilted in such a way that the dying light, falling from the opposite side, casts a shadow over the entire right side of men, trees, and clouds as the sun begins to set). Perhaps the most reliable clue is the shape of the silhouette. Even though he is far off, there is no doubt: that is not the build of a typical jungle Indian, who is usually squat, with short, bowed legs and a broad chest. The one who is talking has an elongated body and I would swear that his skin—he is naked from the waist up—is much lighter than that of his listeners. His hair, however, has that circular cut, like a medieval monk's, of the Machiguengas. I have also decided that the hump on the left shoulder of the storyteller in the photograph is a parrot. Wouldn't it be the most natural thing in the world for a storyteller to travel through the forest with a totemic parrot, companion or acolyte?

After turning the pieces of the puzzle around and around many times and shuffling them this way and that, I see they fit. They outline a more or less coherent story, as long as one sticks strictly to anecdote and does not begin pondering what Fray Luis de León called "the inherent and hidden principle of things."

From that first journey to Quillabamba, where the farmer who was related to his mother lived, Mascarita came into contact with a world that intrigued and attracted him. What must in the beginning have been a feeling of intellectual curiosity and sympathy for the customs and conditions of life of the Machiguengas became, with time, as he got to know them better, learned their language, studied their history, and began to share their existence for longer and longer periods, a conversion, in both the cultural and the religious meaning of the word, an identification with their ways and their traditions, in which, for reasons I can intuit but not entirely understand, Saúl found spiritual sustenance, an incentive and a justification for his life, a commitment that he had not found in those other Peruvian tribes—Jewish, Christian, Marxist, etc.—among which he had lived.

This transformation must have been a very gradual one, taking place unconsciously during the years he spent studying ethnology at San Marcos. That he should have become disillusioned with his studies, that he should consider the scientific outlook of ethnologists a threat to that primitive and archaic culture (adjectives that even that early on he would not have accepted), an intrusion of destructive modern concepts, a form of corruption, is something that I can understand. The idea of an equilibrium between man and the earth, the awareness of the rape of the environment by industrial culture and today's technology, the reevaluation of the wisdom of primitive peoples, forced either to respect their habitat or face extinction, was something that, during those years, although not yet an intellectual fashion, had already begun to take root everywhere, even in Peru. Mascarita must have lived all this with particular intensity, seeing with his own eyes the havoc wreaked by civilized peoples in the jungle, as compared with the way the Machiguengas lived in harmony with the natural world.

The decisive factor that led him to take the final step was, undoubtedly, Don Salomón's death; he was the only person to whom Saúl was attached and to whom he felt obliged to render an account of his life. It is probable, considering how Saúl's conduct changed in his second or third year at the university, that he had already decided that after his father's death he would abandon everything and go to the Alto Urubamba. Up to that point, however, there is nothing extraordinary about his story. In the sixties and seventies—the years of student revolt against a consumer society—many middle-class young people left Lima, motivated partly by adventure-seeking and partly by disgust at life in the capital, and went to the jungle or the mountains, where they lived in conditions that were frequently precarious. One of the Tower of Babel programs—unfortunately ruined, for the most part, by the chronic aberrations of Alejandro Pérez's camera—was, in fact, concerned with a group of kids from Lima who had gone off to the department of Cusco, where they survived by taking up picturesque occupations. That, like them, Mascarita should have decided to turn his back on a bourgeois future and go to Amazonia in search of adventure—a return to fundamentals, to the source—was not particularly remarkable.

But Saúl had not gone off in the same way they had. He erased all trace of his departure and of his intentions, leading those who knew him to believe that he was emigrating to Israel. What else could the alibi of the Jew making the Return mean, except that, on leaving Lima, Saúl Zuratas had irrevocably decided that he was going to change his life, his name, his habits, his traditions, his god, everything he had been up until then? It is evident that he left Lima with the intention of never coming back, of being another person forever.

I am able to follow him this far, though not without difficulty. I believe that his identification with this small, marginal, nomadic community had—as his father conjectured—something to do with the fact that he was Jewish, a member of another community which had also been a wandering, marginal one throughout its history, a pariah among the world's societies, like the Machiguengas in Peru, grafted onto them, yet not assimilated and never entirely accepted. And, surely, his fellow feeling for the Machiguengas was influenced, as I used to tease him, by that enormous birthmark that made of him a marginal among marginals, a man whose destiny would always bear the stigma of ugliness. I can accept that among the worshippers of the spirits of trees and thunder, the ritual users of tobacco and ayahuasca brews, Mascarita would feel more at home—dissolved in a collective being—than among the Jews or the Christians of his country. In a very subtle and personal way, by going to the Alto Urubamba to be born again, Saúl made his *Alyah.*

Where I find it impossible to follow him—an insuperable difficulty that pains and frustrates me—is in the next stage: the transformation of the convert into the storyteller. It is this facet of Saúl's story, naturally, that moves me most; it is what makes me think of it continually and weave and unweave it a thousand times; it is what has impelled me to put it into writing in the hope that if I do so, it will cease to haunt me.

Becoming a storyteller was adding what appeared impossible to what was merely improbable. Going back in time from trousers and tie to a loincloth and tattoos, from Spanish to the agglutinative crackling of Machiguenga, from reason to magic and from a monotheistic religion or Western agnosticism to pagan animism, is a feat hard to swallow, though still possible, with a certain effort of imagination. The rest of the story, however, confronts me only with darkness, and the harder I try to see through it, the more impenetrable it becomes.

Talking the way a storyteller talks means being able to feel and live in the very heart of that culture, means having penetrated its essence, reached the marrow of its history and mythology, given body to its taboos, images, ancestral desires, and terrors. It means being, in the most profound way possible, a rooted Machiguenga, one of that ancient lineage who—in the period in which this Firenze, where I am writing, produced its dazzling effervescence of ideas, paintings, buildings, crimes, and intrigues—roamed the forests of my country, bringing and bearing away those tales, lies, fictions, gossip, and jokes that make a community of that people of scattered beings, keeping alive among them the feeling of oneness, of constituting something fraternal and solid. That my friend Saúl gave up being all that he was and might have become so as to roam through the Amazonian jungle, for more than twenty years now, perpetuating against wind and tide—and, above all, against the very concepts of modernity and progress—the tradition of that invisible line of wandering storytellers, is something that memory now and again brings back to me, and, as on that day when I first heard of it, in the starlit darkness of the village of New Light, it opens my heart more forcefully than fear or love has ever done.

Darkness has fallen and there are stars in the Florentine night, though not as bright as those in the jungle. I have a feeling that at any moment I'll run out of ink (the shops in this city where I might get a refill for my pen are also locked up tight for their chiusura estivale, naturally). The heat is unbearable, and my room in the Pensione Alejandra is alive with mosquitoes buzzing and circling around my head. I could take a shower and go out for a stroll in search of diversion. There might be a breath of a breeze on the Lungarno, and if I walk along it, the spectacle of the floodlit embankments, bridges, and palaces, always beautiful, will lead to another, fiercer, spectacle: the one on the Cascine, by day the respectable promenade of ladies and children, but at this time of night the hangout of whores, gays, and drug dealers. I could mingle with the young people, high on music and marijuana in the Piazza del Santo Spirito or the Piazza della Signoria, become at this hour a motley Cour des Miracles where four, five, even ten different impromptu shows are simultaneously staged: Caribbean maraca players and acrobats, Turkish ropewalkers, Moroccan fire-eaters, Spanish student serenaders, French mimes, American jazz musicians, gypsy fortune-tellers, German guitarists, Hungarian flutists. Sometimes it is enjoyable to lose oneself in this colorful, youthful multitude. But tonight I know that wherever I might wander—on the ocher stone bridges over the Arno, or beneath the trees of the Cascine, each with its waiting prostitute, or the straining muscles of the Neptune fountain, or Cellini's bronze statue of Perseus stained with pigeon droppings—wherever I might try to find refuge from the heat, the mosquitoes, the rapture of my spirit, I would still hear, close by, unceasing, crackling, immemorial, that Machiguenga storyteller.

Firenze, July 1985

London, May 13, 1987